Return from the Stars

ALSO BY STANISLAW LEM

Return from the Stars

BY STANISLAW LEM

TRANSLATED BY BARBARA MARSZAL
AND FRANK SIMPSON

A Helen and Kurt Wolff Book

Harcourt Brace Jovanovich

New York and London

Printed in the United States of America

Library of Congress Cataloging in Publication Data

Lem, Stanisław.
Return from the stars.

Translation of Powrót z gwiazd.
"A Helen and Kurt Wolff book."
I. Title.
PZ4.L537Re [PG7158.L39]   891.8'537   79-3358
ISBN 0-15-177082-4

First edition

B C D E

Return from the Stars

took nothing with me, not even a coat. Unnecessary, they said. They let me keep my black sweater: it would pass. But the shirt I had to fight for. I said that I would learn to do without things gradually. At the very ramp, beneath the belly of the ship, where we stood, jostled by the crowd, Abs offered me his hand with an understanding smile:

"Easy, now . . ."

That, too, I remembered. I didn't crush his fingers. I was quite calm. He wanted to say something more. I spared him that, turning away as if I had not noticed anything, and went up the stairs and inside. The stewardess led me between the rows of seats to the very front. I hadn't wanted a private compartment. I wondered if they had told her. My seat unfolded without a sound. She adjusted the back of it, gave me a smile, and left. I sat down. The cushions were engulfingly soft, as everywhere. The back of my seat was so high that I could barely see the other passengers. The bright colors of the women's clothes I had by now learned to accept, but the men I still suspected, irrationally, of affectation, and I had the secret hope that I would come across some dressed normally—a pitiful reflex. People were seated quickly, no one had luggage. Not even a briefcase or a package. The women, too. There seemed to be more of them. In front of me: two mulatto women in parrot-green furs, ruffled like feathers— apparently, that sort of bird style was in fashion. Farther away, a couple with a child. After the garish selenium lights of the platforms and tunnels, after the unbearably shrill incandescent vegetation of the streets, the light from the concave ceiling seemed practically a glow. I did not know what to do with my hands, so I put them on my knees. Everyone was seated now.

Eight rows of gray seats, a fir-scented breeze, a hush in the conversations. I expected an announcement about takeoff, signals of some sort, the warning to fasten seat belts, but nothing happened. Across the dull ceiling faint shadows began to move from front to rear, like paper cutouts of birds. What the hell is it with these birds? I wondered, perplexed. Does it mean something? I was numb from the strain of trying not to do anything wrong. This, for four days now. From the very first moment. I was invariably behind in everything that went on, and the constant effort to understand the simplest conversation or situation turned that tension into a feeling horribly like despair. I was certain that the others were experiencing the same things, but we did not talk about it, not even when we were alone together. We only joked about our brawn, about that excessive strength that had remained in us, and indeed we had to be on our guard —in the beginning, intending to get up, I would go shooting toward the ceiling, and any object that I held in my hand seemed to be made of paper, empty. But I quickly learned to control my body. In greeting people, I no longer crushed their hands. That was easy. But, unfortunately, the least important.

My neighbor to the left—corpulent, tan, with eyes that shone too much (from contact lenses?)—suddenly disappeared; his seat expanded at the sides, which rose and joined to form a kind of egg-shaped cocoon. A few other people disappeared into such cubicles. Swollen sarcophagi. What did they do in them? But such things I encountered all the time, and tried not to stare, as long as they did not concern me directly. Curiously, the people who gaped at us on learning what we were I treated with indifference. Their dumbfoundedness did not concern me much, although I realized immediately that there was not an iota of admiration in it. What did arouse my antipathy were the ones who looked after us—the staff of Adapt. Dr. Abs most of all, because he treated me the way a doctor would an abnormal patient, pretending, and very well, too, that he was dealing with someone quite ordinary. When that became impossible, he would joke. I had had enough of his direct approach and joviality. If asked about it (or so, at least, I thought), the man on the street would say that Olaf or I was similar to himself—we were not so outlandish to him, it was just our past existence that was unusual. Dr. Abs, on the other hand, and all the workers at Adapt, knew better—that we were decidedly different. This differentness was no mark of distinction but only a barrier to communication, to the simplest exchange of words, hell, to the opening of a door, seeing as doorknobs had ceased to exist—what was it?—some fifty or sixty years earlier.

The takeoff came unexpectedly. There was no change at all in gravity, no sound reached the hermetically sealed interior, the shadows swam evenly across the ceiling—it might have been habit established over many years, an old instinct, that told me that at a certain moment we were in space, because it was certainty, not a guess.

But something else was occupying me. I sat half supine, my legs stretched out, motionless. They had let me have my way too easily. Even Oswamm did not oppose my decision too much. The counterarguments that I heard from him and from Abs were unconvincing—I myself could have come up with better. They insisted on one thing only, that each of us fly separately. They did not even hold it against me that I got Olaf to rebel (because if it had not been for me, he definitely would have agreed to stay there longer). That had been odd. I had expected complications, something that would spoil my plan at the last minute, but nothing happened, and now here I was flying. This final journey was to end in fifteen minutes.

Clearly, what I had devised, and the way, too, that I went before them to argue for an earlier departure, did not surprise them. They must have had a reaction of this type catalogued, it was a behavior pattern characteristic of a stalwart such as myself, assigned an appropriate serial number in their psychotechnical tables. They permitted me to fly—why? Because experience had told them that I would not be able to manage on my own? But how could that be, when this whole "independence" escapade involved flying from one terminal to another, where someone from the Earth branch of Adapt would be waiting and all I had to do was to find him at a prearranged location?

Something happened. I heard raised voices. I leaned out of my seat. Several rows in front of me a woman pushed away the stewardess, who, with a slow, automatic motion, as if from the push—though the push had not been all that hard—went backward down the aisle, and the woman repeated, "I won't have it! Don't let that touch me." I did not see the face of the speaker. Her companion pulled at her arm, was saying something to calm her. What was the meaning of this little scene? The other passengers paid no attention to her. For the hundredth time I was possessed by a feeling of incredible alienation. I looked up at the stewardess, who had stopped by my side and was smiling as before. It was not merely an external smile of official politeness, a smile to cover an upsetting incident. She was not pretending to be calm, she truly was calm.

"Something to drink? Prum, extran, morr, cider?"

A melodious voice. I shook my head. I wanted to say something nice to her, but all I could come up with was the stereotyped question:

"When do we land?"

"In six minutes. Would you care for something to eat? There is no need to hurry. You can stay on after we land."

"No, thank you."

She left. In the air, right before my face, against the background of the seat in front of me, a sign that read STRATO lit up, as though written with the glowing end of a cigarette. I bent forward to see where the sign came from, and flinched. The back of my seat moved with my shoulders and clung to them elastically. I knew already that furniture accommodated every change in position, but I kept forgetting. It was not pleasant—as if someone were following my every move. I wanted to return to my former position but apparently overdid it. The seat misunderstood and nearly flattened itself out like a bed. I jumped up. This was idiotic! More control. I sat, finally. The pink letters of STRATO flickered and flowed into others: TERMINAL. No jolt, no warning, no whistle. Nothing. A distant voice resounded like the horn of a postilion, four oval doors opened at the end of the aisle, and a hollow, all-embracing roar, like that of the sea, rushed in. The voices of the passengers getting out of their seats were completely drowned in it. I remained seated while they exited, a file of silhouettes floating by before the outside lights, green, lilac, purple—a veritable masked ball. Then they were gone. I stood up. Mechanically straightened my sweater. Feeling stupid, somehow, with my hands empty. Through the open door came cooler air. I turned. The stewardess was standing by the partition wall, not touching it with her back. On her face was the same tranquil smile, directed at the empty rows of seats, which now on their own began to roll up, to furl, like fleshy flowers, some faster, some a little more slowly—this was the only movement in the all-embracing, drawn-out roar that flowed in through the oval openings and brought to mind the open sea. "Don't let that touch me!" Suddenly I found something not right in her smile. From the exit I said:

"Good-bye . . ."

"Acknowledged."

The significance of that reply, so peculiar coming from the lips of a beautiful young woman, I did not immediately grasp, for it reached me when my back was turned, as I was halfway out the door. I went to put my foot on a step, but there was no step. Between the metal hull and the edge of the platform yawned a meter-wide crevice. Caught off balance, unprepared for such a trap, I made a clumsy leap and, in midair, felt an invisible flow of force take hold of me as if from below, so that I floated across the void and was set down softly on a white surface, which yielded elastically. In flight, I must have had a none-too-intelligent expression on my face—I felt a number of amused stares, or so it seemed to me. I quickly turned away and walked along the platform. The rocket on which I had arrived was resting in a deep bay, separated from the edge of the platforms by an unprotected abyss. I drew close to this empty space, as if unintentionally, and for the second time felt an invisible resilience that kept me from crossing the white border. I wanted to locate the source of this peculiar force, but suddenly, as if I were waking up, it occurred to me: I was on Earth.

A wave of pedestrians caught me up; jostled, I moved forward in the crowd. It took a moment for me really to see the size of the hall. But was it all one hall? No walls: a glittering white high-held explosion of unbelievable wings; between them, columns, made not of any substance but of dizzying motion. Rushing upward, enormous fountains of a liquid denser than water, illuminated from inside by colored floodlights? No—vertical tunnels of glass through which a succession of blurred vehicles raced upward? Now I was completely at a loss. Constantly pushed and shoved in the swarming crowds, I attempted to work my way to some clear space, but there were no clear spaces here. Being a head taller than those around me, I was able to see that the empty rocket was moving off—no, it was we who were gliding forward with the entire platform. From above, lights flared, and in them the people sparkled and shimmered. Now the flat surface on which we stood close together began to move upward and I saw below, in the distance, double white belts packed with people, and gaping black crevices along inert hulls—for there were dozens of ships like ours. The moving platform made a turn, accelerated, continued to higher levels. Thundering, fluttering the hair of those who were standing with strong gusts of wind, there hurtled past on them, as on impossible (for completely unsupported) viaducts, oval shadows, trembling with speed and trailing long streaks of flame, their signal lights; then the surface carrying us began to branch, dividing along imperceptible seams; my strip passed through an interior filled with people both standing and seated; a multitude of tiny flashes surrounded them, as though they were engaged in setting off colored fireworks.

I did not know where to look. In front of me stood a man in something fluffy like fur, which, when touched by light, opalesced like metal. He supported by the arm a woman in scarlet. What she had on was all in large eyes, peacock eyes, and the eyes blinked. It was no illusion—the eyes on her dress actually opened and closed. The walkway, on which I stood behind the two of them and among a dozen other people, picked up speed. Between surfaces of smoke-white glass there opened colored, lighted malls with transparent ceilings, ceilings trod upon con-

tinuously by hundreds of feet on the floor above; the all-embracing roar now swelled, now was confined, as thousands of human
voices and sounds—meaningless to me, meaningful to them—
were swallowed by each successive tunnel of this journey whose
destination I did not know. In the distance the surrounding
space kept being pierced by streaks of vehicles unknown to me—
aircraft, probably, because now and then they veered up or
down, spiraling into space, so that I automatically expected a
terrible crash, since I saw neither guide wires nor rails, if these
were elevated trains. When the blurred hurricanes of motion
were interrupted for a moment, from behind them emerged
majestically slow, huge surfaces filled with people, like flying
stations, which went in various directions, passed one another,
lifted, and seemed to merge by tricks of perspective. It was hard
to rest the eye on anything that was not in motion, because the
architecture on all sides appeared to consist in motion alone, in
change, and even what I had initially taken to be a vaulted ceiling were only overhanging tiers, tiers that now gave way to other,
higher tiers and levels. Suddenly a heavy purple glare, as though
an atomic fire had flared up somewhere far away in the heart of
the building, filtered its way through the glass of the ceilings, of
those mysterious columns, and was reflected by the silver surfaces; it bled into every corner, into the interiors of the passageways that glided by, into the features of the people. The green
of the incessantly jumping neons became dingy; the milkiness of
the parabolic buttresses grew pink. In this sudden saturation of
the air with redness lay a foreboding of catastrophe, or so it
seemed to me, but no one paid the least attention to the change,
and I could not even say when it cleared away.

At the sides of our ramp appeared whirling green circles, like
neon rings suspended in midair, whereupon some of the people
stepped down onto the approaching branch of another ramp or
walkway; I observed that one could pass through the green lines
of those lights quite freely, as if they were not material.

For a while I let myself be carried along by the white walkway, until it occurred to me that perhaps I was already outside
the station and that this fantastic panorama of sloping glass,

which looked constantly as if on the verge of flight, was in fact the city, and that the one I had left behind existed now only in my memory.

"Excuse me." I touched the arm of the man in fur. "Where are we?"

They both looked at me. Their faces, when they raised them, took on a startled expression. I had the faint hope that it was only because of my height.

"On the polyduct," said the man. "Which is your switch?"

I did not understand.

"Are . . . are we still in the station?"

"Obviously," he replied with a certain caution.

"But . . . where is the Inner Circle?"

"You've already missed it. You'll have to backtrack."

"The rast from Merid would be better," said the woman. All the eyes of her dress seemed to stare at me with suspicion and amazement.

"Rast?" I repeated helplessly.

"Right over there." She pointed to an unoccupied elevation with black-and-silver-striped sides; it resembled the hull of a peculiarly painted vessel lying on its side. This, visible through an approaching green circle. I thanked them and stepped off the walkway, probably at the wrong spot, because the momentum made me stumble. I caught my balance but was spun around, so that I did not know in which direction to go. I considered what to do, but by this time my transfer point had moved considerably from the black-and-silver hill that the woman had shown me, and I could not find it now. Since most of the people around me were stepping onto an upward ramp, I did the same. On it, I noticed a giant stationary sign burning in the air: DUCT CENT. The rest of the letters, on either side, were not visible because of their magnitude. Noiselessly I was carried to a platform at least a kilometer long from which a spindle-shaped craft was just departing, showing, as it rose, a bottom riddled with lights. But perhaps that leviathan shape was the platform and I was on the "rast"—there was not even anyone to ask, for the area around me was deserted. I must have taken a wrong turn. One part of my "platform" held flattened buildings without front walls. Approaching them, I found low, dimly lit cubicles, in which stood rows of black machines. I took these for cars. But when the two nearest me emerged and, before I had time to step back, passed me at tremendous speed, I saw, before they disappeared into the background of parabolic inclines, that they had no wheels, windows, or doors. Streamlined, like huge black drops of liquid. Cars or not—I thought—in any case this appears to be some kind of parking lot. For the "rasts"? I decided that it would be better for me to wait for someone to come along, and go with him: at least I would learn something. My platform lifted lightly, like the wing of an impossible airplane, but remained empty; there were only the black machines, emerging singly or several at a time from their metal lairs and speeding away, always in the same direction. I went down to the very edge of the platform, until once more that invisible, springy force made itself felt, assuring complete safety. The platform truly hung in the air, not supported by anything. Lifting my head, I saw many others like it, hovering motionless in space in the same way, with their great lights out; at some, where craft were arriving, the lights were on. But those rockets or projectiles were not like the one that had brought me in from Luna.

I stood there awhile, until I noticed, against the background of some further hallways—though I did not know whether they were mirrored reflections of this one or reality—letters of fire steadily moving through the air: SOAMO SOAMO SOAMO, a pause, a bluish flash, and then NEONAX NEONAX NEONAX. These might have been the names of stations, or possibly of advertised products. They told me nothing.

It's high time I found that fellow, I thought. I turned on my heel and, seeing a walkway moving in the opposite direction, took it back down. This turned out to be the wrong level, it was not even the hall that I had left: I knew this by the absence of those enormous columns. But, then, they might have gone away somewhere; by now I considered anything possible.

I found myself in a forest of fountains; farther along I came upon a white-pink room filled with women. As I walked by I put my hand, without thinking, into the jet of an illuminated fountain, perhaps because it was pleasant to come across something even a little familiar. But I felt nothing, the fountain was without water. After a moment it seemed to me that I smelled flowers. I put my hand to my nostrils. It smelled like a thousand scented soaps at once. Instinctively I rubbed my hand on my trousers. Now I was standing in front of that room filled with women, only women. It did not appear to me to be a powder room, but I had no way of knowing. I preferred not to ask, so I turned away. A young man, wearing something that looked as though mercury had flowed over him and solidified, puffed-out (or perhaps foamy) on the arms and snug about the hips, was talking with a blonde girl who had her back against the bowl of a fountain. The girl, wearing a bright dress that was quite ordinary, which encouraged me, held a bouquet of pale pink flowers; nestling her face in them, she smiled at the boy with her eyes. At the moment I stood before them and was opening my mouth to speak, I saw that she was eating the flowers—and my voice failed me. She was calmly chewing the delicate petals. She looked up at me. Her eyes froze. But to that I had grown accustomed. I asked where the Inner Circle was.

The boy, it seemed to me, was unpleasantly surprised, even angry, that someone dared to interrupt their tête-à-tête. I must have committed some impropriety. He looked me up and down, as if expecting to find stilts that would account for my height. He did not say a word.

"Oh, there," cried the girl, "the rast on the vuk, your rast, you can make it, hurry!"

I started running in the direction indicated, without knowing to what—I still hadn't the faintest idea what that damned rast looked like—and after about ten steps I saw a silvery funnel descending from high above, the base of one of those enormous columns that had astonished me so much before. Could they be flying columns? People were hurrying toward it from all directions; then suddenly I collided with someone. I did not lose my balance, I merely stood rooted to the spot, but the other person, a stout individual in orange, fell down, and something incredible happened to him: his fur coat wilted before my eyes, collapsed like a punctured balloon! I stood over him, astounded, unable even to mutter an apology. He picked himself up, gave me a dirty look, but said nothing; he turned and marched off, fingering something on his chest—and his coat filled out and lit up again. . . .

By now the place that the girl had pointed out to me was deserted. After this incident I gave up looking for rasts, the Inner Circle, ducts, and switches; I decided to get out of the station. My experiences so far did not encourage me to accost passers-by, so at random I followed a sloping sky-blue arrow upward; without any particular sensation, my body passed through two signs glowing in the air: LOCAL CIRCUITS. I came to an escalator that held quite a few people. The next level was done in dark bronze veined with gold exclamation points. Fluid joinings of ceilings and concave walls. Ceilingless corridors, at the top enveloped in a shining powder. I seemed to be approaching living quarters of some kind, as the area took on the quality of a system of gigantic hotel lobbies—teller windows, nickel pipes along the walls, recesses with clerks; maybe these were offices for currency exchange, or a post office. I walked on. I was now almost certain that this was not the way to an exit and (judging from the length of the ride upward) that I was in the elevated part of the station; nevertheless I kept going in the same direction. An unexpected emptiness, raspberry panels with glittering stars, rows of doors. The nearest was open. I looked in. A large, broad-shouldered man looked in from the opposite side. Myself in a mirror. I opened the door wider. Porcelain, silver pipes, nickel. Toilets.

I felt a little like laughing, but mainly I was nonplused. I quickly turned around: another corridor, bands, white as milk, flowing downward. The handrail of the escalator was soft, warm; I did not count the levels passed; more and more people, who stopped in front of enamel boxes that grew out of the wall at every step; the touch of a finger, and something would fall into their hands; they put this into their pockets and walked on. For some reason I did exactly as the man in the loose violet coat in front of me had done; a key with a small depression for the fingertip, I pressed, and into my palm fell a colored, translucent tube, slightly warm. I shook it, held it up to one eye; pills of some kind? No. A vial? It had no cork, no stopper. What was it for? What were the other people doing? Putting the things in their pockets. The sign on the dispenser: LARGAN. I stood there; I was jostled. And suddenly I felt like a monkey that has been given a fountain pen or a lighter; for an instant I was seized by a blind rage; I set my jaw, narrowed my eyes, and, shoulders hunched, joined the stream of pedestrians. The corridor widened, became a hall. Fiery letters: REAL AMMO REAL AMMO.

Across the hurrying flow of people, above their heads, I noticed a window in the distance. The first window. Panoramic, enormous.

All the firmaments of the night flung onto a flat plane. On a horizon of blazing mist—colored galaxies of squares, clusters of spiral lights, glows shimmering above skyscrapers, the streets: a creeping, a peristalsis with necklaces of light, and over this, in the perpendicular, cauldrons of neon, feather crests and lightning bolts, circles, airplanes, and bottles of flame, red dandelions made of needle signal lights, momentary suns and hemorrhages of advertising, mechanical and violent. I stood and watched, hearing, behind me, the steady sough of hundreds of feet. Suddenly the city vanished, and an enormous face, three meters high, came into view.

"You have been watching clips from newsreels of the seventies, in the series *Views of the Ancient Capitals*. Now the news. Transtel is currently expanding to include cosmolyte studios. . . ."

I practically fled. It was no window. A television screen. I quickened my pace. I was perspiring a little.

Down. Faster. Gold squares of lights. Inside, crowds, foam on glasses, an almost black liquid—not beer, with its virulent, greenish glint—and young people, boys and girls, arms around one another, in groups of six, eight, blocking the way across the entire thoroughfare, came toward me; they had to separate to let me through. I was buffeted. Without realizing it, I stepped onto a moving walkway. Quite close to me, a pair of startled eyes flashed by—a lovely dark girl in something that shone like phosphorized metal. The fabric clung to her: she was as if naked. White faces, yellow, a few tall blacks, but I was still the tallest. People made way for me. High above, behind convex windows, scattered shadows sped by, unseen orchestras played, but here a curious promenade went on; in the dark passages, the headless silhouettes of women: the fluff covering their arms gave off a light, so that only their raised necks showed in it like strange white stems, and the scattered glow in their hair—a luminescent powder? A narrow passage led me to a series of rooms with grotesque—because moving, even active—statues; a kind of wide street with raised sides boomed with laughter. People were being amused, but what was amusing them—the statues?

Huge figures in cones of floodlights; pouring from them was ruby light, honey light, as thick as syrup, an unusual concentration of colors. I walked on passively, squinting, abstracted. A steep green corridor, grotesque pavilions, pagodas reached by little bridges, everywhere small cafés, the sharp, persistent smell of fried food, rows of gas flames behind windows, the clinking of glass, metallic sounds, repeated, incomprehensible. The crowd that had carried me here collided with another, then thinned out; everyone was getting into an open carriage; no, it was only transparent, as if molded in glass, even the seats were like glass, though soft. Without knowing how, I found myself inside—we were moving. The carriage tore along, the people shouted over the sound of a loudspeaker that repeated, "Meridional level, Meridional, change for Spiro, Atale, Blekk, Frosom"; the entire carriage seemed to melt, pierced by shafts of light; walls flew by in strips of flame and color; parabolic arches, white platforms. "Forteran, Forteran, change for Galee, change for outer rasts, Makra," babbled the speaker; the carriage stopped, then sped on. I discovered a remarkable thing: there was no sensation of braking or acceleration, as if inertia had been annulled. How was this possible? I checked, bending my knees slightly, at three consecutive stops. Nothing on the turns, either. People got off, got on. At the front stood a woman with a dog; I had never seen such a dog, it was huge, its head like a ball, very ugly; in its placid hazel eyes were reflected retreating, diminishing garlands of lights. RAMBRENT RAMBRENT. There was a fluttering from white and bluish fluorescent tubes, stairs of crystalline brilliance, black façades; the brilliance gave way slowly to stone; the carriage stopped. I got off and was dumbstruck. Above the amphitheater-like sunken dial of the stop rose a multistory structure that I recognized; I was still in the station, in another place within the same gigantic hall magnified in white sweeping surfaces. I made for the edge of the geometrically perfect depression—the carriage had already left—and received another surprise. I was not at the bottom, as I had thought; I was actually high up, about forty floors above the bands of the walkways visible in the abyss, above the silver decks of the ever-steadily gliding platforms; between them moved long, silent bodies, and people emerged from these through rows of hatches; it was as if monsters, chrome-plated fish, were depositing, at regular intervals, their black and colored eggs. Above all this, through the mist of the distance, I saw words of gold moving in a line:

BACK TODAY GLENIANIA ROON WITH HER MIMORPHIC REAL RECORDING PAYS TRIBUTE IN THE ORATORIUM TO THE MEMORY OF RAPPER KERX POLITR. TERMINAL NEWS BULLETIN: TODAY IN AM-MONLEE PETIFARGUE PRODUCED THE SYSTOLIZATION OF THE FIRST ENZOM. THE VOICE OF THE DISTINGUISHED GRAVISTICIAN WILL BE BROADCAST AT HOUR TWENTY-SEVEN. ARRAKER LEADS. ARRAKER REPEATED HIS SUCCESS AS THE FIRST OBLITERATOR OF THE SEASON AT THE TRANSVAAL STADIUM.

I turned away. So even the way of telling time had changed. Hit by the light of the gigantic letters that flew above the sea of heads like rows of burning tightrope-walkers, the metallic fabrics of the women's dresses flared up in sudden flames. I walked, oblivious, and something inside me kept repeating: So even time has changed. That somehow did me in. I saw nothing, though my eyes were open. I wanted one thing only, to get away, to find a way out of this infernal station, to be under the naked sky, in the open air, to see the stars, feel the wind.

I was attracted to an avenue of elongated lights. On the transparent stone of the ceilings, something was being written—letters—by a sharp flame encased in alabaster: TELETRANS TELEPORT TELETHON. Through a steeply arched doorway(but it was an impossible arch, pried out of its foundation, like the negative image of a rocket prow), I reached a hall upholstered in frozen gold fire. In recesses along the walls were hundreds of booths; people ran into these, burst out again in haste; they threw torn ribbons on the floor, not telegraph tapes, something else, with punched-out projections; others walked over these shreds. I wanted to leave; by mistake I went into a dark room; before I had time to step back something buzzed, a flash like that of a flashbulb, and from a metal-framed slot, as from a mailbox, slipped a piece of shiny paper folded in two. I took it and opened it, a face emerged, the mouth open, the lips slightly twisted, thin; it regarded me through half-closed eyes: myself! I folded the paper in two and the plastic specter vanished. I slowly parted the edges: nothing. Wider: it appeared again, popping out of nowhere, a head severed from the rest of the body, hanging above the paper card with a none-too-intelligent expression. For a moment I contemplated my own face—what was this, three-dimensional photography? I put the paper into my pocket and left. A golden hell seemed to descend on the crowd, a ceiling made of fiery magma, unreal but belching real flames, and no one paid attention; those with business ran from one booth to another; farther back, green letters jumped, columns of numerals flowed down narrow screens; other booths had shutters instead of doors, which lifted rapidly at anyone's approach; at last I found an exit.

A curved corridor with an inclined floor, as sometimes in the theater; from its walls, stylized conches were shooting forth, while above them raced the words INFOR INFOR INFOR without end.

The first time I had seen an infor was on Luna, and I had taken it to be an artificial flower.

I put my face close to the aquamarine cup, which immediately, before I could open my mouth, froze in readiness.

"How do I get out of here?" I asked, none too brightly.

"Where are you going?" a warm alto answered immediately.

"To the city."

"Which district?"

"It doesn't matter."

"Which level?"

"It doesn't matter; I just want to get out of the station!"

"Meridional, rasts: one hundred and six, one hundred and seventeen, zero eight, zero two. Triduct, level AF, AG, AC, circuit M levels twelve, sixteen, the nadir level leads to every direction south. Central level—gleeders, red local, white express, A, B, and V. Ulder level, direct, all escals from the third up . . ." a singsong female voice recited.

I had the urge to tear from the wall the microphone that was inclined with such solicitude to my face. I walked away. Idiot! Idiot! droned in me at every step. EX EX EX EX—repeated a sign that was rising, bordered by a lemon haze. Exit? A way out?

The huge sign said EXOTAL. A sudden rush of warm air made the legs of my trousers flap. I found myself beneath the open sky. But the blackness of the night was kept at a great distance, pushed back by the multitude of lights. An immense restaurant. Tables whose tops blazed with different colors; above them, faces, illuminated from below, therefore somewhat eerie, full of deep shadows. Low armchairs, a black liquid with green foam in glasses, lanterns that spilled tiny sparks, no, fireflies, swarms of burning moths. The chaos of lights extinguished the stars. When I lifted my head I saw only a black void. Yet, strangely enough, at that moment its blind presence gave me courage. I stood and looked. Someone brushed by me; I caught the fragrance of perfume, sharp yet at the same time mild; a young couple passed; the girl turned to the man; her arms and breasts were submerged in a fluffy cloud; she entered his embrace; they danced. They still dance, I thought to myself. That's good. The pair took a few steps, a pale, mercurylike ring lifted them up along with the other couples, their dark red shadows moved beneath its huge plate, which rotated slowly, like a record. It was not supported by anything, did not even have an axis, but, hanging in the air, it turned to the music. I walked among the tables. The soft plastic underfoot ended, gave way to porous rock. I passed through a curtain of light and found myself inside a rocky grotto. It was like ten, fifty Gothic naves formed out of stalactites; veined deposits of pearly minerals surrounded the mouths of the caves; in these people sat, legs dangling; small flames flickered between their knees, and at the bottom lay the unbroken black surface of an underground lake, which reflected the vaults of the rocks. There, too, on flimsy little rafts, people were reclining, all facing the same way. I went down to the water's edge and saw, on the other side, on the sand, a female dancer. She appeared to be naked, but the whiteness of her body was not natural. With short, unsteady steps she ran to the water; when her body was reflected in it, she stretched out her arms suddenly and bowed—the end—but no one applauded; the dancer remained motionless for a few seconds, then slowly went along the shore, following its uneven line. She was perhaps thirty paces from me when something happened to her. One moment I saw her smiling, exhausted face, then, suddenly, as if something had got in the way, her outline trembled and disappeared.

"A raft for you, sir?" came a courteous voice behind me. I turned around; no one, only a streamlined table strutting on comically bowed legs; it moved forward, glasses of sparkling liquid, arranged in rows on side trays, shook, one arm politely offering me this drink, the other reaching for a plate with a fingerhole, something like a small, concave palette—it was a robot. I could see, behind a small glass pane in the center, the glow of its transistorized heart.

I avoided those insect arms stretched out to serve me, loaded with delicacies, which I refused, and I quickly left the artificial cave, gritting my teeth, as if I had somehow been insulted. I crossed the full width of the terrace, among S-shaped tables, under avenues of lanterns, showered with a fine powder of disintegrating, dying fireflies, black, gold. At the very edge, a border of stone, old, covered with a yellowish lichen, and there I felt, at last, a real wind, clean, cool. Nearby stood a vacant table. I sat awkwardly, my back to the people, looking out into the night. Below lay the darkness, vast, formless, and unexpected; only far, very far away, at its perimeter, glowed thin, flickering lights, curiously uncertain, as though not electric, and even farther off, swords of light rose up cold and thin into the sky, whether homes or pillars, I did not know; I would have taken them for the beams of floodlights had they not been traced by a delicate network—a glass cylinder might have looked thus, its base in the earth, its tip in the clouds, filled with alternating concave and convex lenses. They must have been incredibly high; around them, a few lights glimmering, pulsing, so that they were encircled now by an orange haze, now by a nearly white one. That was all, that was how the city looked; I tried to find streets, to guess where they would be, but the dark and seemingly lifeless space below spread out in all directions, not illuminated by a single spark.

"Col . . . ?" I heard; the word had probably been said more than once, but I did not immediately realize that it was addressed to me. I started to turn around, but the chair, quicker than I, did this for me. Standing in front of me was a girl, perhaps twenty years old, in something blue that clung to her like a liquid congealed; her arms and breasts were hidden in a navy-blue fluff that became more and more transparent as it descended. Her slim, lovely belly was like a sculpture in breathing metal. At her ears she had something shining, so large that it covered them completely. A small mouth in an uncertain smile, the lips painted, the nostrils also red inside—I had noticed that this was how most of the women were made up. She held the back of the chair opposite me with both hands and said:

"How goes it, col?"

She sat down.

She was a little drunk, I thought.

"It's boring here," she continued after a moment. "Don't you think so? Shall we take off somewhere, col?"

"I'm not a col . . ." I began. She leaned on the table with her elbows and moved her hand across her half-filled glass, until the end of the golden chain around her fingers dipped into the liquid. She leaned still closer. I could smell her breath. If she was drunk, it was not on alcohol.

"How's that?" she said. "You are. You have to be. Everybody is. What do you say? Shall we?"

If only I knew what all that meant.

"All right," I said.

She stood up. And I got up from my horribly low chair.

"How do you do that?" she asked.

"Do what?"

She stared at my legs.

"I thought you were on your toes. . . ."

I smiled but said nothing. She came up to me, took me by the arm, and was again surprised.

"What have you got there?"

"Where, here? Nothing."

"You're singing," she said and lightly tugged at me. We walked among the tables and I wondered what "singing" meant —perhaps "you're kidding me"?

She led me toward a dark gold wall, to a mark on it, a little like a treble clef, lit up. At our approach the wall opened. I felt a gust of hot air.

A narrow silver escalator flowed down. We stood side by side. She did not even reach my shoulder. She had a catlike head, black hair with a blue sheen, a profile that was perhaps too sharp, but she was pretty. If it were not for those scarlet nostrils . . . She held on to me tightly with her thin hand, the green nails dug into my heavy sweater. I had to smile at the thought of where that sweater had been and how little it had in common with the fingers of a woman. Beneath a circular dome that breathed light—from pink to carmine, from carmine to pink— we went out into the street. That is, I thought it was a street, but the darkness above us was every now and then lit up, as if by a momentary dawn. Farther on, long, low silhouettes sailed past, much like cars, but I knew that there were no more cars. It must have been something else. Even had I been alone, I would have chosen this broad artery, because in the distance blazed the letters TO THE CENTER, although that surely did not mean the center of the city. At any rate, I let myself be led. No matter how this adventure was going to end, I had found myself a guide, and I thought—this time without anger—of that poor fellow who now, three hours after my arrival, was undoubtedly hunting for me through all the infors of this station-city.

We passed a number of half-empty bars, shopwindows in which groups of mannequins were performing the same scene over and over again, and I would have liked to stop and see what they were doing, but the girl hurried along, her slippers clicking, until, at the sight of a neon face with pulsating red cheeks, which continually licked its lips with a comically loose tongue, she cried:

"Oh, bonses! Do you want a bons?"

"Do you?" I asked.

"I think I do."

We entered a small bright room. Instead of a ceiling it had long rows of tiny flames, like pilot lights; from above poured heat, so possibly it was indeed gas. In the walls I saw recesses with counters. When we approached one of these, seats emerged from the wall on either side of us; they seemed first to grow out from the wall in an undeveloped form, like buds, then flattened in the air, turned concave, and became motionless. We sat facing each other; the girl tapped two fingers on the metal surface of the table, and from the wall jumped a nickel claw, which tossed a small plate in front of each of us and with two lightning movements threw on each plate a portion of some white substance that foamed, turned brown, and hardened; meanwhile the plate itself grew darker. The girl then folded it—it was not a plate at all—into the shape of a pancake and began to eat.

"Oh," she said with a full mouth, "I didn't know how hungry I was!"

I did exactly as she. The bons tasted like nothing I had ever eaten. It crackled between the teeth like a freshly baked roll, but immediately crumbled and melted on the tongue; the brown stuff in the middle was sharply seasoned. I was going to like bonses, I decided.

"Another?" I asked, when she had finished hers. She smiled,

shaking her head. On the way out, in the aisle, she put both her hands into a small niche lined with tiles; something in there buzzed. I followed suit. A tickling wind blew on my fingers, and when I withdrew them, they were completely dry and clean. Next we ascended a wide escalator. I did not know if this was still the station but preferred not to ask. She led me to a small cabin inside a wall, not very brightly lit; I had the impression that above it trains of some kind were running, since the floor shook. It got dark for a fraction of a second, something beneath us gave a deep sigh, like a metal monster emptying its lungs of air, the light reappeared, the girl pushed open the door. A real street, apparently. We were quite alone on it. Bushes, trimmed fairly low, grew on either side of the sidewalk; somewhat farther along stood flat black machines, crowded together; a man came out of a shadow, disappeared behind one of the machines—I did not see him open any door, he simply vanished—and the thing took off with such force that it must have flattened him against his seat. I saw no houses, only the roadway, as smooth as a table and covered with strips of dull metal; at the intersections, hanging overhead, were shuttered lights, orange and red; they looked a little like models of wartime searchlights.

"Where shall we go?" asked the girl. She still held me by the arm. She slackened her pace. A red stripe passed across her face.

"Wherever you like."

"My place, then. It isn't worth taking a gleeder. It's nearby." We walked on. Still no houses in sight, and the wind that came rushing out of the darkness, from behind the shrubbery, was the kind you would expect in an open space. Here, around the station, in the Center itself? This seemed odd to me. The wind bore a faint fragrance of flowers, which I inhaled eagerly. Cherry blossom? No, not cherry blossom.

Next we came to a moving walkway; we stood on it, a strange pair; lights swam by; now and then a vehicle shot along, as if cast from a single block of black metal; these vehicles had no windows, no wheels, not even lights, and careered as though blindly, at tremendous speed. The moving lights blazed out of narrow vertical apertures hanging low above the ground. I could not figure out whether they had something to do with the traffic and its regulation.

From time to time, a plaintive whistle high above us rent the unseen sky. The girl suddenly stepped off the flowing ribbon, but only to mount another, which darted steeply upward, and I found myself suddenly high up; this aerial ride lasted maybe half a minute and ended at a ledge covered with weakly fragrant flowers, as if we had reached the terrace or balcony of a dark building by a conveyor belt set against the wall. The girl entered this loggia, and I, my eyes now accustomed to the dark, was able to discern, from it, the huge outlines of the surrounding buildings, windowless, black, seemingly lifeless, for they were without more than light—not the slightest sound reached me, apart from the sharp hiss that announced the passage, in the street, of those black machines. I was puzzled by this blackout, no doubt intentional, as well as by the absence of advertising signs, after the orgy of neon at the station, but I had no time for such reflections. "Come on, where are you?" I heard her whisper. I saw only the pale smudge of her face. She put her hand to the door and it opened, but not into an apartment; the floor moved softly along with us—you can't take a step here, I thought, it's a wonder they still have legs—but this irony was a feeble effort; it came from the constant amazement, from the feeling of unreality of everything that had happened to me in the past several hours.

We were in something like a huge entrance hall or corridor, wide, almost unlit—only the corners of the walls shone, brightened by streaks of luminous paint. In the darkest place the girl again reached out her hand, to place her palm flat against a metal plate on a door, and entered first. I blinked. The hall, brightly lit, was practically empty; she walked to the next door. When I came near the wall, it opened suddenly to reveal an interior filled with small metal bottles of some kind. This happened so suddenly that I froze.

"Don't set off my wardrobe," she said. She was already in the other room.

I followed her.

The furniture—armchairs, a low sofa, small tables—looked as though it had been cast in glass, and inside the semitransparent material swarms of fireflies circulated freely, sometimes dispersed, then joined again into streams, so that a luminous blood seemed to course within the furniture, pale green with pink sparks mixed in.

"Why don't you sit down?"

She was standing far back. An armchair unfolded itself to receive me. I hated that. The glass was not glass at all; the impression I had was of sitting on inflated cushions, and, looking down through the curved, thick surface of the seat, I could, indistinctly, see the floor.

I had thought, upon entering, that the wall opposite the door was of glass, and that through it I was looking into another room, which contained people, as though a party were in progress there; but those people were unnaturally tall—and all at once I realized that what I had in front of me was a wall-sized television screen. The volume was off. Now, from a sitting position, I saw an enormous female face, exactly as if a dark-skinned giantess were peering through a window into the room; her lips moved, she was speaking, and gems as big as shields covered her ears, glittered like diamonds.

I made myself comfortable in the chair. The girl, her hand on her hip—her abdomen really did look like a sculpture in azure metal—studied me carefully. She no longer appeared drunk. Perhaps it had only seemed that way to me before.

"What's your name?" she asked.

"Bregg. Hal Bregg. And yours?"

"Nais. How old are you?"

Curious manners, I thought. But, then, if that's what's done . . .

"Forty—what of it?"

"Nothing. I thought you were a hundred."

I had to smile.

"I can be that, if you insist." The funny thing is, it's the truth, I thought.

"What can I give you?" she asked.

"To drink? Nothing, thank you."

"All right."

She went to the wall, and it opened like a small bar. She stood in front of the opening. When she returned, she was carrying a tray with cups and two bottles. Squeezing one bottle lightly, she filled me a cup to the brim with a liquid that looked exactly like milk.

"Thank you," I said, "not for me . . ."

"But I'm not giving you anything." She was surprised.

Seeing I had made a mistake, although I did not know what kind of mistake, I muttered under my breath and took the cup. She poured herself a drink from the second bottle. This liquid was oily, colorless, and slightly effervescent under the surface; at the same time it darkened, apparently on contact with air. She sat down and, touching the glass with her lips, casually asked:

"Who are you?"

"A col," I answered. I lifted my cup, as if to examine it. This milk had no smell. I did not touch it.

"No, seriously," she said. "You thought I was sending in the dark, eh? Since when! That was only a cals. I was with a six, you see, but it got awfully bottom. The orka was no good and altogether . . . I was just going when you sat down."

Some of this I could figure out: I must have sat at her table by chance, when she was not there; could she have been dancing? I maintained a tactful silence.

"From a distance, you seemed so . . ." She was unable to find the word.

"Decent?" I suggested. Her eyelids fluttered. Did she have a metallic film on them as well? No, it must have been eye shadow. She lifted her head.

"What does that mean?"

"Well . . . um . . . someone you could trust . . ."

"You talk in a strange way. Where are you from?"

"From far away."

"Mars?"

"Farther."

"You fly?"

"I did fly."

"And now?"

"Nothing. I returned."

"But you'll fly again?"

"I don't know. Probably not."

The conversation had trailed off somehow. It seemed to me that the girl was beginning to regret her rash invitation, and I wanted to make things easy for her.

"Maybe I ought to go now?" I asked. I still held my untouched drink.

"Why?" She was surprised.

"I thought that that would . . . suit you."

"No," she said. "You're thinking—no, what for? Why don't you drink?"

"I am."

It was milk after all. At this time of day, in such circumstances! My surprise was such that she must have noticed it.

"What, it's bad?"

"It's milk," I said. I must have looked like a complete idiot.

"What? What milk? That's brit. . . ."

I sighed.

"Listen, Nais . . . I think I'll go now. Really. It will be better that way."

"Then why did you drink?" she asked.

I looked at her, silent. The language had not changed so very much, and yet I didn't understand a thing. Not a thing. It was they who had changed.

"All right," she said finally. "I'm not keeping you. But now this . . ." She was confused. She drank her lemonade—that's what I called the sparkling liquid, in my thoughts—and again I did not know what to say. How difficult all this was.

"Tell me about yourself," I suggested. "Do you want to?"

"OK. And then you'll tell me . . . ?"

"Yes."

"I'm at the Cavuta, my second year. I've been neglecting things a bit lately, I wasn't plasting regularly and . . . that's how it's been. My six isn't too interesting. So really, it's . . . I don't have anyone. It's strange. . . ."

"What is?"

"That I don't have . . ."

Again, these obscurities. Who was she talking about? Who didn't she have? Parents? Lovers? Acquaintances? Abs was right after all when he said that I wouldn't be able to manage without the eight months at Adapt. But now, perhaps even more than before, I did not want to go back, penitent, to school.

"What else?" I asked, and since I was still holding the cup, I took another swallow of that milk. Her eyes grew wide in surprise. Something like a mocking smile touched her lips. She drained her cup, reached out a hand to the fluffy covering on her arms, and tore it—she did not unbutton it, did not slip it off, just tore it, and let the shreds fall from her fingers, like trash.

"But, then, we hardly know each other," she said. She was freer, it seemed. She smiled. There were moments when she became quite lovely, particularly when she narrowed her eyes, and her lower lip, contracting, revealed glistening teeth. In her face was something Egyptian. An Egyptian cat. Hair blacker than black, and when she pulled the furry fluff from her arms and breasts, I saw that she was not nearly so thin as I had thought. But why had she ripped it off? Was that supposed to mean something?

"Your turn to talk," she said, looking at me over her cup.

"Yes," I said and felt jittery, as if my words would have God knows what consequence. "I am . . . I was a pilot. The last time I was here . . . don't be frightened!"

"No. Go on!"

Her eyes were shining and attentive.

"It was a hundred and twenty-seven years ago. I was thirty then. The expedition . . . I was a pilot on the expedition to Fomalhaut. That's twenty-three light years away. We flew there and back in a hundred and twenty-seven years Earth time and ten years ship time. Four days ago we returned. . . . The Prometheus—my ship—remained on Luna. I came from there today. That's all."

She stared at me. She did not speak. Her lips moved, opened, closed. What was that in her eyes? Surprise? Admiration? Fear?

"Why do you say nothing?" I asked. I had to clear my throat.

"So . . . how old are you, really?"

I had to smile; it was not a pleasant smile.

"What does that mean, 'really'? Biologically I'm forty, but by Earth clocks, one hundred and fifty-seven. . . ."

A long silence, then suddenly:

"Were there any women there?"

"Wait," I said. "Do you have anything to drink?"

"What do you mean?"

"Something toxic, you understand. Strong. Alcohol . . . or don't they drink it any more?"

"Very rarely," she replied softly, as if thinking of something else. Her hands fell slowly, touched the metallic blue of her dress.

"I'll give you some . . . angehen, is that all right? But you don't know what it is, do you?"

"No, I don't," I replied, unexpectedly stubborn. She went to the bar and brought back a small, bulging bottle. She poured me a drink. It had alcohol in it—not much—but there was something else, a peculiar, bitter taste.

"Don't be angry," I said, emptying the cup, and poured myself another one.

"I'm not angry. You didn't answer, but perhaps you don't want to?"

"Why not? I can tell you. There were twenty-three of us altogether, on two ships. The second was the *Ulysses*. Five pilots to a ship, and the rest scientists. There were no women."

"Why?"

"Because of children," I explained. "You can't raise children on such ships, and even if you could, no one would want to. You can't fly before you're thirty. You have to have two diplomas under your belt, plus four years of training, twelve years in all. In other words—women of thirty usually have children. And there were . . . other considerations."

"And you?" she asked.

"I was single. They picked unmarried ones. That is—volunteers."

"You wanted to . . ."

"Yes. Of course."

"And you didn't . . ."

She broke off. I knew what she wanted to say. I remained silent.

"It must be weird, coming back like this," she said almost in a whisper. She shuddered. Suddenly she looked at me, her cheeks darkened, it was a blush.

"Listen, what I said before, that was just a joke, really. . . ."

"About the hundred years?"

"I was just talking, just to talk, it had no . . ."

"Stop," I grumbled. "Any more apologizing and I'll really feel all that time."

She was silent. I forced myself to look away from her. Inside that other room, the nonexistent room behind glass, an enormous male head sang without sound; I saw the dark read of the throat quiver at the effort, cheeks glistening, the whole face moving to an inaudible rhythm.

"What will you do?" she asked quietly.

"I don't know. I don't know yet."

"You have no plans?"

"No. I have a little—it's a . . . bonus, you understand. For all that time. When we left, it was put into the bank in my name—I don't even know how much there is. I don't know a thing. Listen, what is this Cavut?"

"The Cavuta?" she corrected me. "It's . . . a sort of school, plasting; nothing great in itself, but sometimes one can get into the reals. . . ."

"Wait . . . then what exactly do you do?"

"Plast. You don't know what that is?"

"No."

"How can I explain? To put it simply, one makes dresses, clothing in general—everything. . . ."

"Tailoring?"

"What does that mean?"

"Do you sew things?"

"I don't understand."

"Ye gods and little fishes! Do you design dresses?"

"Well . . . yes, in a sense, yes. I don't design, I only make . . ."

I gave up.

"And what is a real?"

That truly floored her. For the first time she looked at me as if I were a creature from another world.

"A real is . . . a real . . ." she repeated helplessly. "They are . . . stories. It's for watching."

"That?" I pointed at the glass wall.

"Oh no, that's vision. . . ."

"What, then? Movies? Theater?"

"No. Theater, I know what that was—that was long ago. I know: they had actual people there. A real is artificial, but one can't tell the difference. Unless, I suppose, one got in there, inside . . ."

"Got in?"

The head of the giant rolled its eyes, reeled, looked at me as if it were having great fun, observing this scene.

"Listen, Nais," I said suddenly, "either I'll go now, because it's very late, or . . ."

"I'd prefer the 'or.' "

"But you don't know what I want to say."

"Say it, then."

"All right. I wanted to ask you more about various things. About the big things, the most important, I already know something; I spent four days at Adapt, on Luna. But that was a drop in the bucket. What do you do when you aren't working?"

"One can do a heap of things," she said. "One can travel, actually or by moot. One can have a good time, go to the real, dance, play tereo, do sports, swim, fly—whatever one wants."

"What is a moot?"

"It's a little like the real, except you can touch everything. You can walk on mountains there, on anything—you'll see for yourself, it's not the sort of thing you can describe. But I had the impression you wanted to ask about something else . . . ?"

"Your impression is right. How is it between men and women?"

Her eyelids fluttered.

"I suppose the way it has always been. What can have changed?"

"Everything. When I left—don't take this in bad part—a girl like you would not have brought me to her place at this hour."

"Really? Why not?"

"Because it would have meant only one thing."

She was silent for a moment.

"And how do you know it didn't?"

My expression amused her. I looked at her; she stopped smiling.

"Nais . . . how is it . . . ?" I stammered. "You take a complete stranger and . . ."

She was silent.

"Why don't you answer?"

"Because you don't understand a thing. I don't know how to tell you. It's nothing, you know. . . ."

"Aha. It's nothing," I repeated. I couldn't sit any longer. I got up. I nearly leapt, forgetting myself. She flinched.

"Sorry," I muttered and began to pace. Behind the glass a park stretched out in the morning sunlight; along an alley, among trees with pale pink leaves, walked three youths in shirts that gleamed like armor.

"Are there still marriages?"

"Naturally."

"I don't understand! Explain this to me. Tell me. You see a man who appeals to you, and without knowing him, right away . . ."

"But what is there to tell?" she said reluctantly. "Is it really true that in your day, back then, a girl couldn't let a man into her room?"

"She could, of course, and even with that purpose, but . . . not five minutes after seeing him. . . ."

"How many minutes, then?"

I looked at her. She was quite serious. Well, yes, how was she to know? I shrugged.

"It wasn't a matter of time only. First she had to . . . see something in him, get to know him, like him; first they went out together. . . ."

"Wait," she said. "It seems that you don't understand a thing. After all, I gave you brit."

"What brit? Ah, the milk? What of it?"

"What do you mean, what of it? Was there . . . no brit?"

She began to laugh; she was convulsed with laughter. Then suddenly she broke off, looked at me, and reddened terribly.

"So you thought . . . you thought that I . . . no!"

I sat down. My fingers were unsteady; I wanted to hold something in them. I pulled a cigarette from my pocket and lit it. She opened her eyes.

"What is that?"

"A cigarette. What—you don't smoke?"

"It's the first time I ever saw one. . . . So that's what a cigarette looks like. How can you inhale the smoke like that? No, wait—the other thing is more important. Brit is not milk. I don't know what's in it, but to a stranger one always gives brit."

"To a man?"

"Yes."

"What does it do, then?"

"What it does is make him behave, make him have to. You know . . . maybe some biologist can explain it to you."

"To hell with the biologist. Does this mean that a man to whom you've given brit can't do anything?"

"Naturally."

"What if he doesn't want to drink?"

"How could he not want to?"

Here all understanding ended.

"But you can't force him to drink," I continued patiently.

"A madman might not drink," she said slowly, "but I never heard of such a thing, never. . . ."

"Is this some kind of custom?"

"I don't know what to tell you. Is it a custom that you don't go around naked?"

"Aha. Well, in a sense—yes. But you can undress on the beach."

"Completely?" she asked with sudden interest.

"No. A bathing suit . . . But there were groups of people in my day, they were called nudists. . . ."

"I know. No, that's something else. I thought that you all . . ."

"No. So this drinking is like wearing clothes? Just as necessary?"

"Yes. When there are . . . two of you."

"Well, and afterward?"

"What afterward?"

"The next time?"

This conversation was idiotic and I felt terrible, but I had to find out.

"Later? It varies. To some . . . you always give brit."

"The rejected suitor," I blurted out.

"What does that mean?"

"No, nothing. And if a girl visits a man, what then?"

"Then he drinks it at his place."

She looked at me almost with pity. But I was stubborn.

"And when he doesn't have any?"

"Any brit? How could he not have it?"

"Well, he ran out. Or . . . he could always lie."

She began to laugh.

"But that's . . . you think that I keep all these bottles here, in my apartment?"

"You don't? Where, then?"

"Where they come from, I don't know. In your day, was there tap water?"

"There was," I said glumly. There might not have been. Sure! I could have climbed into the rocket straight from the forest. I was furious for a moment, but I calmed down; it was not, after all, her fault.

"There, you see—did you know in which direction the water flowed before it . . . ?"

"I understand, no need to go on. All right. So it's a kind of safety measure? Very strange!"

"I don't think so," she said. "What do you have there, the white thing under your sweater?"

"A shirt."

"What is that?"

"You never saw a shirt? Sort of, well, clothing. Made of nylon."

I rolled up my sleeve and showed her.

"Interesting," she said.

"It's a custom," I said, at a loss. Actually, they had told me at Adapt to stop dressing in the style of a hundred years ago; I didn't want to. I had to admit, however, that she was right; brit was for me what a shirt was for her. In the final analysis, no one had forced people to wear shirts, but they all had. Evidently, it was the same with brit.

"How long does brit work?" I asked.

She blushed a little.

"You're in such a hurry. You still know nothing."

"I didn't say anything wrong," I defended myself. "I only wanted to know. . . . Why are you looking at me like that? What's the matter with you? Nais!"

She got up slowly. She stood behind the armchair.

"How long ago, did you say? A hundred and twenty years?"

"A hundred and twenty-seven. What about it?"

"And were you . . . betrizated?"

"What is that?"

"You weren't?"

"I don't even know what it means. Nais . . . girl, what's the matter with you?"

"No, you weren't," she whispered. "If you had been, you would know."

I started toward her. She raised her hands.

"Keep away. No! No! I beg you!"

She retreated to the wall.

"But you yourself said that brit . . . I'm sitting now. You see, I'm sitting. Calm yourself. Tell me what it is, this bet . . . or whatever."

"I don't know exactly. But everyone is betrizated. At birth."

"What is it?"

"They put something into the blood, I think."

"To everyone?"

"Yes. Because . . . brit . . . doesn't work without that. Don't move!"

"Child, don't be ridiculous."

I put out my cigarette.

"I am not, after all, a wild animal. Don't be angry, but . . . it seems to me that you've all gone a little mad. This brit . . . well, it's like handcuffing everyone because someone might turn out to be a thief. I mean, there ought to be a little trust."

"You're terrific." She seemed calmer, but still she did not sit. "Then why were you so indignant before, about my bringing home strangers?"

"That's something else."

"I don't see the difference. You're sure you weren't betrizated?"

"I wasn't."

"But maybe now? When you returned?"

"I don't know. They gave me all kinds of shots. Is it so important?"

"It is. They did that? Good."

She sat down.

"I have a favor to ask you," I said as calmly as I could. "You must explain to me . . ."

"What?"

"Your fear. Did you think I would attack you, or what? But that's ridiculous!"

"No. If one looks at it rationally, no, but—it was overwhelming, you see. Such a shock. I never saw a person who was not . . ."

"But surely you can't tell?"

"You can. Oh, you can!"

"How?"

She was silent.

"Nais . . ."

"And if . . ."

"What?"

"I'm afraid."

"To say?"

"Yes."

"But why?"

"You'd understand if I told you. Betrization, you see, isn't done by brit. With the brit, it's only—a side effect. . . . Betrization has to do with something else." She was pale. Her lips trembled. What a world, I thought, what a world this is!

"I can't. I'm terribly afraid."

"Of me?"

"Yes."

"I swear that . . ."

"No, no. I believe you, only . . . no. You can't understand this."

"You won't tell me?"

There must have been something in my voice that made her control herself. Her face became grim. I saw from her eyes the effort it was for her.

"It is . . . so that . . . in order that it be impossible to . . . kill."

"No! People?"

"Anyone."

"Animals, too?"

"Animals. Anyone."

She twisted and untwisted her fingers, not taking her eyes off me, as if with these words she had released me from an invisible chain, as if she had put a knife into my hand, a knife I could stab her with.

"Nais," I said very quietly. "Nais, don't be afraid. Really, there's nothing to fear."

She tried to smile.

"Listen. . . ."

"Yes?"

"When I said that . . ."

"Yes?"

"You felt nothing?"

"And what was I supposed to feel?"

"Imagine that you are doing what I said to you."

"That I am killing? I'm supposed to picture that?"
She shuddered.

"Yes."

"And now?"

"And you feel nothing?"

"Nothing. But, then, it's only a thought, and I don't have the slightest intention . . ."

"But you can? Right? You really can? No," she whispered, as if to herself, "you are not betrizated."

Only now did the meaning of it all hit me, and I understood how it could be a shock to her.

"This is a great thing," I muttered. After a moment, I added, "But it would have been better, perhaps, had people ceased to do it . . . without artificial means."

"I don't know. Perhaps," she answered. She drew a deep breath. "You know, now, why I was frightened?"

"Yes, but not completely. Maybe a little. But surely you didn't think that I . . ."

"How strange you are! It's altogether as though you weren't . . ." She broke off.

"Weren't human?"
Her eyelids fluttered.

"I didn't mean to offend you. It's just that, you see, if it is known that no one can—you know—even think about it, ever, and suddenly someone appears, like you, then the very possibility . . . the fact that there is one who . . ."

"I can't believe that everyone would be—what was it?—ah, betrizated!"

"Why? Everyone, I tell you!"

"No, it's impossible," I insisted. "What about people with dangerous jobs? After all, they must . . ."

"There are no dangerous jobs."

"What are you saying, Nais? What about pilots? And various rescue workers? And those who fight fire, floods . . . ?"

"There are no such people," she said. It seemed to me that I had not heard her right.

"What?"

"No such people," she repeated. "All that is done by robots."

There was silence. It would not be easy for me, I thought, to stomach this new world. And suddenly came a reflection, surprising in that I myself would never have expected it if someone had presented me with this situation purely as a theoretical possibility: it occurred to me that this destruction of the killer in man was a disfigurement.

"Nais," I said, "it's already very late. I think I'll go."

"Where?"

"I don't know. Hold on! A person from Adapt was supposed to meet me at the station. I completely forgot! I couldn't find him, you understand. So I'll look for a hotel. There are hotels?"

"There are. Where are you from?"

"Here. I was born here."

With these words the feeling of the unreality of everything returned, and I was no longer certain either of that city, which existed only within me, or of this spectral one with rooms into which the heads of giants peered, so that for a second I wondered if I might not be on board and dreaming yet another particularly vivid nightmare of my return.

"Bregg." I heard her voice as if from a distance. I started. I had completely forgotten about her.

"Yes?"

"Stay."

"What?"

She did not speak.

"You want me to stay?"

She did not speak. I went up to her, bent over the chair, took hold of her by her cold arms, and lifted her up. She stood submissively. Her head fell back, I saw her teeth glistening; I did not want her, I wanted only to say, "But you're afraid," and for her to say that she was not. Nothing more. Her eyes were closed, but suddenly the whites shone from underneath her lashes; I bent over her face, looked closely into her glassy eyes, as though I wished to know her fear, to share it. Panting, she struggled to break loose, but I did not feel it, it was only when she began to groan "No! No!" that I slackened my grip. She practically fell. She stood against the wall, blocking out part of a huge, chubby face that reached the ceiling, that there, behind the glass, spoke endlessly, with exaggeration, moving its huge lips and meaty tongue.

"Nais . . ." I said quietly. I dropped my hands.

"Don't come near me!"

"But it was you who said . . ."

Her eyes were wild.

I paced the room. She followed me with her eyes, as if I were . . . as if she stood in a cage. . . .

"I'm going now," I announced. She did not speak. I wanted to add something—a few words of apology, of thanks, so as not to leave this way—but I couldn't. Had she been afraid only as a woman is of a man, a strange, even threatening, unknown man, then I wouldn't have given a damn; but this was something else. I looked at her and felt anger growing in me. To grab those naked white arms and shake her . . .

I turned and left. The outer door yielded when I pushed it; the large corridor was almost completely dark. I was unable to find the exit to that terrace, but I did come upon cylinders filled with an attenuated bluish light—elevators. The one I approached was already on its way up; maybe the pressure of my foot on the threshold was enough. The elevator took a long time going down. I saw alternating layers of darkness, and the cross sections of ceilings; white with reddish centers, like fat on muscle, they passed upward, I lost count of them; the elevator fell, fell, it was like a journey to the bottom, as if I had been thrown down a sterile conduit, and this colossal building, deep in its sleep and security, was ridding itself of me. A part of the transparent cylinder opened, I began walking.

Hands in pockets, darkness, a hard long stride, greedily I inhaled the cool air, feeling the movement of my nostrils, my heart working slowly, pumping blood; lights flickered in the low apertures over the road, covered from time to time by the noiseless machines; there was not one pedestrian. Between black silhouettes was a glow, which I thought might be a hotel. It was only an illuminated walkway. I took it. Above me the whitish spans of structures sailed by; somewhere in the distance, above the black edges of the buildings, tripped the steadily shining letters of the news; suddenly the walkway took me into a lighted interior and came to an end.

Wide steps ran down, silvery like a mute waterfall. The desolation surprised me; since leaving Nais, I had not encountered a single passer-by. The escalator was very long. A wide street gleamed below, on either side opened passageways in buildings; beneath a tree with blue leaves—but possibly it was not a real tree—I saw people standing; I approached them, then walked away. They were kissing. I walked toward the muffled sound of music, some all-night restaurant or bar not set off from the street. A few people were sitting there. I wanted to go inside and ask about a hotel. Suddenly I crashed, with my whole body, into an invisible barrier. It was a sheet of glass, perfectly transparent. The entrance was nearby. Inside, someone began laughing and pointed me out to others. I went in. A man in a black undershirt that was actually somewhat similar to my sweater but with a full, inflated collar sat sideways at a table, a glass in his hand, and looked at me. I stopped in front of him. The smile froze on his half-open mouth. I stood still. There was a hush. Only the music played, as though from behind the wall. A woman made a strange, weak noise. I looked around at the motionless faces and left. Not until I was out on the street did I remember that I had intended to ask about a hotel.

I entered a mall. It was filled with displays. Tourist offices, sports shops, mannequins in different poses. These were not exactly displays, for everything stood and lay in the street, on either side of the raised walkway that ran down the middle. Several times I mistook the figures moving within for people. They were puppets, for advertising, performing a single action over and over again. For a while I watched one—a doll almost as large as myself, a caricature with puffed-out cheeks, playing a flute. It did this so well that I had the impulse to call out to it. Farther along were halls for games of some kind; large rainbow wheels revolved, silver pipes hanging loosely from the ceiling struck one another with the sound of sleigh bells, prismatic mirrors glittered, but everything was deserted. At the very end of the mall, in the darkness, flashed a sign: HERE HAHAHA. It disappeared. I went toward it. Again the HERE HAHAHA lit up and disappeared as if blown out. In the next flash I saw an entrance. I heard voices. I entered through a curtain of warm, moving air.

Inside stood two of the wheelless cars; a few lamps shone, and under them three people gesticulated heatedly, as if quarreling. I went up to them.

"Hello!"

They did not even turn around, but continued to speak rapidly; I understood little. "Then sap, then sap," piped the shortest, who had a potbelly. On his head he wore a tall cap.

"Gentlemen, I'm looking for a hotel. Where is there . . . ?"

They paid no attention to me, as if I did not exist. I got furious. Without a word I stepped in their midst. The one nearest me—I saw stupid eyes, whites shining, and trembling lips—lisped:

"I should sap? Sap yourself!"

Just as if he were talking to me.

"Why do you play deaf?" I asked, and suddenly, from the spot where I stood—as if from me, from out of my chest—came a shrill cry:

"I'll show you. So help me!"

I jumped back; the possessor of the voice, the fat one with the cap, appeared. I went to grab him by the arm, but my fingers passed clean through him and closed on air. I stood dumbstruck, and they prattled on; suddenly it seemed to me that from the darkness above the cars, from high up, someone was watching me. I went closer to the edge of the light and saw the pale blotches of faces; there was something like a balcony up there. Blinded by the light, I could not see much; enough, however, to realize what a terrible fool I had made of myself. I fled as if someone were at my heels. The next street headed up and ended at an escalator. I thought that maybe there I would find an infor, and got on the pale gold stairs. I found myself in a circular plaza, fairly small. In the center rose a column, high, transparent as glass; something danced in it, purple, brown, and violet shapes, unlike anything I knew, like abstract sculptures come to life, but very amusing. First one color and then another swelled, became concentrated, took shape in a highly comical way; this melee of forms, although devoid of faces, heads, arms, legs, was very human in character, like a caricature, even. After a while I saw that the violet was a buffoon, conceited, overbearing, and at the same time cowardly; when it burst into a million dancing bubbles, the blue set to work, angelic, modest, collected, but somehow sanctimonious, as if praying to itself. I do not know how long I watched. I had never seen anything remotely like it. Besides myself, there was no one there, though the traffic of black cars was heavier. I did not even know if they were occupied or not, since they had no windows. Six streets led from the circular plaza, some up, some down; they extended far, it seemed, in a delicate mosaic of colored lights. No infor. By now I was exhausted, not only physically—I felt that I could not take in any more impressions. Occasionally, walking, I lost track of things, although I did not doze at all; I do not recall how or when I entered a wide avenue; at an intersection I slackened my pace, lifted my head, and saw the glow of the city on the clouds. I was surprised, for I had thought that I was underground. I went on, now in a sea of moving lights, of displays without glass fronts, among gesticulating mannequins that spun like tops, that furiously did gymnastics; they handed one another shining objects, were inflating something—but I did not even look in their direction. In the distance several people were walking; I was not sure, however, that they were not dolls, and did not try to catch up with them. The buildings parted, and I caught sight of a huge sign—TERMINAL PARK—and a shining green arrow.

An escalator began in the space between the buildings, suddenly entered a tunnel, silver with a gold pulse in the walls, as though underneath the mercury mask of the walls the noble metal truly flowed; I felt a hot gust, everything went out—I stood in a glass pavilion. It was in the shape of a shell, with a ribbed ceiling that glimmered a barely perceptible green; the light was from delicate veins, like the luminescence of a single giant trembling leaf. Doors opened in all directions; beyond them darkness and small letters, moving along the floor: TERMINAL PARK TERMINAL PARK.

I went outside. It was indeed a park. The trees rustled incessantly, invisible in the gloom. I felt no wind; it must have been blowing higher up, and the voice of the trees, steady, stately, encompassed me in an invisible arch. For the first time I felt alone, but not as in a crowd, for the feeling was agreeable. There must have been a number of people in the park: I heard whispers, occasionally the blur of a face shone, once I even brushed by someone. The crowns of the trees came together, so that the stars were visible only through their branches. I recalled that to reach the park I had ridden up, yet back there, in the plaza with the dancing colors and where the streets were filled with displays, I had had a cloudy sky over me; how, then, did it happen that now, a level higher, the sky I was seeing was starry? I could not account for this.

The trees parted, and before I saw the water, I smelled it, the odor of mud, of rotting, or sodden leaves; I froze.

Brushwood formed a black circle around the lake. I could hear the rustling of rushes and reeds, and in the distance, on the other side, rose, in a single immensity, a mountain of luminous, glassy rock, a translucent massif above the plains of the night; spectral radiance issued from the vertical cliffs, pale, bluish, bastion upon bastion, crystal battlements, chasms—and this shining colossus, impossible and unbelievable, was reflected in a long, paler copy on the black waters of the lake. I stood, dumbstruck and enraptured; the wind brought faint, fading echoes of music, and, straining my eyes, I could see the tiers and horizontal terraces of the giant. It came to me in a flash that for the second time I was seeing the station, the mighty Terminal in which I had wandered the day before, and that perhaps I was even looking from the bottom of the dark expanse that had puzzled me so in the place where I met Nais.

Was this still architecture, or mountain-building? They must have understood that in going beyond certain limits they had to abandon symmetry and regularity of form, and learn from what was largest—intelligent students of the planet!

I went around the lake. The colossus seemed to lead me with its motionless, luminous ascent. Yes, it took courage to design such a shape, to give it the cruelty of the precipice, the stubbornness and harshness of crags, peaks, but without falling into mechanical imitation, without losing anything, without falsifying. I returned to the wall of trees. The blue of the Terminal, pale against the black sky, still showed through the branches, then finally disappeared, hidden by the thicket. With my hands I pushed aside the twigs; brambles pulled at my sweater, scraped the legs of my trousers; the dew, shaken from above, fell like rain in my face; I took a few leaves in my mouth and chewed them; they were young, bitter; for the first time since my return, I felt that I no longer desired, was looking for, was in need of a single thing; it was enough to walk blindly forward through this darkness, in the rustling brush. Had I imagined it thus, ten years before?

The shrubbery parted. A winding path. Gravel crunched beneath my feet, shining faintly; I preferred darkness but walked on straight ahead to a stone circle, where a human figure stood. I do not know where the light that bathed it came from; the place was deserted, around it were benches, seats, an overturned table, and sand, loose and deep; I felt my feet sink into it and found it was warm, despite the coolness of the night.

Beneath a dome supported by cracked, crumbling columns stood a woman, as though she had been waiting for me. I saw her face now, the flow of sparks in the diamond disks that hid her ears, the white—in the shadow, silvery—dress. This was not possible. A dream? I was still a few dozen paces from her when she began to sing. Among the unseen trees her voice was weak, childlike almost, I could not make out the words, perhaps there were no words. Her mouth was half open, as if she were drinking, no sign of effort on her face, nothing but a stare, as though she had seen something, something impossible to see, and it was of this that she sang. I was afraid that she might see me, I walked more and more slowly. I was already in the ring of brightness that surrounded the stone circle. Her voice grew stronger, she summoned the darkness, pleaded, unmoving; her arms hung as if she had forgotten she had them, as if she now had nothing but a voice and lost herself in it, as if she had cast off everything, relinquished it, and was saying farewell, knowing that with the last, dying sound more than the song would end. I had not known that such a thing was possible. She fell silent, and still I heard her voice; suddenly light footsteps pounded behind me; a girl ran toward the singer, pursued by someone; with a short, throaty laugh she flew up the steps and ran clean through the singer—then hurried on; the one who was chasing her burst out in front of me, a dark outline; they disappeared, I heard once more the teasing laugh of the girl and stood like a block of wood, rooted in the sand, not knowing whether I should laugh or cry; the nonexistent singer hummed something softly. I did not want to listen. I went off into the darkness with a numb face, like a child who has been shown the falseness of a fairy tale. It had been a kind of profanation. I walked, and her voice pursued me. I made a turn, the path continued, I saw faintly gleaming hedges, wet bunches of leaves hung over a metal gate. I opened it. There was more light behind it. The hedges ended in a wide clearing, from the grass jutted boulders, one of which moved, increased in size; I looked into two pale flames of eyes. I stopped. It was a lion. He lifted himself up heavily, the front first. I saw all of him now, five paces from me; he had a thin, matted mane; he stretched, once, twice; with a slow undulation of his shoulders he approached me, not making the slightest sound. But I had recovered. "There, there, be nice," I said. He couldn't be real—a phantom, like the singer, like the ones down by the black cars—he yawned, one step away, in the dark cavern there was a flash of fangs, he shut his jaws with the snap of a gate bolted, I caught the stench of his breath, what . . .

He snorted. I felt drops of his saliva, and before I had time to be terrified he butted me in the hip with his huge head, he rubbed against me, purring; I felt an idiotic tickling in my chest. . . .

He presented his lower throat, the loose, heavy skin. Semiconscious, I began to scratch him, stroke him, and he purred louder; behind him flashed another pair of eyes, another lion, no, a lioness, who shouldered him aside. There was a rumbling in his throat, a purr, not a roar. The lioness persisted. He struck her with a paw. She snorted furiously.

This will end badly, I thought. I was defenseless, and the lions were as alive, as authentic, as one could imagine. I stood in the heavy fetor of their bodies. The lioness kept snorting; suddenly the lion tore his rough shag from my hands, turned his enormous head toward her, and thundered; she fell flat on the ground.

I must be going now, I told them voicelessly, with my lips only. I began to back off in the direction of the gate, slowly; it was not a pleasant moment, but he seemed not to notice me. He lay down heavily, again resembling an elongated boulder; the lioness stood over him and nudged him with her snout.

When I closed the gate behind me, it was all I could do to keep from running. My knees were a bit weak, and my mouth was dry, and suddenly my throat-clearing turned to mad laughter. I recalled how I had spoken to the lion, "There, there, be nice," convinced that he was only an illusion.

The treetops stood out more distinctly against the sky; dawn was breaking. I was glad of this, because I did not know how to get out of the park. It was now completely empty. I passed the stone circle where the singer had appeared; in the next avenue I came upon a robot mowing the lawn. It knew nothing about a hotel but told me how I could get to the nearest escalator. I rode down several levels, I think, and, getting off on the street at the bottom, was surprised to see the sky above me again. But my capacity for surprise was pretty well exhausted. I had had enough. I walked awhile. I remember that later I sat by a fountain, though perhaps it was not a fountain; I got up, walked on in the spreading light of the new day, until I woke from my stupor in front of large, glowing windows and the fiery letters ALCARON HOTEL.

In the doorkeeper's box, which was like a giant's overturned bathtub, sat a robot, beautifully styled, semitransparent, with long, delicate arms. Without asking a thing, it passed me the guest book; I signed it and rode up, holding a small, triangular ticket. Someone—I have no idea who—helped me open the door or, rather, did it for me. Walls of ice; and in them, circulating fires; beneath the window, at my approach, a chair emerged from nothing, slid under me; a flat tabletop had begun to descend, making a kind of desk, but it was a bed that I wanted. I could not find one and did not even attempt to look. I lay down on the foamy carpet and immediately fell asleep in the artificial light of the windowless room, for what I had at first taken to be a window turned out to be, of course, a television, so that I drifted off with the knowledge that from there, from behind the glass plate, some giant face was grimacing at me, meditating over me, laughing, chattering, babbling. . . . I was delivered by a sleep like death; in it, even time stood still.

TWO

My eyes still closed, I touched my chest; I had my sweater on; if I'd fallen asleep without undressing, then I was on watch duty. "Olaf!" I wanted to say, and sat up suddenly.

This was a hotel, not the *Prometheus*. I remembered it all: the labyrinths of the station, the girl, my initiation, her fear, the bluish cliff of the Terminal above the black lake, the singer, the lions. . . .

Looking for the bathroom, I accidentally found the bed; it was in a wall and fell in a bulging pearly square when something was pressed. In the bathroom there was no tub or sink, nothing, only shining plates in the ceiling and a small depression for the feet, padded with a spongy plastic. It did not look like a shower, either. I felt like a Neanderthal. I quickly undressed, then stood with my clothes in my hands, since there were no hangers; there was instead a small compartment in the wall, and I tossed everything into it. Nearby, three buttons, blue, red, and white. I pushed the white. The light went off. The red. There was a rushing sound, but it was not water, only a powerful wind, blowing ozone and something else; it enveloped me; thick, glittering droplets settled on my skin; they effervesced and evaporated, I did not even feel moisture, it was like a swarm of soft electrodes massaging my muscles. I tried the blue button and the wind changed; now it seemed to go right through me, a very peculiar feeling. I thought that once a person became used to this, he would come to enjoy it. At Adapt on Luna they didn't have this—they had only ordinary bathrooms. I wondered why. My blood was circulating more strongly, I felt good; the only problem was that I did not know how to brush my teeth or with what. I gave up on that in the end. In the wall was still another door, with the sign "Bathrobes" on it. I looked inside. No robes, just three metal bottles, a little like siphons. But by that time I was completely dry and did not need to rub myself down.

I opened the compartment into which I had put my clothes and received a shock: it was empty. A good thing I had put my shorts on the top of the compartment. Wearing my shorts, I went back into the room and looked for a telephone, to find out what had happened to my clothes. A predicament. I discovered the telephone, finally, by the window—in my mind I still called the television screen the window—it leapt from the wall when I began to curse out loud, reacting, I guess, to the sound of my voice. An idiotic mania for hiding things in walls. The receptionist answered. I asked about my clothes.

"You placed them in the laundry," said a soft baritone. "They will be ready in five minutes."

Fair enough, I thought. I sat near the desk, the top of which obligingly moved under my elbow the moment I leaned forward. How did that work? No need to concern myself; the majority of people benefit from the technology of their civilization without understanding it.

I sat naked, except for my shorts, and considered the possibilities. I could go to Adapt. If it were only an introduction to the technology and the customs, I would not have hesitated, but I had noticed on Luna that they tried at the same time to instill particular approaches, even judgments of phenomena; in other words, they started off with a prepared scale of values, and if one did not adopt them, they attributed this—and, in general, everything—to conservatism, subconscious resistance, ingrained habits, and so on. I had no intention of giving up such habits and resistance until I was convinced that what they were offering me was better, and my lessons of the previous night had done nothing to change my mind. I didn't want nursery school or rehabilitation, certainly not with such politeness and not right away. Curious, that they had not given me that betrization. I would have to find out why.

I could look for one of us; for Olaf. That would be in clear contravention of the recommendations of Adapt. Ah, because they never ordered; they repeated continually that they were acting in my best interest, that I could do what I liked, even jump straight from the Moon to Earth (jocular Dr. Abs) if I was in such a hurry. I was choosing to ignore Adapt, but that might not suit Olaf. In any case I would write him. I had his address.

Work. Try to get a job? As what, a pilot? And make Mars-Earth-Mars runs? I was an expert at that sort of thing, but . . .

Suddenly I remembered that I had some money. It wasn't exactly money, for it was called something else, but I failed to see the difference, inasmuch as everything could be obtained with it. I asked the receptionist for a city connection. In the receiver, a distant singing. The telephone had no numbers, no dial; would I need to give the name of the bank? I had it written on a card; the card was with my clothes. I looked into the bathroom, and there they lay in the compartment, freshly laundered; in the pockets were my odds and ends, including the card.

The bank was not a bank—it was called Omnilox. I said the name, and, quickly, as if my call had been expected, a rough voice responded:

"Omnilox here."

"My name is Bregg," I said, "Hal Bregg, and I understand that I have an account with you. . . . I would like to know how much is in it."

Something crackled, and another, higher, voice said:

"Hal Bregg?"

"Yes."

"Who opened the account?"

"Cosnav—Cosmic Navigation—by order of the Planetological Institute and the Cosmic Affairs Commission of the United Nations, but that was a hundred and twenty-seven years ago."

"Do you have any identification?"

"No, only a card from Adapt on Luna, from Director Oswamm . . ."

"That's in order. The state of the account: twenty-six thousand, four hundred and seven ets."

"Ets?"

"Yes. Do you require anything further?"

"I would like to withdraw a little mon—some ets, that is."

"In what form? Perhaps you would like a calster?"

"What is that? A checkbook?"

"No. You will be able to pay cash right away."

"Yes. Good."

"How high should the calster be?"

"I really don't know—five thousand. . . ."

"Five thousand. Good. Should it be sent to your hotel?"

"Yes. Wait—I've forgotten the name of this hotel."

"Is it not the one from which you are calling?"

"It is."

"That is the Alcaron. We will send you the calster right away. But there is one more thing: your right hand has not changed, has it?"

"No. Why?"

"Nothing. If it had, we would need to change the calster. You will receive it very soon."

"Thank you," I said, putting down the receiver. Twenty-six thousand, how much was that? I did not have the faintest idea. Something began to hum. A radio? It was the phone. I picked up the receiver.

"Bregg?"

"Yes," I said. My heart beat stronger, but only for a moment. I recognized her voice. "How did you know where I was?" I asked, for she did not speak immediately.

"From an infor. Bregg . . . Hal . . . listen, I wanted to explain to you. . . ."

"There is nothing to explain, Nais."

"You're angry. But try to understand. . . ."

"I'm not angry."

"Hal, really. Come over to my place today. You'll come?"

"No, Nais; tell me, please—how much is twenty-six thousand ets?"

"What do you mean, how much? Hal, you have to come."

"Well . . . how long can one live on that much?"

"As long as you like. Living costs nothing, after all. But let's forget about that. Hal, if you wanted to . . ."

"Wait. How many ets do you spend in a month?"

"It varies. Sometimes twenty, sometimes five, or nothing."

"Aha. Thank you."

"Hal! Listen!"

"I'm listening."

"Let's not end it this way. . . ."

"We're not ending a thing," I said, "because nothing ever began. Thanks for everything, Nais."

I put down the receiver. Living costs nothing? That interested me most at the moment. Did that mean that there were some things, some services, free of charge?

The telephone again.

"Bregg here."

"This is reception. Mr. Bregg, Omnilox has sent you a calster. I am sending it up."

"Thank you—hello!"

"Yes?"

"Does one pay for a room?"

"No, sir."

"Nothing?"

"Nothing, sir."

"And is there a restaurant in the hotel?"

"Yes, there are four. Do you wish to have breakfast in your room?"

"All right, and . . . does one pay for meals?"

"No, sir. You now have the calster. Breakfast will be served in a moment."

The robot hung up, and I did not have time to ask where I was supposed to look for the calster. I had no idea what it looked like. Getting up from the desk, which, abandoned, immediately shrank and shriveled up, I saw a kind of stand growing out of the wall next to the door; on it lay a flat object wrapped in transparent plastic and resembling a small cigarette case. On one side it had a row of little windows, in them showed the number 1100 1000. At the bottom were two tiny buttons labeled "1" and "0." I looked at it, puzzled, until I realized that the sum of five thousand had been entered in the binary system. I pressed the "1" and a small plastic triangle with the number 1 stamped on it fell into my hand. This, then, was a kind of stamping machine or press for money, up to the amount indicated in the windows—the number at the top decreased by a unit.

I was dressed and ready to leave when I remembered about Adapt. I phoned and told them that I had been unable to find their man at the Terminal.

"We were getting worried about you," said a woman's voice, "but we learned this morning that you were staying at the Alcaron. . . ."

They knew where I was. Why, then, had they not found me at the station? Planned that way, no doubt. I was supposed to get lost, so as to realize how rash my "rebellion" on Luna had been.

"Your information is correct," I replied politely. "At present I am going out to see the city. I'll report to you later."

I left the room; corridors flowed, silver and in motion, and the wall along with them—something new to me. I took an escalator down and on successive floors passed bars; one of them was green, as if submerged in water; each level had its own dominant color, silver, gold, already this had begun to annoy me. And after a single day! Odd that they liked it. Strange tastes. But then I recalled the view of the Terminal at night.

I needed to get myself some clothes. With that decision I stepped out into the street. The sky was overcast, but the clouds were bright, high up, and the sun shone through them occasionally. Only now did I see—from the boulevard, down the center of which ran a double line of huge palms with leaves as pink as tongues—a panorama of the city. The buildings stood like islands, set apart, and here and there a spire soared to the heavens, a frozen jet of some liquid material, its height incredible. They were no doubt measured in whole kilometers. I knew— someone had told me back on Luna—that no one built them any more and that the rush to construct tall buildings had died a natural death soon after these had been put up. They were monuments to a particular architectural epoch, since, apart from their immensity, offset only by their slimness of form, there was nothing in them to appeal to the eye. They looked like pipes, brown and gold, black and white, transversely striped, or silver, serving to support or trap the clouds, and the landing pads that jutted out from them against the sky, hanging in the air on tubular supports, were reminiscent of bookshelves.

Much more attractive were the new buildings, without windows, so that all their walls could be decorated. The entire city took on the appearance of a gigantic art exhibit, a showcase for masters of color and form. I cannot say that I liked everything that adorned those twenty- and thirty-floor heights, but for a hundred-and-fifty-year-old character I was not, I dare say, overly stuffy. To my mind the most attractive were the buildings divided in half by gardens. Maybe they were not houses—the fact that the structures were cut in the middle and seemed to rest on cushions of air (the walls of those high-level gardens being of glass) gave an impression of lightness; at the same time pleasantly irregular belts of ruffled green cut across the edifices.

On the boulevards, along those lines of fleshlike palms, which I definitely did not like, flowed two rivers of black automobiles. I knew now that they were called gleeders. Above the buildings flew other machines, though not helicopters or planes; they looked like pencils sharpened at both ends.

On the walkways were a few people, but not as many as there had been in the city a hundred years earlier. There had been a marked easing of traffic, pedestrian especially, perhaps because of the multiplication of levels, for beneath the city that I had seen spread successive, lower, subterranean tiers, with streets, squares, stores—a corner infor told me, for example, that it was best to shop at the Serean level. It was a first-rate infor, or maybe by now I was expressing myself better, because it gave me a little plastic book with four fold-outs, maps of the city's transit system. When I wanted to go somewhere, I touched the silver-printed name—street, level, square—and instantly on the map a circuit of all the necessary connections lit up. I could also travel by gleeder. Or by rast. Or—finally—on foot; therefore, four maps. But I realized now that traveling on foot (even with the moving walkways and escalators) often took many hours.

Serean, unless I was mistaken, was the third level. And again the city astounded me: coming out of the tunnel, I found myself not underground but on a street beneath the open sky, in the full light of the sun; in the center of a square grew great pines, farther off the striped spires took on a blue tint, and, in the other direction, behind a small pool in which children were splashing, riding the water with colorful little bikes, there stood a white skyscraper, cut by palm-green bands and with a most peculiar caplike structure, shining like glass, on its summit. I regretted that there was no one I could ask about this curiosity; then suddenly I remembered—or, rather, my stomach reminded me—that I had not eaten breakfast, for I had completely forgotten that it was to be sent to my room at the hotel, and I had left without waiting for it. Perhaps the robot at reception had made a mistake.

Back, then, to the infor; I no longer did anything without first checking out exactly what and how, and in any event the infor could also reserve a gleeder for me, although I was not about to ask for one yet, since I did not know how to get inside the thing, let alone what to do after that; but I had time.

In the restaurant, one look at the menu and I saw that it was complete Greek to me. I firmly asked for breakfast, a normal breakfast.

"Ozote, kress, or herma?"

Had the waiter been human, I would have asked him to bring what he himself preferred, but it was a robot. It could not matter to a robot.

"Is there coffee?" I asked uneasily.

"There is. Kress, ozote, or herma?"

"Coffee, and . . . well, whatever goes best with coffee, that, uh . . ."

"Ozote" it said and went away.

Success.

It must have had everything prepared, for it returned immediately, and with such a heavily loaded tray that I supected some trick or joke. But the sight of the tray made me realize, apart from the bons I had eaten the day before, and a cup of the notorious brit, I had eaten nothing since my return.

The only familiar thing was the coffee, which was like boiled tar. The cream was in tiny blue specks and definitely came from no cow. I wished I could have observed someone, to see how to eat all this, but apparently the time for breakfast was over, because I was alone. Small plates, crescent-shaped, contained steaming masses from which protruded things like matchsticks, and in the middle was a baked apple; not an apple, of course, and not matchsticks, and what I took for oatmeal began to rise at the touch of a spoon. I ate everything; I was, it turned out, ravenous, so that the nostalgia for bread (of which there was not a trace) came to me only later, as an afterthought, when the robot appeared and waited at a distance.

"What do I pay?" I asked it.

"Nothing, thank you," it said. It was more a piece of furniture than a mannequin. It had one round eye of crystal. Something moved about inside, but I could not bring myself to peer into its stomach. There was not even anyone for me to tip. I doubted that it would understand me if I asked it for a paper; perhaps there were none now. So I went out shopping. But first I found the travel agency—a revelation. I went in.

The large hall, silver with emerald consoles (I was getting tired of these colors), was practically empty. Frosted-glass windows, enormous color photographs of the Grand Canyon, the Crater of Archimedes, the cliffs of Deimos, Palm Beach, Florida —done in such a way that, looking at them, one had the impression of depth, and even the waves of the ocean moved, as if these were not photographs but windows opening onto actual scenes. I went to the counter with the sign EARTH.

Sitting there, of course, was a robot. This time a gold one. Rather, gold-sprinkled.

"What can we do for you?" it asked, It had a deep voice. If I closed my eyes, I could have sworn that the speaker was a muscular, dark-haired man.

"I want something primitive," I said. "I've just returned from a long journey, a very long one. I don't want too much comfort. I want peace and quiet, water, trees, there could be mountains, too. Only it should be primitive and old-fashioned. Like a hundred years ago. Do you have anything like that?"

"If you desire it, we must have it. The Rocky Mountains. Fort Plumm. Majorca. The Antilles."

"Something closer," I said. "Yes . . . within a radius of a thousand kilometers. Is there anything?"

"Clavestra."

"Where is that?"

I had noticed that I had no difficulty conversing with robots, because absolutely nothing surprised them. They were incapable of surprise. A very sensible quality.

"An old mining settlement near the Pacific. The mines have not been in use for almost four hundred years. Interesting excursions on walkways underground. Convenient ulder and gleeder connections. Rest homes with medical care, villas to rent, with gardens, swimming pools, climate conditioning; our local office organizes all kinds of activities, excursions, games, social gatherings. Also available—real, moot, and stereon."

"Yes, that might suit me," I said. "A villa with a garden. And there has to be water. A swimming pool, you said?"

"Naturally, sir. A swimming pool with diving boards. There are also artificial lakes with underwater caves, a well-equipped facility for divers, underwater shows. . . ."

"Never mind about the shows. What does it cost?"

"A hundred and twenty ets a month. But if you share with another party, only forty."

"Share?"

"The villas are very spacious, sir. From twelve to eighteen rooms—automatic service, cooking done on the premises, local or exotic, whichever you prefer . . ."

"Yes. I just might . . . all right. My name is Bregg. I'll take it. What is the name of the place? Clavestra? Do I pay now?"

"As you wish."

I handed it my calster.

It turned out that only I could operate the calster, but the robot was not in the least surprised by my ignorance. More and more I was beginning to like them. It showed me what I had to do so that only one disc, with the correct number stamped on it, came out. The numbers in the windows at the top were reduced by the same amount, showing the balance of the account.

"When can I go there?"

"Whenever you wish. At any moment."

"But—with whom am I sharing the villa?"

"The Margers. He and she."

"Can you tell me what sort of people they are?"

"Only that they are a young married couple."

"Hm. And I won't disturb them?"

"No. Half of the villa is up for rent, and you will have an entire floor to yourself."

"Good. How do I get there?"

"By ulder would be best."

"How do I do that?"

"I will have the ulder for you on the day and hour you designate."

"I'll phone from my hotel. Is that possible?"

"Certainly, sir. The payment will be reckoned from the moment you enter the villa."

When I left, I already had the vague outline of a plan. I would buy books and some sports equipment. Most important were the books. I should also subscribe to some specialized journals. Sociology, physics. No doubt a mass of things had been done in the past hundred years. And yes, I had to buy myself some clothes.

But again I was sidetracked. Turning a corner, I saw—I didn't believe my eyes—a car. A real car. Perhaps not exactly as I remembered it: the body was designed all in sharp angles. It was, however, a genuine automobile, with tires, doors, a steering wheel, and behind it stood others. Behind a large window; on it, in big letters: ANTIQUES. I went inside. The owner, or salesman, was a human. A pity, I thought.

"May I buy a car?"

"Of course. Which one would you like?"

"Do they cost much?"

"From four hundred to eight hundred ets."

Stiff, I thought. Well, antiques weren't cheap.

"And can one travel in it?" I asked.

"Naturally. Not everywhere, true—there are local restrictions —but in general it's possible."

"And what about fuel?" I asked cautiously, for I had no idea what lay beneath the hood.

"No problem there. One charge will last you for the life of the car. Including, of course, the parastats."

"All right," I said. "I would like something strong, durable. It doesn't have to be big, just fast."

"In that case I would suggest this giabile or that model there. . . ."

He led me down a big hall, along a row of machines, which shone as if they were really new.

"Of course," the salesman continued, "they can't compare with gleeders, but, then, the automobile today is no longer a means of transportation. . . ."

What is it, then? I wanted to ask, but said nothing.

"All right," I said, "how much does this one cost?" I pointed to a pale blue limousine with silver recessed headlights.

"Four hundred and eighty ets."

"But I want to have it at Clavestra," I said. "I have rented a villa there. You can get the exact address from the travel office, here, on this street."

"Excellent sir. It can be sent by ulder; that will not cost anything."

"Really? I'll be going there by ulder."

"Give us the date, then, and we will put it in your ulder. That would be simplest. Unless you would prefer . . ."

"No, no. Let it be as you say."

I paid for the car—the calster was not at all a bad thing to have—and left the antique store full of the smell of leather and rubber. Exquisite.

With the clothes I had no luck. Of what I knew, almost nothing existed. At any rate, I discovered the secret of those mysterious bottles at the hotel, in the compartment with the sign "Bathrobes." Not only robes of that kind, but suits, socks, sweaters, underwear—everything was sprayed on. I could see how that might appeal to women, because by discharging from a few or a few dozen bottles a liquid that immediately set into fabrics with textures smooth or rough—velvet, fur, or pliable metal—they could have a new creation every time, each for one occasion only. Of course, not every woman did this for herself: there were special plasting salons (so that was what Nais did!), but the tight-fitting fashion that resulted from this process did not much appeal to me. And getting dressed by operating a siphon bottle seemed to me unnecessarily bothersome. There were a few ready-to-wear items, but they did not fit; even the largest were four sizes too small for my height and width. In the end I decided on clothes in bottles, because I saw that my shirt would not hold out much longer. Of course, I could have sent for the rest of my things from the *Prometheus*, but on board the ship I had had no suits or white shirts, there being little need for such in the vicinity of the Fomalhaut constellation. So I bought, in addition, a few pairs of denimlike trousers that resembled gardening overalls, only they had relatively wide legs and could be lengthened. For everything together I paid one et; that was what the trousers cost. For the rest, no charge. I asked to have the clothes sent to my hotel, and let myself be talked into going to a fashion salon, simply out of curiosity. There I was received by a fellow with the bearing of an artist, who first of all appraised me and agreed that I ought to wear loose-fitting clothes; I could see that he was not especially delighted with me. Nor was I with him. I ended up with a few sweaters, which he made for me while I waited. I stood with my arms raised and he set to work, spraying from four bottles at once. The liquid in the air, white like foam, set almost instantaneously. From it arose sweaters of various colors; one had a stripe across the chest, red on black; the most difficult part, I noticed, was finishing off the collar and sleeves. For that, skill was clearly needed.

Richer for the experience, which in any case had not cost a thing, I found myself on the street in the full noonday sun. There were fewer gleeders; above the roofs, however, were many of the cigar-shaped machines. People streamed down the escalators to the lower levels; everyone was in a hurry, only I had time. For about an hour I warmed myself in the sun, under a rhododendron with woody husks left by dead leaves, and then I returned to the hotel. In the hall downstairs I obtained an apparatus for shaving; when I began to shave in the bathroom, I noticed that I had to bend over slightly to use the mirror, although I remembered that previously I had been able to see myself in it standing upright. The difference was minimal, but a moment before, when taking off my shirt, I had observed something strange: the shirt was shorter. As if it had shrunk. I now examined it carefully. Neither the sleeves nor the collar showed any change. I laid it on the table. It was the same shirt, and yet, when I put it on, it barely came below my waist. It was I who had changed, not the shirt. I had grown.

An absurd thought; nevertheless, it worried me. I phoned the hotel infor, requesting the address of a doctor, a specialist in cosmic medicine. I preferred not to go running to Adapt, if at all possible. After a brief silence, almost as if the automaton at the other end were hesitating, I heard the address. A doctor lived on the very same street, a few blocks down. I went to see him. A robot led me into a large, darkened room. Besides me, no one was there.

Soon the doctor entered. He looked as though he had stepped out of a family portrait in my father's study. He was short but not slight, gray-haired; he wore a tiny white beard and gold-rimmed glasses—the first glasses I had seen on a human face since I landed. His name was Dr. Juffon.

"Hal Bregg?" he said. "Is that you?"

"It is."

Silent, he studied me.

"What's bothering you?"

"Nothing really, doctor, it's just that . . ." I told him of my strange observations.

Without a word he opened a door in front of me. I entered a small examination room.

"Undress, please."

"Everything?" I asked when only my trousers were left.

"Yes."

He examined me naked.

"Such men as you no longer exist," he muttered, as if to himself. He listened to my heart, putting a cold stethoscope to my chest. And in a thousand years that will not change, I thought, and the thought gave me a small pleasure. He measured my height, then told me to lie down. He inspected the scar under my right collarbone, but said nothing. He examined me for nearly an hour.

Reflexes, lung capacity, electrocardiogram—everything. When I was dressed, he sat down behind a small black desk. The drawer squeaked as he pulled it open to look for something. After all the furniture that followed a person around as if possessed, this old desk appealed to me.

"How old are you?"

I explained the situation.

"You have the body of a man in his thirties," he said. "You hibernated?"

"Yes."

"For long?"

"A year."

"Why?"

"We returned on increased thrust. It was necessary to lie in water. Shock absorption, you understand, doctor, and therefore, because it would be hard to lie conscious in water for a year . . ."

"Of course. I thought that you had hibernated longer. We can easily subtract that year. Not forty, only thirty-nine."

"And . . . the other thing?"

"That's nothing, Bregg. How much did you have?"

"Acceleration? Two g's."

"So there you are. You thought that you were growing? No. You aren't growing. It's simply the intervertebral disks. Do you know what they are?"

"Yes, bits of cartilage in the spine . . ."

"Exactly. They are expanding now that you are out from under all that weight. What is your height?"

"When I took off, one hundred and ninety-seven centimeters."

"And after that?"

"I don't know. I didn't measure myself; there were other things to think about, you know."

"Now you are two meters two."

"Marvelous," I said, "and will this go on for long?"

"No. Probably it is all over now. . . . How do you feel?"

"Fine."

"Everything seems too light, doesn't it?"

"Less and less so, now. At Adapt on Luna, they gave me pills to reduce muscle tension."

"They degravitized you?"

"Yes. For the first three days. They said that it was not enough after so many years; on the other hand, they didn't want to keep us shut up any more, after everything. . . ."

"And your state of mind?"

"Well . . ." I hesitated. "There are moments. . . . I have the feeling that I'm a Neanderthal that has been brought to the city. . . ."

"What do you intend to do?"

I told him about the villa.

"You could do worse, perhaps," he said, "but . . ."

"Adapt would be better?"

"I am not saying that. You . . . I remember you, do you know?"

"How can that be? Surely you couldn't be . . ."

"No. But I heard about you from my father. When I was twelve."

"That must have been years after we started out," I said. "And they still remembered us? That's strange."

"I don't think so. On the contrary, it's strange that they should have forgotten. But you knew, didn't you, how the return would look, even though you obviously could not picture it?"

"I knew."

"Who referred you to me?"

"No one. That is . . . the infor at the hotel. Why?"

"It's amusing," he said. "I am not actually a doctor."

"How is that?"

"I have not practiced for forty years. I am working on the history of cosmic medicine, because it is history now, Bregg, and outside of Adapt there is no longer any work for us specialists."

"I'm sorry; I didn't know. . . ."

"Nonsense. I am the one who should be grateful to you. You are living proof against the Millman school's thesis concerning the harmful effects of increased acceleration on the human body. You do not even exhibit hypertrophy of the left ventricle, nor is there a trace of emphysema . . . and the heart is excellent. But you know this?"

"Yes."

"As a doctor, I really have nothing more to tell you, Bregg; however . . ."

He hesitated.

"Yes?"

"You are coping in our . . . present way of life?"

"Muddling along."

"Your hair is gray, Bregg."

"That means something?"

"Yes. Gray hair signifies age. No one turns gray now before eighty, and even then, rarely."

It was the truth, I realized: I had seen no old people.

"Why?" I asked.

"There are preparations, medicines that halt graying. One can also restore the original color of the hair, although that is a little more trouble."

"Fine," I said, "but why are you telling me this?"

I saw that he was undecided.

"Women, Bregg," he said abruptly.

I winced.

"Is that supposed to mean that I look like . . . an old man?"

"Like an old man—no, more like an athlete . . . but, then, you don't walk about naked. It is mainly when you sit that you look . . . that an average person would take you for an old man who has had a rejuvenation operation, hormone treatments, et cetera."

"I don't mind," I said. I do not know why his calm gaze made me feel so awful. He took off his glasses and put them on his desk. He had blue, slightly watery eyes.

"There is a great deal you do not understand, Bregg. If you intended to live like a monk for the remainder of your days, your 'I don't mind' might be in order, but . . . the society to which you have returned is not enthusiastic about what you gave more than your life for."

"Don't say that, doctor."

"I am saying what I think. To give one's life, what is that? People have been doing it for centuries. But to give up all one's friends, parents, kin, acquaintances, women—you did sacrifice them, Bregg!"

"Doctor . . ."

The word hardly left my throat. I rested an elbow on the old desk.

"Apart from a handful of specialists, no one cares about it, Bregg. You know that?"

"Yes. They told me on Luna, at Adapt, only they put it . . . more delicately."

We were silent for a while.

"The society to which you have returned is stabilized. Life is tranquil. Do you understand? The romance of the early days of astronautics is gone. It is like the achievements of Columbus. His expedition was something extraordinary, but who took any interest in the captains of galleons two hundred years after him? There was a two-line note about your return in the real."

"But, doctor, that is not important," I said. His sympathy was beginning to irritate me more than the indifference of others, though I could not tell him that.

"It is, Bregg, although you do not want to face it. If you were someone else, I would be silent, but you deserve the truth. You are alone. A man cannot live alone. Your interests, the ones you have returned with, are an island in a sea of ignorance. I doubt if many people would want to hear what you could tell them. I happen to be one of the interested ones, but I am eighty-nine years old. . . ."

"I have nothing to tell," I said, angry. "Nothing sensational. We did not discover any galactic civilization, and anyway, I was only a pilot. I flew the ship. Someone had to do it."

"Yes?" he said quietly, raising his white eyebrows.

On the surface I was calm, but inside furious.

"Yes! A thousand times, yes! And that indifference, now—if you must know—affects me only on account of the ones who were left behind. . . ."

"Who was left behind?" he asked quietly.

I cooled down.

"There were many. Arder, Venturi, Ennesson. Doctor, what point . . . ?"

"I don't ask out of mere curiosity. This was—and believe me, I do not like grand words, either—a part of my own youth. It was because of you people that I took up these studies. We are equal in our uselessness. You may not, of course, accept this. I won't belabor the point. But I would like to know. What happened to Arder?"

"No one knows exactly," I answered. Suddenly it didn't matter. And why shouldn't I speak about it? I looked at the cracked black polish of the desk. I had never imagined that it would be like this.

"We were flying two probes over Arcturus. I lost contact with him. I couldn't find him. It was his radio that had gone dead, not mine. When my oxygen ran out, I returned."

"You waited?"

"Yes. That is, I circled Arcturus. Six days. A hundred and fifty-six hours, to be exact."

"By yourself?"

"Yes. I had bad luck, because Arcturus developed new spots and I completely lost contact with the *Prometheus*. With my ship. Static. He could not return alone, without a radio. Arder, I mean. Because in the probes the directional teleran is connected to the radio. He could not return without me, and he didn't return. Gimma ordered me back. He was quite right: to kill time, I later calculated the chances of my finding Arder by visual means, on the radar—I don't remember exactly now, but it was something like one in a trillion. I hope he did the same as Arne Ennesson."

"What did Arne Ennesson do?"

"He lost beam focalization. His thrust began to go on him. He could have stayed in orbit, I don't know, another twenty-four hours; he would have spiraled, then finally fallen into Arcturus, so he chose to enter the protuberance at once. Burned up before my eyes."

"How many pilots were there besides you?"

"On the *Prometheus*, five."

"How many came back?"

"Olaf Staave and myself. I know what you're thinking, doctor —that this was heroism. I, too, thought that way once, reading books about such people. But it isn't so. Do you hear? If I could have, I would have left Arder and returned at once, but I couldn't. He would not have returned, either. None of us would have. Including Gimma . . ."

"Why do you protest so much?" he asked softly.

"Because there is a difference between heroism and necessity. I did what anyone would have done. Doctor, to understand it you would have had to be there. A man is a bubble of fluid. All it takes is a defocalized drive or a demagnetized field, vibrations are set up, and in an instant the blood coagulates. Bear in mind that I'm not talking about outside causes, such as meteors, but only about malfunctions, defects. The least damned thing, a burned-out filament in the transmitter—and that's it. If people were to let one another down under such conditions, the expeditions would amount to suicide. You understand?" I closed my eyes for a second. "Doctor—they don't fly now? How can that be?"

"You want to fly?"

"No."

"Why?"

"I'll tell you. None of us would have flown had he known. What it is like, no one knows. No one who wasn't there. We were a group of mortally frightened, desperate animals."

"How do you reconcile this with what you said a moment ago?"

"I don't. That is how it was. We were afraid. Doctor, while I was orbiting that sun, waiting for Arder, I conjured up various people and spoke with them. I spoke for myself and for them, and toward the end I believed that they were there with me. Each saved himself the best way he knew how. Think about it, doctor. Here I sit before you. I've rented myself a villa, I've bought an old car; I want to learn, read, swim; but I have all that inside me. That space, that silence, and how Venturi cried for help, and I, instead of saving him, went into full reverse!"

"Why?"

"I was piloting the *Prometheus*; his pile broke down. He could have blown us all up. It did not blow up; it would not have blown up. Perhaps we would have had time to pull him out, but I did not have the right to risk it. Then, with Arder, it was the other way around. I wanted to save him, but Gimma ordered me in, because he was afraid that we would both die."

"Bregg . . . tell me, what did you all expect of us? Of Earth?"

"I have no idea. I never thought about it. It was like someone talking about the hereafter or heaven: it would come, but none of us could picture it. Doctor—enough. Let's not talk about it. I did want to ask you one thing. This betrization . . . what exactly is it?"

"What do you know about it?"

I told him, but said nothing of how or from whom I had acquired my knowledge.

"Yes," he said, "that is more or less so, in the popular conception."

"And I . . . ?"

"The law makes an exception in your case, because the betrization of adults can affect the health and even be dangerous. Besides which, it is considered—rightly, in my opinion—that you have passed a test . . . of moral attitude. And, in any event, there are so few of you."

"Doctor, one more thing. You mentioned women. Why did you say that to me? But perhaps I am taking up too much of your time."

"No, you're not. Why did I say that? Who can a man be close to, Bregg? To his parents. His children. Friends. A woman. You have neither parents nor children. You cannot have friends."

"Why?"

"I was not thinking of your comrades, although I don't know if you would want to be constantly in their company, to remember. . . ."

"God, no! Never!"

"And so? You know two eras. In the first you spent your youth, and the second you will get to know soon enough. If we include those ten years, your experience cannot be compared with that of people your age. You cannot be on an equal footing with them. What then? Are you to live among old people? That leaves women, Bregg. Only women."

"Perhaps just one," I muttered.

"Ah, just one is difficult nowadays."

"How so?"

"Ours is a period of prosperity. Translated into the language of sexual matters this means: arbitrariness. Because you cannot acquire love or women for . . . money. Material factors have ceased to exist here."

"And this you call arbitrariness? Doctor!"

"Yes. No doubt you think—since I spoke of buying love—that I meant prostitution, whether concealed or in the open. No. That now belongs to the distant past. Once, success used to attract a woman. A man could impress her with his salary, his professional qualifications, his social position. In an egalitarian society that is not possible. With one or two exceptions. If, for example, you were a realist . . ."

"I am a realist."

The doctor smiled.

"The word has another meaning now. A realist is an actor appearing in the real. Have you been to the real?"

"No."

"Take in a couple of melodramas and you will understand what the criteria for sexual selection are today. The most important thing is youth. That is why everyone struggles for it so much. Wrinkles and gray hair, especially when premature, evoke the same kind of feelings as leprosy did, centuries ago. . . ."

"But why?"

"It is hard for you to understand. But arguments based on reason are powerless against prevailing customs. You fail to appreciate how many factors, once decisive in the erotic sphere, have vanished. Nature abhors a vacuum; other factors had to take their place. Consider, for example, something you have become accustomed to, so accustomed that you no longer see the exceptional nature of the phenomenon: risk. It does not exist any more, Bregg. A man cannot impress a woman with heroics, with reckless deeds, and yet literature, art, our whole culture for centuries was nourished by this current: love in the face of adversity. Orpheus went to Hades for Eurydice. Othello killed for love. The tragedy of Romeo and Juliet . . . Today there is no tragedy. Not even the possibility of it. We eliminated the hell of passion, and then it turned out that in the same sweep, heaven, too, had ceased to be. Everything is now lukewarm, Bregg."

"Lukewarm?"

"Yes. Do you know what even the unhappiest lovers do? They behave sensibly. No impetuosity, no rivalry . . ."

"You mean to say all that has disappeared?" I asked. For the first time I felt a kind of superstitious dread of this world. The old doctor was silent.

"Doctor, it's not possible. Really?"

"Yes, really. And you must accept it, Bregg, like air, like water. I said that it is difficult to have just one woman. For a lifetime it is practically impossible. The average length of a marriage is roughly seven years. And that represents progress. Half a century ago, it was less than four. . . ."

"Doctor, I don't want to take up your time. What do you advise me to do?"

"What I mentioned before: restore the original color of your hair. It sounds trivial, I know. But it is important. I am embarrassed to be giving you such advice. Embarrassed not for myself. But what can I . . . ?"

"Thank you. Really. One last thing. Tell me, how do I look out on the street? To the people on the street? What is there about me . . . ?"

"Bregg, you are different. First, there is your size. Something out of the *Iliad*. Antediluvian proportions. It could even be an opportunity, although you know, don't you, the fate of those who are too different?"

"I know."

"You are a little too big. I do not remember such people even in my youth. You look now like a very tall man dressed terribly, but it is not that the clothes hang badly on you, it is just because you are so incredibly well muscled. Before the voyage, too?"

"No, doctor. It was the two g's, you understand."

"That is possible. . . ."

"Seven years. Seven years of doubled weight. My muscles had to become enlarged, the respiratory, the abdominal, and I know the size of my neck. But otherwise I would have suffocated like a rat. They were working even while I slept. Even in hibernation. Everything weighed twice as much. That was the reason."

"The others, too? Excuse me for asking, it is my medical curiosity. . . . Yours was the longest expedition there ever was, you know."

"I know. The others? Olaf is pretty much like me. No doubt it depends on the skeleton; I was always broad. Arder was larger. Over two meters. Yes, Arder . . . What was I saying? The others—well, I was the youngest and therefore able to adapt better. That at least is what Venturi said. . . . Are you familiar with the work of Janssen?"

"Am I? It is a classic for us, Bregg."

"Really? That's funny. He was one lively little doctor. . . . I took seventy-nine g's for a second and a half for him, did you know that?"

"Are you serious?"

I smiled.

"I have it in writing. But that was a hundred and thirty years ago. Now forty would be too much for me."

"Bregg, today no one could take twenty!"

"Why? Because of the betrization?"

He was silent. It seemed to me that he knew something but did not want to tell me. I got up.

"Bregg," he said, "since we are on the subject: be careful."

"Of what?"

"Of yourself and of others. Progress never comes free. We've rid ourselves of a thousand dangers, conflicts, but for that we had to pay. Society has softened, while you are . . . you can be hard. Do you understand me?"

"I do," I said, thinking of the man in the restaurant the night before who had laughed but fell silent when I walked up to him.

"Doctor," I said suddenly, "I just remembered . . . I met a lion last night. Two lions, in fact. Why did they do nothing to me?"

"There are no predators now, Bregg. . . . Betrization . . . You met them last night? And what did you do?"

"I scratched their necks," I said and showed him how. "But that *Iliad* business, doctor, is an exaggeration. I was badly frightened. What do I owe you?"

"I wouldn't think of it. And if you ever need . . ."

"Thank you."

"But don't put if off too long," he added, almost to himself, as I was leaving. Only on the stairs did I realize what that meant: he was nearly ninety.

I went back to the hotel. In the hall was a barber. A robot, of course. I had it cut my hair. I was pretty shaggy, with a lot of hair over the ears. The temples were the grayest. When it was done, it seemed to me that I looked a little less savage. In a melodious voice the robot asked if it should darken the hair.

"No," I said.

"Aprex?"

"What is that?"

"For wrinkles."

I hesitated. I felt stupid, but perhaps the doctor had been right.

"Go ahead," I agreed. It covered my face with a layer of sharp-smelling jelly that hardened into a mask. Afterward I lay under compresses, glad that my face was covered.

I went upstairs; the packages with the liquid clothing were already lying in my room. I stripped and went into the bathroom, where there was a mirror.

Yes. I could strike terror. I had not known that I looked like a circus strongman. Indented pectorals, torso, I was knotted all over. When I lifted my arm and flexed the chest, a scar as wide as the palm of my hand appeared on it. I tried to see the other, near the shoulder blade, for which I had been called a lucky bastard, because if the splinter had gone three centimeters more to the left it would have shattered my spine. I punched the plank of my stomach.

"Animal," I said to the mirror. I wanted a bath, a real one, not in the ozone wind, and looked forward to the swimming pool at the villa. I decided to dress in one of my new things, but somehow could not part with my trousers. So I put on only the white sweater, although I much preferred my old black one tattered at the elbows, and went to the restaurant.

Half the tables were occupied. I passed through three rooms to reach the terrace; from there I could see the great boulevards, the endless streams of gleeders; under the clouds, like a mountain peak, blue in the distant air, stood the Terminal.

I ordered lunch.

"What will you have?" asked the robot. It wanted to give me a menu.

"It doesn't matter," I replied. "A regular lunch."

It was only when I began to eat that I noticed that the tables around me were vacant. I had automatically sought seclusion. I had not even realized it. I did not know what I was eating. I was no longer certain that what I had decided on was good. A vacation, as if I wanted to reward myself, seeing as no one else had thought of it. The waiter approached noiselessly.

"Mr. Bregg?"

"Yes."

"You have a visitor—in your room."

"A visitor?"

I thought at once of Nais. I drank the rest of the dark, bubbling liquid and got up, feeling stares at my back as I left. It would have been nice to saw off about ten centimeters. In my room sat a young woman I had never seen before. A fluffy gray dress, a red whimsy around her arms.

"I am from Adapt," she said. "I spoke with you today."

"Ah, so that was you?"

I stiffened a little. What did they want of me now?

She sat down. And I sat down slowly.

"How are you feeling?"

"Fine. I went to a doctor today, and he examined me. Everything is in working order. I have rented myself a villa. I want to do a little reading."

"Very wise. Clavestra is ideal for that. You will have mountains, quiet. . . ."

She knew that it was Clavestra. Were they spying on me, or what? I sat motionless, waiting.

"I brought you . . . something from us."

She pointed to a small package on the table.

"It is our latest thing." She spoke with an animation that seemed artificial. "Before going to sleep you set this machine, and in the course of a dozen nights or so you learn, in the easiest possible way, without any effort, a great many useful things."

"Really? That's good," I said. She smiled at me. And I smiled, the well-behaved pupil.

"You are a psychologist?"

"Yes. You guessed."

She hesitated. I saw that she wanted to say something.

"Go ahead."

"You won't be angry with me?"

"Why should I be angry?"

"Because . . . you see . . . the way you are dressed is a bit . . ."

"I know. But I like these trousers. Maybe in time . . ."

"Ah, no, not the trousers. The sweater."

"The sweater?" I was surprised. "They made it for me today. It's the latest word in fashion, isn't it?"

"Yes. Except that you shouldn't have inflated it. May I?"

"Please," I said quite softly. She leaned forward in her chair, poked me lightly in the chest with straightened fingers, and let out a faint cry.

"What do you have there?"

"Other than myself, nothing," I answered with a crooked smile.

She clutched the fingers of her right hand with her left and stood up. Suddenly my calm, invested with a malicious satisfaction, became like ice.

"Why don't you sit down?"

"But . . . I'm terribly sorry, I . . ."

"Forget it. Have you been with Adapt long?"

"It's my second year."

"Aha—and your first patient?" I pointed a finger at myself. She blushed a little.

"May I ask you something?"

Her eyelids fluttered. Did she think that I would ask her out? "Certainly."

"How do they work it so that the sky is visible at every level of the city?"

She perked up.

"Very simple. Television—that is what they called it, long ago. On the ceilings are screens. They transmit what is above the Earth—the sky, the clouds. . . ."

"But surely the levels are not that high," I said. "Forty-story buildings stand there. . . ."

"It is an illusion," she said, smiling. "The buildings are only partly real; their continuation is an image. Do you understand?"

"I understand how it's done, but not the reason."

"So that the people living on each level do not feel deprived. Not in any way."

"Aha," I said. "Yes, that's clever. One more thing. I'll be shopping for books. Could you suggest a few works in your field? An overview . . . ?"

"You want to study psychology?" She was surprised.

"No, but I'd like to know what has been accomplished in all this time."

"I'd recommend Mayssen," she said.

"What is that?"

"A school textbook."

"I would prefer something larger. Abstracts, monographs—it's always better to go to the source."

"That might be too . . . difficult."

I smiled politely.

"Perhaps not. What would the difficulty be?"

"Psychology has become very mathematical. . . ."

"So have I. At least, up to the point where I left off, a hundred or so years ago. Do I need to know more?"

"But you are not a mathematician."

"Not by profession, but I studied the subject. On the *Prometheus*. There was a lot of spare time, you know."

Surprised, disconcerted, she said no more. She gave me a piece of paper with a list of titles. When she had gone, I returned to

the desk and sat down heavily. Even she, an employee of Adapt
. . . Mathematics? How was it possible? A wild man. I hate
them, I thought. I hate them. I hate them. Whom did I hate?
I did not know. Everyone. Yes, everyone. I had been tricked.
They sent me out, not knowing themselves what they were doing. I should not have returned, like Venturi, Arder, Thomas,
but I did return, to frighten them, to walk about like a guilty
conscience that no one wants. I am useless, I thought. If only I
could cry. Arder knew how. He said you should not be ashamed
of tears. Maybe I had lied to the doctor. I had never told anyone about that, but I was not sure whether I would have done
it for anyone else. Perhaps I would have. For Olaf, later. But I
was not completely sure of that. Arder! They destroyed us and
we believed in them, feeling the entire time that Earth was by
us, present, had faith in us, was mindful of us. No one spoke of
it. Why speak of what is obvious?

I got up. I couldn't sit still. I walked from corner to corner.

Enough. I opened the bathroom door, but there was no water,
of course, to splash on my face. Stupid. Hysterics.

I went back to the room and started to pack.

spent the afternoon in a bookstore. There were no books in it. None had been printed for nearly half a century. And how I had looked forward to them, after the microfilms that made up the library of the *Prometheus!* No such luck. No longer was it possible to browse among shelves, to weigh volumes in the hand, to feel their heft, the promise of ponderous reading. The bookstore resembled, instead, an electronic laboratory. The books were crystals with recorded contents. They could be read with the aid of an opton, which was similar to a book but had only one page between the covers. At a touch, successive pages of the text appeared on it. But optons were little used, the sales-robot told me. The public preferred lectons—lectons read out loud, they could be set to any voice, tempo, and modulation. Only scientific publications having a very limited distribution were still printed, on a plastic imitation paper. Thus all my purchases fitted into one pocket, though there must have been almost three hundred titles. A handful of crystal corn—my books. I selected a number of works on history and sociology, a few on statistics and demography, and what the girl from Adapt had recommended on psychology. A couple of the larger mathematical textbooks—larger, of course, in the sense of their content, not of their physical size. The robot that served me was itself an encyclopedia, in that—as it told me—it was linked directly, through electronic catalogues, to templates of every book on Earth. As a rule, a bookstore had only single "copies" of books, and when someone needed a particular book, the content of the work was recorded in a crystal.

The originals—crystomatrices—were not to be seen; they were kept behind pale blue enameled steel plates. So a book was printed, as it were, every time someone needed it. The question of printings, of their quantity, of their running out, had ceased to exist. Actually, a great achievement, and yet I regretted the passing of books. On learning that there were secondhand bookshops that had paper books, I went and found one. I was disappointed; there were practically no scientific works. Light reading, a few children's books, some sets of old periodicals.

I bought (one had to pay only for the old books) a few fairy tales from forty years earlier, to find out what were considered fairy tales now, and I went to a sporting-goods store. Here my disappointment had no limit. Athletics existed in a stunted form. Running, throwing, jumping, swimming, but hardly any combat sports. There was no boxing now, and what they called wrestling was downright ridiculous, an exchange of shoves instead of a respectable fight. I watched one world-championship match in the projection room of the store and thought I would burst with anger. At times I began laughing like a lunatic. I asked about American free-style, judo, ju-jitsu, but no one knew what I was talking about. Understandable, given that soccer had died without heirs, as an activity in which sharp encounters and bodily injuries came about. There was hockey, but it wasn't hockey! They played in outfits so inflated that they looked like enormous balls. It was entertaining to see the two teams bounce off each other, but it was a farce, not a match. Diving, yes, but from a height of only four meters. I thought immediately of my own (my own!) pool and bought a folding springboard, to add on to the one that would be at Clavestra. This disintegration was the work of betrization. That bullfights, cockfights, and other bloody spectacles had disappeared did not bother me, nor had I ever been an enthusiast of professional boxing. But the tepid pap that remained did not appeal to me in the least. The invasion of technology in sports I had tolerated only in the tourist business. It had grown, especially, in underwater sports.

I had a look at various equipment for diving: small electric torpedoes one could use to travel along the bottom of a lake; speedboats, hydrofoils that moved on a cushion of compressed air; water microgleeders, everything fitted with special safety devices to guard against accidents.

The racing, which enjoyed a considerable popularity, I could not consider a sport; no horses, of course, and no cars—remote-control machines raced one another, and bets could be placed on them. Competition had lost its importance. It was explained to me that the limits of man's physical capability had been reached and the existing records could be broken only by an abnormal person, some freak of strength or speed. Rationally, I had to agree with this, and the universal popularity of those athletic disciplines that had survived the decimation, deserved praise; nevertheless, after three hours of inspecting, I left depressed.

I asked that the gymnastic equipment I had selected be sent on to Clavestra. After some thought, I decided against a speed-boat; I wanted to buy myself a yacht, but there were no decent ones, that is, with real sails, with centerboards, only some miserable boats that guaranteed such stability that I could not understand how sailing them could gratify anyone.

It was evening when I headed back to the hotel. From the west marched fluffy reddish clouds, the sun had set already, the moon was rising in its first quarter, and at the zenith shone another—some huge satellite. High above the buildings swarmed flying machines. There were fewer pedestrians but more gleeders, and there appeared, streaking the roadways, those lights in apertures, whose purpose I still did not know. I took a different route back and came upon a large garden. At first I thought it was the Terminal park, but that glass mountain of a station loomed in the distance, in the northern, higher part of the city.

The view was unusual, for although the darkness, cut by street lights, had enveloped the whole area, the upper levels of the Terminal still gleamed like snow-covered Alpine peaks.

It was crowded in the park. Many new species of trees, especially palms, blossoming cacti without spines; in a corner far from the main promenades I was able to find a chestnut tree that must have been two hundred years old. Three men of my

size could not have encircled its trunk. I sat on a small bench
and looked at the sky for some time. How harmless, how friendly
the stars seemed, twinkling, shimmering in the invisible cur-
rents of the atmosphere that shielded Earth from them. I
thought of them as "little stars" for the first time in years. Up
there, no one would have spoken in such a way—we would have
thought him crazy. Little stars, yes, hungry little stars. Above the
trees, which were now completely dark, fireworks exploded in the
distance, and suddenly, with astounding reality, I saw Arcturus,
the mountains of fire over which I had flown, teeth chattering
from the cold, while the frost of the cooling equipment, melting, ran red with rust down my suit. I was collecting samples
with a corona siphon, one ear cocked for the whistle of the compressors, in case of any loss of rotation, because a breakdown of
a single second, their jamming, would have turned my armor,
my equipment, and myself into an invisible puff of steam. A
drop of water falling on a red-hot plate does not vanish so
quickly as a man evaporates then.

The chestnut tree was nearly out of bloom. I had never cared
for the smell of its flowers, but now it reminded me of long ago.
Above the hedges the glare of fireworks came and went in
waves, a noise swelled, orchestras mingling, and every few seconds, carried by the wind, returned the choral cry of participants
in some show, perhaps of passengers in a cable car. My little
corner, however, remained undisturbed.

Then a tall, dark figure emerged from a side path. The
greenery was not completely gray, and I saw the face of this
person only when, walking extremely slowly, a step at a time,
barely lifting his feet off the ground, he stopped a few meters
away. His hands were thrust into funnellike swellings from
which extended two slender rods that ended in black bulbs. He
leaned on these, not like a paralytic, but like someone in an extremely weakened state. He did not look at me, or at anything
else—the laughter, the shouting, the music, the fireworks seemed
not to exist for him. He stood for perhaps a minute, breathing
with great effort, and I saw his face off and on in the flashes of
light from the fireworks, a face so old that the years had wiped

all expression from it, it was only skin on bone. When he was about to resume his walk, putting forward those peculiar crutches or artificial limbs, one of them slipped; I jumped up from the bench to support him, but he had already regained his balance. He was a head shorter than I, though still tall for a man of the time; he looked at me with shining eyes.

"Excuse me," I muttered. I wanted to leave, but stayed: in his eyes was something commanding.

"I've seen you somewhere. But where?" he said in a surprisingly strong voice.

"I doubt it," I replied, shaking my head. "I returned only yesterday . . . from a very long voyage."

"From . . . ?"

"From Fomalhaut."

His eyes lit up.

"Arder! Tom Arder!"

"No," I said. "But I was with him."

"And he?"

"He died."

He was breathing hard.

"Help me . . . sit down."

I took his arm. Under the slippery black material were only bones. I eased him down gently onto the bench. I stood over him.

"Have . . . a seat."

I sat. He was still wheezing, his eyes half closed.

"It's nothing . . . the excitement," he whispered. After a while he lifted his lids. "I am Roemer," he said simply.

This took my breath away.

"What? Is it possible . . . you . . . you . . . ? How old . . . ?"

"A hundred and thirty-four," he said dryly. "Then, I was . . . seven."

I remembered him. He had visited us with his father, the brilliant mathematician who worked under Geonides—the creator of the theory behind our flight. Arder had shown the boy the huge testing room, the centrifuges. That was how he remained in my memory, as lively as a flame, seven years old, with his father's dark eyes; Arder had held him up in the air so the little one could see from close up the inside of the gravitation chamber, where I was sitting.

We were both silent. There was something uncanny about this meeting. I looked through the darkness with a kind of eager, painful greed at his terribly old face, and felt a tightness in my throat. I wanted to take a cigarette from my pocket but could not get to it, my fingers fumbled so much.

"What happened to Arder?" he asked.

I told him.

"You recovered—nothing?"

"Nothing there is ever recovered . . . you know."

"I mistook you for him. . . ."

"I understand. My height and so forth," I said.

"Yes. How old are you now, biologically?"

"Forty."

"I could have . . ." he murmured.

I understood what he was thinking.

"Do not regret it," I said firmly. "You should not regret it. You should not regret a thing, do you understand?"

For the first time he lifted his gaze to my face.

"Why?"

"Because there is nothing for me to do here," I said. "No one needs me. And I . . . no one."

He didn't seem to hear me.

"What is your name?"

"Bregg. Hal Bregg."

"Bregg," he repeated. "Bregg . . . No, I don't remember. Were you there?"

"Yes. At Apprenous, when your father came with the corrections Geonides made in the final month before takeoff . . . It turned out that the coefficients of refraction for the dark dusts had been too low. . . . Does that mean anything to you?" I broke off uncertainly.

"It does. Of course," he replied with special emphasis. "My

father. Of course. At Apprenous? But what were you doing there? Where were you?"

"In the gravitation chamber, at Janssen's. You were there then, Arder brought you in, you stood high up, on the platform, and watched while they gave me forty g's. When I climbed out, my nose was bleeding. You gave me your handkerchief."

"Ah! That was you?"

"Yes."

"But that person in the chamber had dark hair, I thought."

"Yes. My hair isn't light. It's gray. It's just that you can't see well now."

There was a silence, longer than before.

"You are a professor, I suppose?" I said, to say something.

"I was. Now . . . nothing. For twenty-three years. Nothing." And once more, very quietly, he repeated, "Nothing."

"I bought some books today, and among them was Roemer's topology. Is that you or your father?"

"I. You are a mathematician?"

He stared at me, as if with renewed interest.

"No," I said, "but I had a great deal of time . . . there. Each of us did what he wanted. I found mathematics helpful."

"How did you understand it?"

"We had an enormous number of microfilms: fiction, novels, whatever you like. Do you know that we had three hundred thousand titles? Your father helped Arder compile the mathematical part."

"I know about that."

"At first, we treated it as . . . a diversion. To kill time. But then, after a few months, when we had completely lost contact with Earth and were hanging there—seemingly motionless in relation to the stars—then, you see, to read that some Peter nervously puffed his cigarette and was worried about whether or not Lucy would come, and that she walked in and twisted her gloves, well, first you began to laugh at this like an idiot, and then you simply saw red. In other words, no one would touch it."

"And mathematics?"

"No. Not right away. At first I took up languages, and I stuck with that until the end, even though I knew it might be futile, for when I returned, some might have become archaic dialects. But Gimma—and Thurber, especially—urged me to learn physics. Said it might be useful. I tackled it, along with Arder and Olaf Staave, but we three were not scientists. . . ."

"You did have a degree."

"Yes, a master's degree in information theory and cosmodromia, and a diploma in nuclear engineering, but all that was professional, not theoretical. You know how engineers know mathematics. So, then, physics. But I wanted something more— of my own. And, finally, pure mathematics. I had no mathematical ability. None. I had nothing but persistence."

"Yes," he said quietly. "One would have to have that to fly. . . ."

"Particularly to become a member of the expedition," I corrected him. "And do you know why mathematics had this effect? I only came to understand this there. Because mathematics stands above everything. The works of Abel and Kronecker are as good today as they were four hundred years ago, and it will always be so. New roads arise, but the old ones lead on. They do not become overgrown. There . . . there you have eternity. Only mathematics does not fear it. Up there, I understood how final it is. And strong. There was nothing like it. And the fact that I had to struggle was also good. I slaved away at it, and when I couldn't sleep I would go over, in my mind, the material I had studied that day."

"Interesting," he said. But there was no interest in his voice. I did not even know whether he was listening to me. Far back in the park flew columns of fire, red and green blazes, accompanied by roars of delight. Here, where we sat, beneath the trees, it was dark. I fell silent. But the silence was unbearable.

"For me it had the value of self-preservation," I said. "The theory of plurality . . . what Mirea and Averin did with the legacy of Cantor, you know. Operations using infinite, transfinite quantities, the continua of discrete increments, strong . . . it was wonderful. The time I spent on this, I remember it as if it were yesterday."

"It isn't so useless as you think," he muttered. He was listening, after all. "You haven't heard of Igalli's studies, I suppose?"

"No, what are they?"

"The theory of the discontinuous antipole."

"I don't know anything about an antipole. What is it?"

"Retronihilation. From this came parastatics."

"I never even heard of these terms."

"Of course, for it originated sixty years ago. But that was only the beginning of gravitology."

"I can see that I will have to do some homework," I said. "Gravitology—that's the theory of gravitation?"

"Much more. It can only be explained using mathematics. Have you studied Appiano and Froom?"

"Yes."

"Well, then, you should have no difficulty. These are metagen expansions in an n-dimensional, configurational, degenerative series."

"What are you saying? Didn't Skriabin prove that there are no metagens other than the variational?"

"Yes. A very elegant proof. But this, you see, is transcontinuous."

"Impossible! That would . . . but it must have opened up a whole new world!"

"Yes," he said dryly.

"I remember one paper by Mianikowski . . ." I began.

"Oh, that is not related. At the most, a similar direction."

"Would it take me long to catch up with everything that has been done in all this time?" I asked.

He was silent for a moment.

"What use is it to you?"

I did not know what to say.

"You are not going to fly any more?"

"No," I said. "I'm too old. I couldn't take the sort of accelerations that . . . and anyway . . . I would not fly now."

After these words we were silent for good. The unexpected

elation with which I had talked about mathematics had suddenly evaporated, and I sat beside him, feeling the weight of my own body, its unnecessary size. Outside of mathematics we had nothing to say to each other, and we both knew it. Then it occurred to me that the emotion with which I had spoken of the blessed role of mathematics on the voyage was a deception. I had been deceiving myself with the modesty, the serious heroism of the pilot who occupies himself, in the gaps of the nebulae, with theoretical studies of infinity. Hypocrisy. For what had it been, really? If a castaway, adrift for months at sea, has a thousand times counted the number of wood fibers that make up his raft, in order to keep sane, should he boast about it when he reaches land? That he had the tenacity to survive? And what of it? Who cared? Why should it matter to anyone how I had filled my poor brain those ten years, and why was that more important than how I had filled my stomach? I must stop playing the quiet hero, I thought. I will be able to allow myself that when I look the way he does. I must concentrate on the future.

"Help me get up," he said in a whisper.

I led him to a gleeder that stood in the street. We went very slowly. Where there were lights, among the hedges, people followed us with their eyes. Before he got into the gleeder he turned to say good-bye to me. Neither he nor I could find anything to say. He made an unintelligible motion with his hand, from which one of the canes jutted like a sword, shook his head, and got inside; the dark vehicle floated off noiselessly. I stood with my arms hanging until the black gleeder had disappeared in a stream of others. I stuck my hands in my pockets and moved on, unable to answer the question of which of us had chosen better.

That nothing remained of the city that I had left behind me, not one stone upon another, was a good thing. As if I had been living, then, on a different Earth, among different men; that had begun and ended once and for all, and this was new. No relics, no ruins to cast doubt on my biological age; I could forget about its Earthly reckoning, so contrary to nature—until that incredible coincidence brought me together with a person whom

I had last seen as a small child; the whole time, sitting next to him, looking at his hands, dry as a mummy's, and at his face, I had felt guilt and knew he was aware of this. What an improbable accident, I repeated over and over again, inanely, until I realized that he could have been drawn to this place by the same thing that had drawn me: growing there, after all, was that chestnut tree, older than either of us. I had no idea yet how far they had gone in increasing the span of human life, but I could see that Roemer's age was something exceptional: he must have been the last or one of the last of his generation. If I had not left Earth, I would no longer be alive, I thought, and for the first time I saw an unexpected reverse side to our expedition: the subterfuge, the cruel trick that I had played on others. I walked on blindly. Around me was the noise of a crowd, a stream of pedestrians bore me along and pushed me—then I stopped, suddenly awake.

There was an indescribable racket; in the midst of mingled shouts and music, volleys of fireworks burst into the sky, hanging high above in colorful bouquets; burning spheres rained on the tops of the nearby trees; at regular intervals came the piercing sound of many voices, a howl of terror mixed with laughter, exactly as if somewhere close by there was a roller coaster, but I looked in vain for the trestles. In the middle of the park stood a large building with towers and battlements, like a fortified castle transported from the Middle Ages; the cold flames of neon lights, licking its roof, arranged themselves every few seconds into the words MERLIN'S PALACE. The crowd that had led me here made for the side, toward the crimson wall of a pavilion, unusual in that it resembled a human face, with smoldering eyes for windows, and a huge, distorted mouth, full of teeth, opened to swallow the next helping of jostling people, to the accompaniment of general merriment; each time, the mouth consumed the same number—six. At first my intention was to get out of the crowd and leave; but that would not have been easy, and besides, I had nowhere to go, and the thought came to me that out of all the possible ways of spending the rest of the evening, this one, unknown, might not be the worst. I appeared to be the only one by myself—there were mostly couples, boys and girls, men and women, lined up two by two—and when my turn came, heralded by the white flash of the huge teeth and the gaping crimson darkness of the mysterious throat, I found myself in a predicament, because I did not know whether I could join an already completed six. At the last moment the decision was made for me by a woman who stood with a young dark-haired man dressed more extravagantly than all the others: she grabbed me by the hand and without ceremony pulled me after her.

It grew almost completely dark; I felt the warm, strong hand of the unknown woman, the floor moved, the light returned, and we found ourselves in a spacious grotto. The last dozen or so steps led uphill, over loose gravel, between piles of crushed stone. The unknown woman let go of my hand—and, one by one, we stooped through the narrow exit from the cave.

Although I had been prepared for a surprise, my jaw dropped. We were standing on the broad, sandy bank of a big river, under the burning rays of a tropical sun. The far bank of the river was overgrown with jungle. In the still backwaters were moored boats, or, rather, dugouts; against the background of the brownish-green river that flowed lazily behind them, immensely tall blacks stood frozen in hieratic poses, naked, gleaming with oil, covered with chalk-white tattoos; each leaned with his spatulate oar against the side of the boat.

One of the boats was just leaving, full; its black crew, with blows from the paddles and terrifying yells, was dispersing crocodiles that lay in the mud, half immersed, like logs; these turned over and weakly snapped their tooth-lined jaws as they slid into deeper water. The seven of us descended along the steep bank; the first four took places in the next boat. With visible effort the blacks set the oars against the shore and pushed the unsteady boat away, so that it turned around; I remained in the rear, in front of me there was now only the couple to whom I owed my presence and the journey that was about to take place, for now appeared the next boat in line, about ten meters long; the black oarsmen called to us and, fighting the current, docked skillfully. We jumped into the rotting interior of the boat, kicking up a dust that smelled of charred wood. The young man in the fanciful outfit—a tiger skin, actually a costume, for the upper half of the predator's skull, slung over his shoulder, could serve as a hood—helped his companion to a seat. I took a seat opposite them. We had already been moving a good while, and although a few minutes earlier I had been in the park, in the middle of the night, now I was not so sure of that. The tall black standing at the sharp prow of the boat gave a wild cry every few seconds, two rows of backs bent, gleaming, oars hit the water with brief, violent strokes, the boat scraped over the sand, drifted, then suddenly entered the main current of the river.

There was the heavy, heated smell of the water, of the mud, of the rotting vegetation that floated past us around the sides of the boat, which were hardly a hand's breadth above the surface of the water. The banks receded; we passed bush, characteristically gray-green, as though burned; from sun-baked sandy shoals crocodiles slid from time to time like animated logs, with a splash; one of them remained for quite a while at our stern, its elongated head on the surface; slowly water began to encroach upon the bulging eyes, and then there was only its snout, dark as a river stone, gliding swiftly, cleaving the brown water. Between the rhythmically swaying backs of the black rowers one could see humps in the river, where it flowed over submerged obstacles—the man at the bow would then let out a harsh cry, the oars on one side began to strike the water more vigorously, and the boat turned. It is difficult to say when the hollow grunts made by the blacks as they leaned on their oars began to merge in an inexpressibly gloomy, endlessly repeating song, a kind of angry cry that changed to grievance, whose chorus was the lapping of the water broken by the oars. Thus we proceeded, as if actually transported into the heart of Africa, on an enormous river in the middle of a gray-green wild. The solid wall of jungle receded finally and disappeared in a shimmering mass of sweltering air; the black helmsman quickened the tempo; on the distant savannah antelopes grazed; and at one point a herd of giraffes passed in a cloud of dust, at a languorous trot; then I felt the gaze of the woman seated opposite me, and I looked at her.

Her loveliness took me by surprise. I had noticed earlier that she was attractive, but that had been just in passing and had not arrested my attention. Now I was too close to her to make the same mistake: she was not attractive, she was beautiful. She had dark hair with a coppery sheen, a white, indescribably tranquil face, and dark, motionless lips. She captivated me. Not as a woman—rather, in the same way as this vast expanse mute beneath the sun. Her beauty had that perfection that had always frightened me a little. Possibly because I had, on Earth, experienced too little and thought too much about it; in any case, here before me was one of those women who seem cast of a different clay from that of ordinary mortals, although this magnificent life is produced only by a certain configuration of features and is entirely on the surface—but who, looking, thinks of that? She smiled, with only her eyes; her lips preserved an expression of scornful indifference. Not to me—to her own thoughts, perhaps. Her companion sat on a recessed ledge in the dugout; he let his left hand hang limply over the side, so that his fingers trailed in the water, but he did not look in that direction, or at the panorama of wild Africa unfolding all around; he simply sat, as in a dentist's waiting room, completely bored.

Ahead of us gray rocks came into view, strewn across the entire river. The helmsman began to shout, as if cursing, with a penetrating, powerful voice; the blacks struck furiously with their oars, and when the rocks turned out to be diving hippopotamuses, the boat picked up speed; the herd of thick-skinned animals was left behind, and through the rhythmic splash of the oars, through the hoarse, heavy song of the rowers, one could hear a hollow roar that came from an unknown source. Far off, where the river disappeared between increasingly steeper banks, I saw two rainbows, immense, flickering, bending toward each other.

"Age! Annai! Annai! Agee!" bellowed the helmsman frantically. The blacks redoubled their strokes, the boat flew as if it had acquired wings; the woman reached out her hand, without looking, for the hand of her companion.

The helmsman howled. The dugout moved at an amazing speed. The bow lifted, we descended from the crest of a huge, seemingly motionless wave, and between the rows of black backs that labored at a furious pace I saw a great bend in the river: the suddenly darkened waters pounded at a gate of rock. The current split in two; we kept to the right, where the water rose in whiter and whiter crests of foam, while the left arm of the river disappeared as if chopped off, and only a monstrous thunder and columns of whirling mist indicated that those rocks concealed a waterfall. We avoided it and reached the other arm of the river, but here it was not peaceful, either. The dugout now bucked like a horse among black boulders, each of which held in check a high wall of roaring water; the banks drew near, the blacks on the right side of the boat stopped rowing and held the blunted handles of their oars to their chests; then, with a shock whose force could be judged by the hollow thud it sent through them, the boat rebounded from the rock and gained the center of the current. The bow flew upward, the helmsman standing on it kept his balance by some miracle; I felt the cold from the spray that streamed off the edges of the rocks as the dugout, quivering like a spring, sped downward. Our shooting of the rapids was extraordinary. On either side flashed black rocks with flowing manes of water; time and time again the dugout, with an echoing jolt, was kept off the rocks by the oars, bounced off, and went into the throat of the fastest water, an arrow released across white foam. I looked up and saw, high among the branching crowns of sycamores, tiny monkeys scampering. I had to grab the sides of the boat, so powerful was the next jolt, a heave, and in the thunder of water that rushed in on us from either side, so that in an instant we were soaked to the skin, we went down at an even steeper angle—we were falling, the boulders of the bank flew past like statues of monstrous birds in a welter of sharp wings, thunder, thunder. Against the sky, the taut silhouettes of the oarsmen, like guardians at a cataclysm—we were headed straight for a pillar of stone dividing the narrows in half, and in front of it swirled a black vortex of water. We flew toward the barrier, I heard a woman's scream.

The blacks struggled with the frenzy of desperation, and the helmsman lifted his arms; I saw his lips open wide in a shout, but I heard no voice. He danced on the bow, the dugout went sideways, a rebounding wave held us, for a second we stood in place, then, as if the work of the oars counted for nothing, the boat turned right around and went backward, faster and faster.

In an instant the two rows of blacks, throwing down their oars, disappeared; without hesitation they jumped overboard on both sides of the boat. The last to make the deadly leap was the helmsman.

The woman cried out a second time; her companion held fast with his feet against the opposite side of the boat and she clung to him; I watched, entranced, the spectacle of tumbling water, roaring rainbows; the boat struck something, a scream, a piercing scream. . . .

Across the path of the downward-rushing torrent that carried us lay, just above the surface, a tree, a giant of the forest, which had fallen to form a kind of bridge. The other two dropped to the bottom of the boat. In the fraction of a second left to me, I debated whether I should do the same. I knew that everything—the blacks, this shooting of the rapids, the African waterfall—was only an amazing illusion, but to sit still while the bow of the boat slid under the dripping, resinous trunk of the huge tree was beyond me. I threw myself down but at the same time lifted a hand, which passed through the trunk without touching it; I felt nothing, as I had expected, but in spite of this, the illusion that we had miraculously escaped catastrophe remained intact.

Yet this was not all; with the next wave the boat stood on end, an enormous roller caught us and turned us around, and for the next few heartbeats the dugout went in a hellish circle, heading for the center of the whirlpool. If the woman screamed, I did not hear it, I would not have heard a thing; I felt the crash, the splitting of the boat, with my whole body, my ears were as if stopped by the bellow of the waterfall; the dugout, hurled upward with enormous force, got wedged between the boulders. The other two jumped out onto a foam-covered rock; they scrambled up, with me behind them.

We found ourselves on a crag between two arms of trembling whiteness. The right bank was quite distant; to the left led a footbridge anchored in crevices in the rock, a kind of elevated passage above the waves that went plunging into the depths of that hellish cauldron. The air was chilly from the mist, the spray; the narrow bridge hung—without handrails, slippery from the dampness—above the wall of sound; one had to set one's feet on the rotting planks, loosely joined by knotted ropes, and walk a few steps to reach the bank. The others were on their knees in front of me and apparently arguing about who should go first. I heard nothing, of course. It was as if the air itself had hardened from the constant thunder. At last the young man got up and said something to me, pointing downward. I saw the dugout; its stern, broken off, danced on a wave and disappeared, spinning faster and faster, pulled in ' by the whirlpool. The young man in the tiger suit was less indifferent or sleepy than at the beginning of the journey, but seemed annoyed, as if there against his will. He grasped the woman by the arm, and I thought that he had gone insane, for unmistakably he was pushing her straight into the roaring gorge. She said something to him, I saw indignation flash in her eyes. I put my hands on their shoulders, gestured for them to let me pass, and stepped onto the bridge. It swung and danced; I walked, not too quickly, keeping my balance by moving my shoulders; in the middle I reeled once or twice, and suddenly the bridge began to shake, so that I almost fell. Without waiting for me to get across, the woman walked out on the bridge. Afraid that I would fall, I leapt forward; I landed on the very edge of the rock and immediately turned around.

The woman did not cross: she had gone back. The young man went first, holding her by the hand; the strange shapes created by the waterfall, black and white phantoms, provided the background for their unsteady passage. He was near; I gave him my hand; at the same time the woman stumbled, the footbridge began to sway, I pulled as if I would have sooner torn off his arm than let him fall; the impetus carried him two meters, and he landed behind me, on his knees—but he let go of her.

She was still in the air when I jumped, feet first, having aimed so that I would enter the water at an angle, between the bank and the vertical face of the closest rock. I thought about all this later, when I had time. Essentially I knew that the waterfall and the crossing of the bridge were an illusion, the proof of which was the tree trunk that my hand had gone straight through. Nevertheless, I jumped as if she had been in real peril of her life, and I even recall that, quite by instinct, I braced myself for the icy impact with the water, whose spray had been continually dousing our faces and clothes.

I felt nothing, however, but a strong gust of air, and I landed in a spacious room, my legs slightly bent, as though I had jumped from a height of one meter at the most. I heard a chorus of laughter.

I stood on a soft, plasticlike floor, surrounded by other people, some still in soaked clothes; with their heads turned up, they were roaring with laughter.

I followed their gaze—it was extraordinary.

No trace of waterfalls, cliffs, the African sky. I saw an illuminated ceiling and, beneath it, a dugout just arriving; actually it was a kind of decoration, since it resembled a boat only from above and from the sides; the base was some sort of metal construction. Four people lay flat inside it, but there was nothing around them—no black oarsmen, no rocks, no river, only thin jets of water spurted now and then from concealed nozzles. . . . Somewhat farther away stood the obelisk of rock at which our journey had come to an end; it rose like a tethered balloon, for it was not supported by anything. From it the footbridge led to a stone exit that jutted out from the metal wall. A little higher, small steps with a handrail, and a door. That was all. The dugout with the people tossed, rose, fell sharply, without the slightest sound; I heard only the bursts of hilarity that accompanied each successive stage of the adventure of the waterfall that did not exist. After a while the dugout collided with the rock, the people jumped out, they had to cross the footbridge. .... .

Twenty seconds, perhaps, had gone by since my leap. I looked for the woman. She was watching me. I grew confused. I did not know whether I should go over to her. But the crowd began to leave, and the next moment we found ourselves next to each other.

"It's always the same," she said then. "I always fall!"

The night in the park, the fireworks, and the music were, somehow, not entirely real. We left with the crowd, which was agitated after the terrors it had just experienced. I saw the woman's companion pushing his way toward her. Again he was lethargic. He did not appear to notice me at all.

"Let's go to Merlin's," the woman said, so loudly that I heard. I had not intended to eavesdrop. But a new wave of exiting people pushed us together even closer. For this reason, I continued to stand near them.

"You look like you are trying to escape," she said, smiling. "What, are you afraid of witchcraft . . . ?"

She spoke to him but looked at me. I could have elbowed my way out, of course, but, as always in such situations, I was most afraid of appearing ridiculous. They moved on, leaving a gap in the crowd. Others, next to me, suddenly decided to visit Merlin's Palace, and when I headed in that direction, with a few people separating us, I knew that I had not been mistaken a moment before.

We moved a step at a time. On the lawn stood pots of tar fluttering with flame; their light revealed steep bricked bastions. We crossed a drawbridge over a moat and stepped under the bared teeth of a portcullis, the dimness and chill of a stone entrance hall embraced us, a spiral staircase ascended, full of the echoes of thumping feet. But the arched corridor of the upper level contained fewer people. It led to a gallery with a view of a yard, where a noisy mob mounted on caparisoned horses pursued some black monstrosity; I went on, hesitant, not knowing where to go, among several people whom I was beginning to recognize; the woman and her companion passed by me between columns; empty suits of armor stood in recesses in the walls. Farther on, a door with copper fittings, a door for giants, opened up, and we entered a chamber upholstered in red damask, lit by torches whose resinous smoke irritated the nose. At tables a boisterous company was feasting, either pirates or knights-errant, huge sides of meat turned on spits, licked by flames, a reddish light played on sweating faces, bones crunched between the teeth of the armored revelers, who from time to time got up from their tables and mingled with us. In the next room several giants were playing skittles, using skulls for balls; the whole thing struck me as awfully naïve, mediocre; I had stopped beside the players, who were as tall as I, when someone bumped into me from behind and cried out in surprise. I turned and met the éyes of some youth. He stammered an apology and left quickly with a foolish expression on his face; only the look of the dark-haired woman who was the reason for my being in this palace of cheap wonders made me realize what had happened: the youth had tried to walk right through me, taking me for one of Merlin's unreal banqueters.

Merlin himself received us in a distant wing of the palace, surrounded by a retinue of masked men who assisted him passively in his feats of magic. But I had had enough of this and watched indifferently the demonstrations of the black art. The show was soon over, and the audience had begun to leave when Merlin, gray, magnificent, barred our way and silently pointed to the door opposite, covered with a shroud.

He invited only the three of us inside. He himself did not go in. We found ourselves in a fairly small room, very high, with one of the walls a mirror from the ceiling to the black-and-white stone floor. The impression was of a room twice the size that contained six people standing on a stone chessboard.

There was no furniture—nothing but a tall alabaster urn with a bouquet of flowers, which were like orchids but had unusually large calyxes. Each was a different color. We stood facing the mirror.

Then my image looked at me. The movement was not a reflection of my own. I froze, but the other, large, broad-shouldered, slowly looked first at the dark-haired woman, then at her companion. None of us moved, and only our images, grown independent of us in some mysterious way, came to life, played out a silent scene among themselves.

The young man in the mirror went up to the woman and looked into her eyes; she shook her head in refusal. She took the flowers from the white vase, sorted through them with her fingers, selected three—a white, a yellow, and a black. The white she gave to him, and with the other two she came to me. To me—in the mirror. She offered both flowers. I took the black. Then she returned to her place and all three of us—there, in the mirror room—assumed exactly the positions that we really occupied. When that happened, the flowers disappeared from the hands of our doubles, and they were once more ordinary reflections, faithfully repeating every moment.

A door in the far wall opened up; we went down spiral stairs. Columns, alcoves, vaults changed imperceptibly into the silver and white of plastic corridors. We walked on in silence, not separately, not together; the situation was becoming intolerable, but what was I to do? Step forward and introduce myself in the time-honored fashion, with an antiquated *savoir-vivre*?

The muffled sound of an orchestra. It was as if we were in the wings, behind an unseen stage; there were a few empty tables with the chairs pushed back. The woman stopped and asked her companion:

"You won't dance?"

"I don't want to," he said. I heard his voice for the first time.

He was handsome, but filled with an inertia, an unaccountable passivity, as if he cared about nothing in the world. He had beautiful lips, almost the lips of a girl. He looked at me. Then at her. He stood there, saying nothing.

"Well, then, go, if you like," she said. He parted a curtain that formed one of the walls, and left. I started to follow him.

"Please?" I heard her voice.

I stopped. From behind the curtain came applause.

"Won't you have a seat?"

Without a word I sat down. She had a magnificent profile. Her ears were covered by little shields of pearl.

"I am Aen Aenis."

"Hal Bregg."

She seemed surprised. Not by my name—it meant nothing to her—but by the fact that I had received her name so indifferently. Now I could get a close look at her. Her beauty was perfect and merciless, as was the calm, controlled carelessness of her movements. She wore a pink-gray dress, more gray than pink; it set off the whiteness of her face and arms.

"You don't like me?" she asked quietly.

"I don't know you."

"I am Ammai—in *The True Ones*."

"What is that?"

She regarded me with curiosity.

"You haven't seen *The True Ones*?"

"I don't even know what it is."

"Where did you come from?"

"I came here from my hotel."

"Really. From your hotel . . ." There was open mockery in her tone. "And where, may I ask, were you before you got to your hotel?"

"In Fomalhaut."

"What is that?"

"A constellation."

"What do you mean?"

"A star system, twenty-three light years from here."

Her eyelids fluttered. Her lips parted. She was very pretty.

"An astronaut?"

"Yes."

"I understand. I am a realist—rather well known."

I said nothing. We were silent. The music played.

"Do you dance?"

I nearly laughed out loud.

"What they dance now—no."

"A pity. But you can learn. Why did you do that?"

"Do what?"

"There—on the footbridge."

I did not answer immediately.

"It was . . . a reflex."

"You were familiar with it?"

"That make-believe journey? No."

"No?"

"No."

A moment of silence. Her eyes, for a moment green, now became almost black.

"Only in very old prints can one see that sort of thing," she
said, as if involuntarily. "No one would play . . . It isn't possible. When I saw it, I thought that . . . that you . . ."

I waited.

". . . might be able to. Because you took it seriously. Yes?"

"I don't know. Perhaps."

"Never mind. I know. Would you be interested? I'm friends
with Frenet. But you don't know who he is, do you? I must tell
him. . . . He is the chief producer of the real. If you are
interested . . ."

I burst out laughing. She gave a start.

"I'm sorry. But—ye gods and little fishes, you thought of
giving me a job as . . ."

"Yes."

She did not seem to be offended. Quite the contrary.

"Thank you, but no. I really don't think so."

"But can you tell me how you did it? Is it a secret?"

"What do you mean, how? Didn't you see . . . ?"

I broke off.

"You want to know how I was able to do it."

"You are most perceptive."

She knew how to smile with the eyes alone like no one else.
Wait, in a minute you won't be wanting to seduce me, I
thought.

"It's simple. And no secret. I'm not betrizated."

"Ooh . . ."

For a moment I thought that she would get up, but she controlled herself. Her eyes became once more large and avid. She

looked at me as at a beast that lay a step away, as though she found a perverse pleasure in the terror that I aroused in her. To me it was an insult worse than if she had been merely frightened.

"You can . . . ?"

"Kill?" I replied, smiling politely. "Yes. I can."

We were silent. The music played. Several times she raised her eyes to me. She did not speak. Nor did I. Applause. Music. Applause. We must have sat like that for a quarter of an hour. Suddenly she got up.

"Will you come with me?"

"Where?"

"To my place."

"For some brit?"

"No."

She turned and left. I sat without moving. I hated her. She walked without looking about, walked like no woman I had ever seen. She did not walk: she floated. Like a queen.

I caught up with her among hedges, where it was almost dark. The last traces of light from the pavilions blended with the bluish glow of the city. She must have heard my footsteps, but on she went, not looking, as if she were alone, even when I took her by the arm. She walked on; it was like a slap. I grabbed her shoulders, turned her to me; she lifted her face, white in the darkness; she looked into my eyes. She did not try to break away. But she could not have done so. I kissed her roughly, full of hatred; I felt her tremble.

"You . . . " she said in a low voice, when we separated.

"Be quiet."

She tried to free herself.

"Not yet," I said and began to kiss her again. Suddenly my rage turned into self-disgust, and I released her. I thought that she would flee. She remained. She tried to look me in the face. I turned away.

"What is the matter?" she asked quietly.

"Nothing."

She took me by the arm.

"Come."

A couple passed us and vanished in the shadows. I followed her. There, in the darkness, it had seemed that anything was possible, but when it grew lighter, my outburst of a moment before—which was supposed to have been in reprisal for an insult—became merely amusing. I felt that I was walking into something false, false as the danger had been, the wizardry, everything—and I walked on. No anger, no hatred, nothing. I did not care. I found myself among high-hanging lights and felt this huge, heavy presence of mine, which made my every step by her side grotesque. But she seemed unaware of this. She walked along a rampart, behind which stood rows of gleeders. I wanted to stay behind, but she slid her hand down my arm and grasped my hand. I would have had to tear it away, becoming even more comical—an image of astronautical virtue in the clutches of Potiphar's wife. I climbed in after her, the machine trembled and took off. It was my first trip in a gleeder, and I understood now why they had no windows. From the inside they were entirely transparent, as if made of glass.

We traveled a long time, in silence. The buildings of the city center gave way to bizarre forms of suburban architecture—under small artificial suns, immersed in vegetation, lay structures with flowing lines, or inflated into odd pillows, or winged, so that the division between the interior of a home and its surroundings was lost; these were products of a phantasmagoria, of tireless attempts to create without repeating old forms. The gleeder left the wide runway, shot through a darkened park, and came to rest by stairs folded like a cascade of glass; walking up them, I saw an orangery spread out beneath my feet.

The heavy gate opened soundlessly. A huge hall enclosed by a high gallery, pale pink shields of lamps neither supported nor suspended; in the sloping walls, windows that seemed to look out into a different space, niches containing not photographs, not dolls, but Aen herself, enormous, directly ahead—Aen in the arms of a dark man who kissed her, above the undulating staircase; Aen in the white, endless shimmer of a dress; and, to the side, Aen bent over flowers, lilies as large as her face. Walking behind her, I saw her again in another window, smiling girlishly, alone, the light trembling on her auburn hair.

Green steps. A suite of white rooms. Silver steps. Corridors from end to end, and in them, slow, incessant movement, as if the space were breathing; the walls slid back silently, making way wherever the woman before me directed her steps. One might think that an imperceptible wind were rounding off the intersections of the galleries, sculpturing them, and that everything I had seen so far were only a threshold, an introduction, a vestibule. Through a room, illuminated from without by the most delicate veining of ice, so white that even the shadows in it seemed milky, we entered a smaller room—after the pure radiance of the other, its bronze was like a shout. There was nothing here but a mysterious light from a source that seemed to be inverted, so that it shone on us and our faces from below; she made a motion of the hand, it dimmed; she stepped to the wall and with a few gestures conjured from it a swelling that immediately began to open out to make a kind of wide double bed— I knew enough about topology to appreciate the research that must have gone into the line of the headrest alone.

"We have a guest," she said, pausing. From the open paneling a low table emerged, all set, and ran to her like a dog. The large lights went out when, over a niche with armchairs—I cannot describe what sort of armchairs they were—she gestured for a small lamp to appear, and the wall obeyed. She seemed to have had enough of these budding, blooming pieces of furniture; she leaned across the table and asked, not looking in my direction:

"Blar?"

"All right," I said. I asked no questions; I could not help being a savage, but at least I could be a silent savage.

She handed me a tall cone with a tube in it; it glittered like a ruby but was soft, as though I had touched the fuzzy skin of a fruit. She took one herself. We sat down. Uncomfortably soft, like sitting on a cloud. The liquid had a taste of unknown fresh fruits, with tiny lumps that unexpectedly and amusingly burst on the tongue.

"Is it good?" she asked.

"Yes."

Perhaps this was a ritual drink. For example, for the chosen ones; or, on the contrary, to pacify the especially dangerous. But I had decided to ask no questions.

"It's better when you sit."

"Why?"

"You're awfully large."

"That I know."

"You work at being rude."

"No. It comes to me naturally."

She began to laugh, quietly.

"I am also witty," I said. "All sorts of talents."

"You're different," she said. "No one talks like that. Tell me, how is it? What do you feel?"

"I don't understand."

"You're pretending. Or perhaps you lied—no, that isn't possible. You wouldn't have been able to . . ."

"Jump?"

"I wasn't thinking of that."

"Of what, then?"

Her eyes narrowed.

"You don't know?"

"Ah, that!" I said. "And isn't that done any more?"

"It is, but not like that."

"I do it so well?"

"No, certainly not . . . but it was as if you had wanted to . . ." She did not finish.

"To what?"

"You know. I felt it."

"I was angry," I confessed.

"Angry!" she said contemptuously. "I thought that . . . I don't know what I thought. No one would dare to, you know."

I began to smile a little.

"And you liked it."

"You don't understand a thing. This is a world without fear, but you, one can be afraid of you."

"You want more?" I asked. Her lips parted, again she looked at me as at an imaginary beast.

"I do."

She moved toward me. I took her hand, placed it against my own, flat—her fingers barely reached beyond my palm.

"What a hard hand you have," she said.

"It's from the stars. They're sharp-edged. And now say: What large teeth you have."

She smiled.

"Your teeth are quite ordinary."

Then she lifted my hand, and was so careful doing it that I remembered the encounter with the lion, but instead of feeling offended I smiled, because it was awfully stupid.

She got up, stood over me, poured herself a drink from a small dark bottle, and drank it down.

"Do you know what that is?" she asked, screwing up her face as if the liquid burned. She had enormous lashes, no doubt false. Actresses always have false lashes.

"No."

"You won't tell anyone?"

"No."

"Perto."

"Well," I said noncommittally.

She opened her eyes.

"I saw you before. You were walking with a horrible old man, and then you came back alone."

"That was the son of a young colleague of mine," I replied. The odd thing was, it was pretty much the truth.

"You attract attention—do you know?"

"What can I do?"

"Not only because you're so big. You walk differently—and you look around as though you . . ."

"What?"

"Were on your guard."

"Against what?"

She did not answer. Her expression changed. Breathing more heavily, she examined her own hand. The fingers trembled. "Now . . ." she said softly and smiled, though not at me. Her smile became inspired, the pupils dilated, engulfing the irises, she leaned back slowly until her head was on the gray pillow, the auburn hair fell loose, she gazed at me in a kind of jubilant stupor.

"Kiss me."

I embraced her, and it was awful, because I wanted to and I didn't want to. It seemed to me that she had ceased to be herself—as though at any moment she could change into something else. She sank her fingers into my hair; her breathing, when she tore herself away from me, was like a moan. One of us is false, contemptible, I thought, but who, she or I? I kissed her, her face was painfully beautiful, terribly alien, then there was only pleasure, unbearable, but even then the cold, silent observer remained in me; I did not lose myself. The back of the chair, obedient, became a rest for our heads, it was like the presence of a third person, degradingly attentive, and, as though aware of this, we did not exchange a single word during the entire time. Then I was dozing, my arms around her neck, and still it seemed to me that someone stood and watched, watched. . . .

When I awoke, she was asleep. It was a different room. No, the same. But it had changed somehow—a part of the wall had moved aside to reveal the dawn. Above us, as if it had been forgotten, a narrow lamp burned. Straight ahead, above the tops of the trees, which were still almost black, day was breaking. Carefully I moved to the edge of the bed; she murmured something like "Alan," and went on sleeping.

I walked through huge, empty rooms. In them were windows facing east. A red glow entered and filled the transparent furniture, which flickered with the fire of red wine. Through the suite of rooms I saw the silhouette of someone walking—a pearly-gray robot without a face, its torso giving off a weak light; inside it glowed a ruby flame, like a small lamp before an icon.

"I wish to leave," I said.

"Yes, sir."

Silver, green, sky-blue stairs. I bade farewell to all the faces of Aen in the hall as high as a cathedral. It was day now. The robot opened the gate. I told it to call a gleeder for me.

"Yes, sir. Would you like the house one?"

"It can be the house one. I want to get to the Alcaron Hotel."

"Very good, sir. Acknowledged."

Someone else had addressed me in this way. Who? I could not recall.

Down the steep steps—so that to the very end it would be remembered that this was a palace, not a home—we both went; in the light of the rising sun I got into the machine. When it began to move, I looked back. The robot was still standing in a subservient pose, a little like a mantis with its thin, articulated arms.

The streets were almost empty. In the gardens, like strange, abandoned ships, the villas rested, yes, rested, as if they had only alighted for a moment among the hedges and trees, folding their angular, colored wings. There were more people in the center of the city. Spires with their summits ablaze in the sun, palm-garden houses, leviathan houses on widely spread stilts—the street cut through them, flew off into the blue horizon; I did not look at anything more. At the hotel I took a bath and telephoned the travel office. I reserved an ulder for twelve. It amused me a little, that I could toss the name around so easily, having no idea what an ulder was.

I had four hours. I called the hotel infor and asked about the Breggs. I had no descendants, but my father's brother had left two children, a boy and a girl. Even if they were not living, their children . . .

The infor listed eleven Breggs. I then asked for their genealogy. It turned out that only one of them, an Atal Bregg, belonged to my family. He was my uncle's grandson, not young, either: he was now almost sixty. So I had found out what I wanted to know. I even picked up the receiver with the intention of phoning him, but put it down again. What, after all, did I have to say to him? Or he to me? How my father had died? My mother? I had died to them earlier and now had no right, as their surviving child, to ask. It would have been—or so I felt at that moment—an act of treachery, as if I had tricked them, evading fate in a cowardly escape, hiding myself within time, which had been less mortal for me than for them. It was they who had buried me, among the stars, not I them, on Earth.

However, I did lift the receiver. The phone rang a long time. At last the house robot answered and informed me that Atal Bregg was off Earth.

"Where?" I asked quickly.

"On Luna. He is away for four days. What shall I tell him?"

"What does he do? What is his profession?" I asked. "Because . . . I am not sure he is the one I want, perhaps there has been a mistake. . . ."

It was easier, somehow, to lie to a robot.

"He is a psychopedist."

"Thank you. I will call back in a few days."

I put the receiver down. At least he was not an astronaut; good.

I got the hotel infor again and asked what it could recommend as entertainment for two or three hours.

"Try our realon," it said.

"What's there?"

"*The Fiancée*. It is the latest real of Aen Aenis."

I went down; it was in the basement. The show had already begun, but the robot at the entrance told me that I had missed practically nothing—only a few minutes. It led me into the darkness, drew out an egg-shaped chair, and, after seating me in it, disappeared.

My first impression was of sitting near the stage of a theater, or no—on the stage itself, so close were the actors. As though one could reach out and touch them. I was in luck, because it was a story from my time, in other words, a historical drama; the years during which the action took place were not specified exactly, but, judging from certain details, it was a decade or two after my departure.

Right away I was delighted by the costumes; the scenario was naturalistic, but for that very reason I enjoyed myself, because I caught a great number of mistakes and anachronisms. The hero, a handsome swarthy man with brown hair, came out of his house in a dress suit (it was early morning) and went by car to meet his beloved; he even had on a top hat, but a gray one, as if he were an Englishman riding at the Derby. Later, a romantic roadhouse came into view, with an innkeeper like none that I had ever seen—he looked like a pirate; the hero seated himself on the tails of his jacket and drank beer through a straw; and so on.

Suddenly I stopped smiling; Aen had entered. She was dressed absurdly, but that became irrelevant. The viewer knew that she loved another and was deceiving the young man; the typical, melodramatic role of the treacherous woman, sentimentality, cliché. But Aen did it differently. She was a girl devoid of thought, affectionate, heedless, and, because of the limitless naïveté of her cruelty, an innocent creature, one who brought unhappiness to everyone because she did not want to make anyone unhappy. Falling into the arms of one man, she forgot about the other, and did this in such a way that one believed in her sincerity—for the moment.

But this nonsense did not hold together, and there remained only Aen the great actress.

The real was more than just a film, because whenever I concentrated on some portion of the scene, it grew larger and expanded; in other words, the viewer himself, by his own choice, determined whether he would see a close-up or the whole picture. Meanwhile the proportions of what remained on the periphery of his field of vision underwent no distortion. It was a diabolically clever optical trick producing an illusion of an extraordinarily vivid, an almost magnified reality.

Afterward I went up to my room to pack my things, for in a few minutes I would be setting off. It turned out that I had more things than I thought. I was not ready when the telephone sang out: my ulder was waiting.

"I'll be down in a minute," I said. The robot porter took my bags, and I was on my way out when the telephone sounded again. I hesitated. The soft signal repeated itself untiringly. Just so it doesn't look like I'm running away, I thought, and lifted the receiver, not altogether sure, however, why I was doing it.

"Is that you?"

"Yes. You're up?"

"A long time ago. What are you doing?"

"I saw you. In the real."

"Yes?" was all she said, but I sensed the satisfaction in her voice. It meant: he is mine.

"No," I said.

"No what?"

"Girl, you are a great actress. But I am not at all the person you imagine me to be."

"Did I imagine last night, too?" she interrupted. In her voice, a quiver of amusement—and suddenly the ridiculousness returned. I was unable to avoid it: the Quaker from the stars who has fallen once, stern, desperate, and modest.

"No," I said, controlling myself, "you didn't imagine it. But I am going away."

"Forever?"

She was enjoying the conversation.

"Girl," I began, and did not know what to say. For a moment I heard only her breathing.

"And what next?" she asked.

"I don't know." I quickly corrected myself: "Nothing. I'm going away. There is no sense to this."

"None whatever," she agreed, "and that is why it can be splendid. What did you see? *The True Ones?*"

"No, *The Fiancée.* Listen. . . ."

"That's a complete bomb. I can't look at it. My worst thing. See *The True Ones,* or no, come this evening. I'll show it to you. No, no, today I can't. Tomorrow."

"Aen, I'm not coming. I really am leaving in a minute. . . ."

"Don't say 'Aen' to me, say 'girl,'" she begged.

"Girl, go to hell!" I put down the receiver, felt terribly

ashamed of myself, picked it up, put it down once more, and ran out of the room as if someone were after me. Downstairs, I learned that the ulder was on the roof. And so up again.

On the roof there was a garden restaurant and an airport. Actually, a restaurant-airport, a mixture of levels, flying platforms, invisible windows—I would not have found my ulder in a year. But I was led to it, practically by the hand. It was smaller than I expected. I asked how long the flight would last, for I planned to do some reading.

"About twelve minutes."

It was not worth starting anything. The interior of the ulder reminded me a little of the experimental Thermo-Fax rocket that I had piloted once, except that it was more comfortable, but when the door closed on the robot that wished me a pleasant trip, the walls instantly became transparent, and because I had taken the first of the four seats (the others were unoccupied), the impression was of flying in an armchair mounted inside a large glass.

It's funny, but the ulder had nothing in common with a rocket or an airplane; it was more like a magic carpet. The peculiar vehicle first moved vertically, without the least vibration, giving off a long whistle, then it sped horizontally, like a bullet. Again the thing that I had observed once before: acceleration was not accompanied by an increase in inertia. The first time, at the station, I had thought that I might be the victim of an illusion; now, however, I was sure of myself. It is difficult to put into words the feeling that came over me—because if they had truly succeeded in making acceleration independent of inertia, then all the hibernations, tests, selections, hardships, and frustrations of our voyage turned out to be completely needless; so that, at that moment, I was like the conqueror of some Himalayan peak who, after the indescribable difficulty of the climb, discovers that there is a hotel full of tourists at the top, because during his lonely labor a cable car and amusement arcades had been installed on the opposite side. The fact that had I remained on Earth I would probably not have lived to see this amazing discovery was small consolation to me: a consolation would be, rather, the thought that perhaps this contrivance did not lend itself to cosmic navigation. That was, of course, pure egoism on my part, I admitted it, but the shock was too great for me to be able to show the proper enthusiasm.

Meanwhile the ulder flew, now without a sound; I looked down. We were passing the Terminal. It moved slowly to the rear, a fortress of ice; on the upper levels, not visible from the city, huge rocket pads showed black. Then we flew fairly close to the needle tower, the one with black and silver stripes; it loomed above the ulder. From the Earth, its height could not be appreciated. It was a bridge of pipe joining the city and the sky, and the "shelves" that protruded from it were crowded with ulders and other, bigger, machines. The people on these landing strips looked like poppy seeds spilled on a silver plate. We flew over white and blue colonies of houses, over gardens; the streets got wider and wider, their surfaces were also colored—pale pink and ocher predominated. A sea of buildings extended to the horizon, broken occasionally by belts of green, and I feared that this would continue all the way to Clavestra. But the machine picked up speed, the houses became scattered, dispersed among the gardens, there appeared instead enormous loops and straight stretches of roads; these ran at numerous levels, merged, criss-crossed, plunged beneath the ground, converged in star-shaped arrangements, and shot away in strips along a flat gray-green plane beneath the high sun, swarming with gleeders. Then, amid quadrangles of trees, emerged huge structures with roofs in the shape of concave mirrors; in their centers burned something red. Farther along, the roads separated and green prevailed, now and then interrupted by squares of a different vegetation—red, blue —they could not have been flowers, the colors were too intense.

Dr. Juffon would be proud of me, I thought. The third day, and already . . . And what a beginning. Not just anyone. A brilliant actress, famous. She had not been afraid, and if afraid, then she had got pleasure from the fear, too. Just keep it up. But why had he spoken of intimacy? Was that what their intimacy looked like? How heroically I jumped into the waterfall. The noble gorilla. And then a beauty, worshiped by the masses, lavishly rewarded him; how generous of her!

My face burned all over. All right, cretin, I said to myself mildly, what exactly do you want? A woman? You've had a woman. You've had everything it's possible to have here, including an offer to appear in the real. Now you will have a house, you will take walks in a garden, read books, look at the stars, and tell yourself, quietly, in your modesty: I was there. I was there and I came back. And even the laws of physics worked in your favor, lucky man, you have half a lifetime ahead of you, and do you remember how Roemer looked, a hundred years older than yourself?

The ulder began its descent, the whistling started up, the ground, crossed by white and blue roads whose surfaces gleamed like enamel, grew larger. Great ponds and small square pools threw up sparks of sun. Houses scattered on the slopes of gentle hills became progressively more real. On the blue horizon stood a chain of mountains with whitened peaks. I saw gravel paths, lawns, flower beds, the cool green of water in cement-rimmed pools, lanes, bushes, a white roof; all this turned slowly, surrounded me, and became motionless, as if it had taken possession.

he door opened. A white-and-orange robot was waiting on the lawn. I stepped out.

"Welcome to Clavestra," it said, and its white belly unexpectedly began to sing: tinkling notes, as though it had a music box inside.

Still laughing, I helped it unload my things. Then the rear hatch of the ulder, which lay on the grass like a small silver zeppelin, opened, and two orange robots rolled out my car. The heavy blue body sparkled in the sun. I had completely forgotten about it. And then all the robots, carrying my suitcases, boxes, and packages, moved in single file toward the house.

The house was a large cube with glass walls. One entered through a panoramic solarium, and farther on were a hall, a dining room, and a wooden staircase going up; the robot, the one with the music box, did not fail to point out to me this rarity.

Upstairs there were five rooms. I did not pick one with the best—an eastern—exposure because in them, particularly in the room with the view of the mountains, there was too much gold and silver, whereas mine had only streaks of green, like crushed leaves on a cream background.

Efficiently and quietly, the robots put all my belongings away in closets while I stood at the window. A port, I thought. A haven. Leaning forward, I could see the blue mist of the mountains. Below lay a flower garden with a dozen or so old fruit trees farther back; they had twisted, tired boughs and probably no longer yielded anything.

Off to the side, toward the road (I had seen it earlier from the ulder, it was obscured by hedges), the tower of a diving board rose above the brush. The pool. When I turned around, the robots had already left. I moved the desk, light as if inflated, over to the window; on it I set my packs of scientific journals, the bags of crystal books, and the reading machine; I arranged the still-unused notebooks and the pen separately. It was my old pen—under the increased gravity it had started leaking and blotted everything, but Olaf had fixed it. I put covers on the notebooks, labeled them "History," "Mathematics," and "Physics"—all in a rush, because I was anxious to get into the water. I didn't know if I could go outside in my trunks, I had forgotten a bathrobe. So I went to the bathroom in the corridor, and there, maneuvering a bottle of foam, I produced a horrible monstrosity that bore no resemblance to anything. I tore it off and tried again. The second bathrobe turned out a little better, but even so it was a fright; I cut away the larger irregularities of the sleeves and hem with a knife, and then it was more or less presentable.

I went downstairs, still not sure if anyone was home. The hall was empty. The garden, too. There was only an orange robot trimming the grass by the rosebushes, which were already out of bloom.

I practically ran to the pool. The water gleamed and shimmered. An invisible freshness hung over it. I threw my robe on the golden sand that burned my feet, then pounded up the metal steps and ran to the top of the diving board. It was low, but fine for a start. I kicked off, did a single somersault—I wouldn't attempt more after such a long time!—and entered the water like a knife.

I swam happily. I began to pull myself with large strokes, first in one direction, then a turn, the other direction. The pool was about fifty meters long; I did eight laps without slowing down, climbed out dripping like a seal, and lay on the sand, my heart hammering. It was good. Earth had its attractions! In a few minutes I was dry. I stood up, looked around: no one. Splendid. I ran up on the springboard. First I did a back somersault; it came off, although I had kicked too hard: instead of a plank there was a section of plastic, which worked like a spring. Then a double; not too successful, I hit the water with my thighs. The skin reddened for a moment, as though it had been burned. And again. A little better, still not right. On the second turn I did not straighten out in time and screwed up with my feet. But I was stubborn and I had the time, plenty of time! A third dive, a fourth, a fifth. I had begun to feel a buzzing in my ears when —after one more look around, just in case—I tried a somersault with a twist. It was a complete bust, a fiasco; the impact knocked the wind out of me, I swallowed water, and, coughing and sputtering, crawled out onto the sand. I sat under the azure ladder of the diving board, mortified and angry, until suddenly I burst out laughing. Then I swam four hundred meters more, took a break, and did another four hundred.

When I returned to the house the world looked different. That was what I had been missing the most, I thought. A white robot was waiting at the door.

"Will you eat in your room or in the dining room?"

"Will I be eating alone?"

"Yes, sir. The others arrive tomorrow."

"The dining room, then."

I went upstairs and changed. I still did not know where to begin my studies. Probably with history; that would be the most sensible, yet I wanted to do everything at once, and most of all to attack the mystery of how gravity had been conquered. A musical tone sounded—not the telephone—and because I did not know what it was, I called the house infor.

"Lunch is served," explained a melodious voice.

The dining room was bathed in a light filtered through greenery; the curved panes in the ceiling glittered like crystal. On the table lay one setting. A robot brought the menu.

"No, no," I said, "anything will do."

The first course was like a cold fruit soup. The second was not like anything. I would have to say good-bye to meat, potatoes, and vegetables, apparently.

It was a good thing that I ate alone, because my dessert exploded on me. A slight exaggeration, perhaps; in any case I ended up with cream on my knees and on my sweater. It had been a complicated structure, hard only at the surface, and I had poked it carelessly with my spoon.

When a robot appeared, I asked if I could have coffee in my room.

"Of course," it said. "Now?"

"Please. But a lot of coffee."

I said this because I was feeling a little sleepy, no doubt as a result of my swim, and suddenly I regretted the time that I had been wasting. How completely different it was here from on board the spacecraft! The afternoon sun beat down on the old trees, the shadows were short, they joined together at the trunks, the air quivered in the distance, but the room remained cool. I sat at the desk, took up the books. The robot brought me coffee. The transparent thermos held at least three liters. I said nothing. Clearly, it had overcompensated for my dimensions.

I intended to begin with history, but I started in on sociology, because I wanted to learn as much as possible right away. I soon discovered, however, that I was in over my head. The subject was loaded with a difficult—since specialized—mathematics, and, what was worse, the authors referred to facts unknown to me. In addition, I did not understand many words and had to look them up in the encyclopedia. So I set up a second opton for myself—I had three—then gave this up, because it took too long. I swallowed my pride and opened an ordinary school textbook on history.

Something had got into me and I did not have an ounce of patience—I, whom Olaf had called the last incarnation of the Buddha. Instead of taking things in order, I turned immediately to the chapter on betrization.

The theory had been worked out by three people: Bennett, Trimaldi, and Zakharov. Hence the name. I was surprised to learn that they were of my generation—they had announced their discovery a year after our departure. The resistance to it, of course, was tremendous. At first no one even wanted to take the project seriously. Then it reached the forum of the UN. For some time it went from subcommittee to subcommittee—it seemed that the project would be buried in endless deliberation. In the meantime the research was making rapid progress, improvements were introduced, large-scale experiments were carried out on animals, then on humans (the first to submit to the procedure were the originators themselves—Trimaldi was paralyzed for some time, the dangers of betrization to adults having not been discovered yet, and this stopped the project for the next eight years). But in the seventeenth year after zero (my personal reckoning: zero was the takeoff of the *Prometheus*) a resolution for the universal implementation of betrization was passed; and this was only the beginning of the struggle for the humanization of mankind (as the textbook put it). In many countries parents refused to have their children treated, and attacks were made on the first betrization centers; fifty or sixty of them were completely destroyed. A period of turmoil, of repression, of coercion and resistance, lasted some twenty years. The textbook passed over this with a few generalities, for perfectly obvious reasons. I resolved to consult source materials for more detailed information, but meanwhile continued my reading. The new order became firmly established only when the first betrizated generation had children. About the biological aspect of the process the book said nothing. There were a great many paeans, on the other hand, for Bennett, Zakharov, and Trimaldi. A proposal was made to number the years of the New Era from the time of the introduction of betrization, but was not accepted. The reckoning of dates did not change. The people changed. The chapter concluded with a ringing encomium to the New Epoch of Humanism.

I looked up the monograph on betrization by Ullrich. It, too, was full of mathematics, but I was determined to stick with it. The procedure was not carried out on the hereditary plasm, as I had secretly feared. But, then, had it been, it would not have been necessary to betrizate each new generation. That was encouraging: there remained, at least in theory, the possibility of return. Betrization acted on the developing prosencephalon at an early stage in life by means of a group of proteolytic enzymes. The effects were selective: the reduction of aggressive impulses by 80 to 88 percent in comparison with the nonbetrizated; the elimination of the formation of associative links between acts of aggression and the sphere of positive feelings; a general 87-percent reduction in the possibility of accepting personal risk to life. The greatest achievement cited was the fact that these changes did not influence negatively the development of intelligence or the formation of personality, and, what was even more important, that the resulting limitations did not operate on the principle of fear conditioning. In other words, a man refrained from killing not because he feared the act itself. Such a result would have psychoneuroticized and infected with fear all of mankind. Instead, a man did not kill because "it could not enter his head" to do so.

One sentence in Ullrich struck me particularly: "Betrization causes the disappearance of aggression through the complete absence of command, and not by inhibition." Thinking this over, I concluded, however, that it did not explain the most important thing, the thought process of a man subjected to betrization. They were, after all, completely normal people, able to imagine absolutely anything, and therefore murder, too. What, then, made doing it impossible?

I searched for the answer to that question until it grew dark outside. As was usually the case with scientific problems, what seemed clear and simple in an abstract or a summary became more complicated the more precise an explanation I required. The musical signal announced dinner—I asked that it be brought to my room, but I did not even touch it. The explanations that I found at last did not entirely agree. A repulsion, similar to disgust; a supreme aversion, magnified in a manner incomprehensible to one not betrizated; most interesting were testimonies from people who, eighty years before, as subjects in an experiment at the Tribaldi Institute near Rome, had attempted to override the invisible barrier established in their minds. This was the most striking thing that I read. None of them had succeeded, but each gave a different account of the sensations that accompanied his attempt. For some, psychological symptoms predominated: a desire to escape, to avoid the situation in which they had been placed. In this group, continued testing caused severe headaches and, if persisted in, led finally to neurosis, which, however, could be quickly cured. In others, physical symptoms prevailed: shortness of breath, a feeling of suffocation; the condition resembled the manifestations of fear, but these people did not complain of fear, only of their physical discomfort.

The work of Pilgrin showed that 18 percent of those betrizated were able to perform a simulated murder, for example on a dummy, but the belief that they were dealing with an inanimate doll had to take the form of absolute certainty.

The prohibition was extended to all the higher animals, but amphibians and reptiles did not count as such, nor did insects. Of course, those betrizated had no scientific knowledge of zoological taxonomy. The prohibition simply applied according to the degree of similarity to man, as generally accepted. Because everyone, educated or not, considers a dog to be closer to a man than is a snake, the problem was in this way resolved.

As I went through many other papers, I had to agree with those who said that a betrizated individual could be understood introspectively only by one who was himself betrizated. I set aside this reading with mixed feelings. What disturbed me most was the lack of any critical work done in the spirit of opposition, of satire even, the lack of any analysis summarizing the negative aspects of the procedure. For I did not doubt for a minute that such existed, not because I questioned the scientists but simply because this is the nature of all human enterprise: there is never good without evil.

Murwick's brief sociographic sketch provided me with a number of interesting facts about the resistance to betrization in its early days. This appears to have been strongest in countries with a long tradition of conflict and bloodshed, such as Spain and certain Latin-American states. But illegal organizations to combat betrization were formed throughout the world—in South Africa, in Mexico, on several islands in the Pacific. All kinds of methods were employed, from the forging of medical certificates stating that the operations had been performed, to the assassination of the doctors who performed them. The period of large-scale violence was followed by an apparent calm. Apparent, because it was then that the conflict of the generations began. The betrizated young, growing up, rejected a considerable part of humanity's achievement, and customs, traditions, art, the entire cultural heritage underwent a radical re-evaluation. The change included a large number of areas—sexuality, social mores, the attitude toward war.

Of course, this great division of the people had been anticipated. The law was not enacted until five years after its passage, because enormous cadres had to be assembled—educators, psychologists, various specialists—to chart the proper course of development for the new generation. Total reform was necessary in schooling, in the content of plays, reading material, films. Betrization—to convey the scope of the transformation in a few words—during the first ten years consumed about 40 percent of national revenues throughout the world, in all its ramifications and exigencies.

It was a time of great tragedies. Young people, betrizated, became strangers to their own parents, whose interests they did not share. They abhorred their parents' bloody tastes. For a quarter of a century it was necessary to have two types of periodicals, books, plays: one for the old generation, one for the new. But all this had taken place eighty years earlier. Children born now were of the third betrizated generation, and only a handful of the nonbetrizated were still alive; these were people one hundred and thirty years old. The substance of their youth seemed to the new generation as remote as the Paleolithic.

In the history textbook I finally found information on the second great event of the last century, the harnessing of gravitation. The century was even called the "age of parastatics." My generation had dreamed of conquering gravity in the hope that that would bring about a revolution in space travel. It turned out differently. The revolution came, but its primary effect was on Earth.

The problem of "peacetime death" caused by transportation accidents had become the menace of my day. I remember how some of the best minds strove, by relieving the perpetual congestion of the roads and highways, to reduce even a little the ever-mounting statistics; each year hundreds of thousands of lives were claimed in disasters, the problem seemed insoluble, like squaring the circle. There was no way to return, it was said, to the safety of traveling on foot; the best airplane, the most powerful automobile or train could slip from human control; automata were more dependable than people, but they, too, broke down; every technology, even the most advanced, had a certain margin, a percentage of error.

Parastatics, gravitation engineering, provided a solution, one as necessary as it was unexpected: necessary because a betrizated world had to be a world of complete safety; otherwise, the virtues of this medical procedure would have been pointless.

Roemer had been right. The essence of the discovery could be expressed only through mathematics—and, I must add, an infernal mathematics. The general solution, holding "for all possible universes," was given by Emil Mitke, the son of a post-office clerk, a crippled genius who did with the theory of relativity what Einstein had done with Newton. It was a long, unusual story and, like all true stories, improbable, a mixture of matters trivial and momentous, of the ridiculous and the colossal in man, and it culminated at last, after forty years, in the "little black boxes."

Every vehicle, every craft on water or in the air, had to have its little black box; it was a guarantee of "salvation now," as Mitke jokingly put it toward the end of his life; at the moment of danger—a plane crash, a collision of cars or trains—the little black box released a "gravitational antifield" charge that combined with the inertia produced by the impact (more generally, by the sudden braking, the loss of speed) and gave a resultant of zero. This mathematical zero was a concrete reality; it absorbed all the shock and all of the energy of the accident, and in this way saved not only the passengers of the vehicle but also those whom the mass of the vehicle would otherwise have crushed.

The black boxes were to be found everywhere: in elevators, in hoists, in the belts of parachutists, in ocean-going vessels and motorcycles. The simplicity of their construction was as astounding as the complexity of the theory that produced them.

Daybreak was reddening the walls of my room when I fell exhausted on my bed.

I was awakened by a robot entering the room with breakfast. It was almost one o'clock. Sitting up in bed, I made sure that nearby was the book I had put aside the previous night—On Interstellar Flight by Starck.

"You have to eat, Mr. Bregg," the robot said reprovingly. "Otherwise, you will become weak. Also, reading until dawn is inadvisable. Doctors are very much against it."

"I am sure they are, but how do you know this?" I asked.

"It is my duty, Mr. Bregg."

It handed me a tray.

"I will try to mend my ways," I said.

"I hope that you do not misinterpret my good will and think me importunate," it replied.

"Ah, not at all," I said. Stirring the coffee and feeling the lumps of sugar crumble beneath the spoon, I was amazed, in a way both serene and profound, not only by the fact that I was actually on Earth, that I had returned, not only by the reading I had done all night, which still agitated me and fermented in my head, but also simply because I was sitting on a bed, my heart was beating—I was alive. I wanted to do something in honor of this discovery, but, as usual, nothing particularly sensible came to mind.

"Listen," I addressed the robot, "I have a favor to ask you."

"I am at your command."

"Do you have a moment? Then play me that tune, the one from yesterday, all right?"

"With pleasure," it answered. To the merry sound of the music box I drank my coffee in three gulps; as soon as the robot left the room, I changed and ran to the pool. I cannot say why I was in such a constant hurry. Something drove me, as if I sensed that at any moment this peace would come to an end, undeserved as it was and unbelievable. In any case, my endless urgency made me cut across the garden at a run, without looking around me, and in a few bounds I was at the top of the diving-board tower; I had already kicked off when I noticed two people coming out from behind the house. For obvious reasons I could not study them closely. I did a somersault, not the best, and dove to the bottom. I opened my eyes. The water was like shimmering crystal, green, with the shadows of waves dancing on the sunlit bottom. I swam low above it, in the direction of the steps, and when I surfaced there was no one in the garden. But my skilled eyes had fixed a picture in my mind, perceived upside down and in a fraction of a second—of a man and a woman. Apparently I had neighbors now. I debated whether to swim one more length, but Starck won out. The introduction to the book—where he spoke of flights to the stars as a mistake of the early days of astronautics—had so angered me that I was ready to close it and not return to it. But I forced myself. I went upstairs, changed; coming down, I saw on the hall table a bowl full of pale pink fruit somewhat similar to pears; I stuffed the pockets of my gardening overalls with them, then found a secluded spot surrounded on three sides by hedges, climbed an old apple tree, selected a fork in the branches that could take my weight, and there set about studying this obituary on my life's work.

After an hour, I was not so sure of myself. Starck employed arguments difficult to refute. He based them on the meager data brought back by the two expeditions that had preceded ours; we had called them the "pinpricks," for they were probes over a distance of only several light years. Starck drew up statistical tables of the probability distribution or "habitation density" of the entire galaxy. The probability of encountering intelligent beings, he concluded, was one in twenty. In other words, for every twenty expeditions—within a radius of a thousand light years—one expedition had a chance of discovering an inhabited planet. This conclusion, however, odd as it may sound, was considered by Starck to be quite encouraging; he demolished the idea of establishing cosmic contacts in a later part of his exposition.

I bridled, reading what an author, unknown to me, had written about expeditions like ours—that is, initiated before the discovery of the Mitke effect and the phenomenon of parastatics—because he regarded them as absurd. But I learned from him, in black and white, that, in principle at least, it was possible to construct a ship that could reach an acceleration on the order of 1,000, perhaps even 2,000 g's. The crew of such a craft would feel no acceleration or braking; on board, the gravitation would be constant, equal to a fraction of Earth's. Thus, Starck admitted that flights to the ends of the galaxy, and even to other galaxies—the transgalactodromia of which Olaf had dreamed—were possible, and possible in the span of a single lifetime. At a speed a tiny fraction of a percent less than the speed of light, a crew would age by several or a couple of dozen months in the time it took to reach the depths of the metagalaxy and return to Earth. But in that time not hundreds but millions of years would have elapsed on Earth. The civilization found by those who returned would not be able to assimilate them. It would be easier for a Neanderthal to adapt to life in our time. That was not all. The fate of a group of people was not the issue here. They were the envoys of humanity. Humanity posed—through them—a question, to which they were to bring back an answer. If the answer concerned problems connected with the level of development of the civilization, then humanity would surely obtain it before their return. Because from the posing of the question to the arrival of the answer, millions of years would have passed. The answer, moreover, would be out of date, defunct, for they would be bringing news of the state of the other civilization at the time when they had reached that far shore of the stellar sea. During their journey back, however, that other world would not be standing still, it would move forward a million, two million, three million years. The questions and answers, then, would miss one another, would suffer hundred-century delays, which would nullify them and make any exchange of experiences, values, and ideas impossible. Futile. The astronauts were thus purveyors of dead information, and their work an act of utter and irreversible separation from human history; space expeditions were an unprecedented and expensive—the most expensive possible—desertion of the realm of historical change. And for such a fantasy, a never profitable, always futile madness, Earth was to labor with the utmost effort and give up her best people?

The book ended with a chapter on the possibilities of exploration with the aid of robots. Robots, too, would transmit dead information, but this approach would at least avoid human sacrifices.

And there was a three-page appendix, an attempt to answer the question of the possible existence of travel faster than light, and even of the so-called instantaneous cosmic conjunction, that is, the crossing of space with little or no passage of time, thanks to still-undiscovered properties of matter and space, through a sort of "hyperjump"; this theory, or, rather, speculation, not based on any facts to speak of, had a name—teletaxis. Starck believed that he had an argument to cancel this last remaining hope. If such a thing existed, he maintained, undoubtedly it would have been discovered by one of the more highly developed civilizations of our or another galaxy. In which case, the representatives of that civilization would have been able, in an incredibly short time, to visit in succession every planetary system and sun, including our own. But Earth had not experienced any such visit so far, which was proof that this lightning-fast method of penetrating the cosmos could be imagined but never turned into reality.

I went back to the house stunned, with the almost childish feeling that I had been personally injured. Starck, a man whom I had never met, had dealt me a blow as no one else ever had. My clumsy summary does not convey the ruthless logic of his reasoning. I do not know how I got to my room, how I changed my clothes—at one point I felt like having a cigarette and realized that I was smoking one already, sitting hunched on my bed as if I were waiting for something. True: lunch. Lunch for three. The fact was, I was afraid of people. I had not admitted this to myself, but that was why I had agreed so hurriedly to share the villa with strangers; perhaps anticipation of their arrival was even the reason for my unnatural haste, as if I had been working to get ready for their presence, to initiate myself, through the books, into the mysteries of the new life. I would not have considered this in the morning of that day, but after Starck's book my nervousness suddenly fell away from me. From the reading apparatus I removed the seedlike bluish crystal, and in awe placed it on the table. This was what had sent me reeling. For the first time since my return I thought of Thurber and Gimma. I would have to see them. Maybe the book was right, but we represented a different truth. No one had the whole truth. That was not possible. I was roused from my trance by the musical signal. I straightened my sweater and went downstairs, in control of myself, already calmer. The sun streamed through the vines of the veranda; the hall, as always in the afternoon, was filled with a diffuse greenish glow. On the table in the dining room lay three settings. As I entered, the door opposite opened and they appeared. They were tall by present standards. We met in the middle of the room, like diplomats. I gave my name, we shook hands and sat at the table.

A numbness possessed me, like that of a boxer who has picked himself up off the floor after a technical knockout. From my depression, as from a theater box, I looked at the young couple.

The girl was probably not even twenty. I was to conclude, later, that she did not lend herself to description; she certainly would not resemble a photograph of herself—and even on the second day I had no idea what kind of nose she had, straight or upturned. The way she held out her hand for a plate delighted me like something precious, a surprise that did not happen every day; she smiled rarely and with composure, as if slightly distrustful of herself, as if she felt she was insufficiently self-possessed, too merry by nature or maybe too willful, and she judiciously tried to remedy this, but her strictness toward herself was constantly being undermined, she knew of it, and it even amused her.

She drew my gaze, and I had to fight this. Every moment I was staring at her, at her hair, which challenged the wind; I bowed my head over my plate, I glanced furtively, reaching for a dish, so that twice I nearly knocked over a vase of flowers; in other words, I made a perfect ass of myself. But it was as if they did not see me at all. Their eyes were only for each other, and invisible threads of comprehension linked them. During the entire time I am sure we exchanged no more than twenty words, about how the weather was good, the place was nice, perfect for a vacation.

Marger was no more than a head shorter than I but was as slender as a boy, although he must have been thirty. He wore dark clothing, was blond, and had a long face and a high forehead. At first he seemed exceptionally handsome, but that was only when he kept his face immobile. He hardly said a word to his wife; when he did, usually with a smile, the conversation consisted of allusions and hints, completely cryptic to an outsider, and he became almost ugly. Not ugly, exactly. It was as if his facial proportions deteriorated; the mouth bent a little to the left and lost its expression, and even his smile became neutral, although he had beautiful white teeth. And when he was animated, the eyes were too blue, the jaw too pronounced, and altogether he was like an impersonal model of masculine charm, out of a fashion magazine.

In other words, from the first I felt an aversion to him.

The girl—I could not think of her as his wife, no matter how I tried—did not have pretty eyes or lips, or unusual hair; she had nothing unusual. She was in her entirety unusual. With one like her, carrying a tent on her back, I could cross the Rockies twice, I thought. Why mountains, exactly? I didn't know. She brought to mind nights spent in pine forests, the labor of scaling a cliff, the seashore, where there is nothing but the sand and the waves. Was this only because she wore no lipstick? I felt her smile, felt it across the table, even when she was not smiling at all. Then, in a sudden rush of boldness, I decided to look at her neck—as if committing a theft. This was near the end of the meal. Marger turned to me unexpectedly; I believe I blushed.

He had been speaking for some time before I caught the sense of what he was saying: that the house had only one gleeder, that he, unfortunately, had to take it, because he was going to the city. Therefore, if I, too, intended to go and did not want to wait until evening, perhaps I would accompany him? He could, of course, send me another gleeder from the city, or . . .

I interrupted him. I started to say that I had no intention of going anywhere, but I checked myself, as if I had remembered something, then heard my own voice saying that indeed I had planned to travel to the city and if he didn't mind . . .

"Well, then, that is perfect," he said. We got up from the table. "What time would be most convenient for you?"

We stood on ceremony awhile, then I got him to admit that he was in something of a hurry, and I said that I could go at any time. We agreed to leave in half an hour.

I went back upstairs, confounded by this turn of events. He meant nothing to me. And there was absolutely nothing that called me to the city. What, then, was the point of this escapade? I had the impression, besides, that his politeness toward me was a bit exaggerated. Anyway, if I had really been in a hurry to get to the city, the robots certainly would have seen to it. I would not have had to go on foot. Did he want something from me? But what? He didn't know me from Adam. I was puzzling over this, again for no good reason, when the agreed-upon time arrived and I went downstairs.

His wife was nowhere to be seen, nor did she appear at the window to say good-bye to him once more. Inside the spacious machine we were silent at first, watching curves appear as the road snaked among the hills. Slowly a conversation was struck up. I learned that Marger was an engineer.

"Today I have to inspect the city selex-station," he said. "You, too, I understand, are a cyberneticist?"

"From the Stone Age," I replied. "Excuse me . . . but how did you know that?"

"The travel office told me. I was naturally curious about who our neighbor would be."

"Aha."

We said nothing for a while; the increasing density of colored plastic outgrowths indicated our approach to the suburbs.

"If you don't mind . . . I wanted to ask you if you, the crew, had any problems with your automata," he said suddenly;

it was not so much from the question itself as from his tone that
I realized my answer was important to him. Was this what he
was after? But what exactly did he want?

"You mean malfunctions? We had hundreds. But that was
only natural; our models, in comparison with yours, were so
primitive. . . ."

"No, not malfunctions," he hastened to reply. "Rather, per-
formance fluctuation in such variable conditions . . . Today,
unfortunately, we do not have the opportunity to test automata
in so thorough a way."

It boiled down to a purely technical question. He was interested merely in certain function parameters of electronic brains,
how these behaved in the context of powerful magnetic fields,
in nebulae, in funnels of gravitational perturbation, and he
thought that this information might belong to expedition records
temporarily withheld from publication. I told him what I knew,
and for data more specialized I advised him to contact Thurber,
who had been the assistant to the scientific director of the
voyage.

"And might I give your name . . . ?"

"Of course."

He thanked me warmly. I was a little disappointed. So that
was all? But the conversation had established a professional bond
between us, and I asked him, in turn, about his work. What was
this selex-station that he had to inspect?

"Ah, nothing very interesting. A scrap dump . . . What I
would really like to do is devote myself to theoretical work; this
is in the nature of practical experience, and not terribly useful
experience, at that."

"Practical experience? Work in a scrap dump? How can that
be? After all, you are a cyberneticist. . . ."

"It is cybernetic scrap," he explained with a wry smile. And
added, somewhat contemptuously, "For we are very thrifty, you
see. The idea is that nothing should go to waste. At my institute
I could show you one or two interesting things, but here—
well . . ."

He shrugged; the gleeder pulled off the main road, passed

through a high metal gate, and entered the large yard of a factory; I saw rows of conveyors, gantries, something like a modernized furnace.

"Now you can have this machine," said Marger. From an opening in the wall near which we had stopped, a robot leaned out and said something to him. Marger got out, I saw him gesticulating, then he turned to me, annoyed.

"Wonderful," he said. "Gloor is sick. That's my colleague—I'm not permitted to work on my own—now what am I supposed to do?"

"What is the problem?" I asked, and also got out.

"The inspection has to be carried out by two people, at least two," he explained. Suddenly his face lit up. "Mr. Bregg! You are a cyberneticist! If only you would agree!"

"Ha," I said, smiling, "a cyberneticist. Add: ancient. I know nothing."

"But it's only a formality!" he interrupted me. "I'll take care of the technical side, of course. All we need is a signature, nothing more!"

"Really?" I said slowly. I could understand his hurry to get back to his wife, but I didn't like pretending to be what I wasn't; I am not cut out to be a figurehead; I told him this, though perhaps in gentler language. He raised his arms, as if to defend himself.

"Please, don't misunderstand me! But you must be in a hurry, aren't you? You had business in the city. In that case, I . . . somehow . . . forgive me for . . ."

"My business can wait," I replied. "Go ahead, please. If I am able, I will help you."

We went into a white building that stood to one side; Marger led me down a strangely empty corridor; several motionless robots stood in alcoves. In a small, simply furnished office he took a sheaf of papers from a wall cabinet, spread them on the table, and began to explain the nature of his—or, rather, our—job. He was not much of a lecturer, and I soon had doubts about his chances for a scientific career: he kept assuming I had knowledge of things that were completely unknown to me. I had to interrupt him repeatedly to ask embarrassingly elementary questions, but he, understandably not wanting to offend me, received all these proofs of my ignorance as if they were virtues.

In the end I learned that for the past fifty years or so there had existed a total separation between work and life. All production was automated and took place under the supervision of robots, which were overseen by other robots; there was no longer any place in this realm for people. Society led its own life, and the robots and automata theirs; except that, to prevent unforeseen aberrations in the established order of this mechanical army of labor, periodic inspections were necessary, and they were carried out by specialists. Marger was one of these.

"There can be no doubt," he explained, "that we will find everything normal; then we take a look at particular links in the processes, then leave our signatures, and that is all."

"But I do not even know what is produced here." I indicated the buildings through the window.

"Nothing whatever!" he exclaimed. "That is the whole point. Nothing. This is simply a dump for scrap, as I told you."

I didn't particularly care for this role unexpectedly imposed on me, but I could not keep objecting.

"All right. What exactly am I supposed to do?"

"What I do: we make a tour of the complexes. . . ."

We left the papers in the office and went out on the inspection. First was a huge sorting plant, where automatic scoops took hold of piles of sheet metal, twisted, broken trunks, crushed them, and threw them into compactors. The blocks ejected from these traveled by belts to the main conveyor. At the entrance Marger put on a small mask with a filter and handed one to me; we could not speak to each other on account of the din. The air was filled with a rust-colored dust that burst in red clouds out of the compactors. We continued through the next hall, also filled with noise, and took a moving walkway to a floor where rows of presses consumed the scrap, which, now more finely broken down and quite featureless, was poured from hoppers. On an overhead gallery leading to a building opposite, Marger checked readings on control meters; then we went to the factory yard, where our way was blocked by a robot that said that Engineer Gloor wanted Marger on the phone.

"Excuse me, I'll be back in a minute!" called Marger, and ran up a winding stairway to a glass annex not far away. I stood alone on the pavement, which was hot from the sun. I looked around. The buildings at the far end of the lot we had already seen; they held the compactors and presses. What with the distance and the soundproofing, not a murmur reached me from there. Off by itself, behind the annex into which Marger had vanished, was a low and unusually long building, a kind of tin barracks; I headed for it to find some shade, but the heat from the metal walls was unbearable. I was about to leave when I heard a peculiar sound coming from inside the barracks, difficult to identify, not at all like the noise of machines at work. Thirty paces farther and I reached a steel door. In front of it stood a robot. At the sight of me, the robot opened the door and stepped aside. The curious sounds became stronger. I looked inside; it was not as dark as I had thought at first. Because of the murderous heat from the sheet metal I could hardly breathe, and would have backed out immediately had it not been for the voices. For they were human voices—distorted, merging in a hoarse chorus, blurred, babbling, as though in the gloom a pile of defective telephones were talking. I took two uncertain steps, something crunched beneath my feet, and clearly, from the floor, it spoke:

"Pleash . . . shir . . . haff . . ."

I stood rooted to the spot. The stifling air tasted of iron. The whisper came from below.

"Pleash . . . haff . . . look ar-round . . . pleash . . ."

It was joined by a second, monotonous voice, steadily reciting:

"O anomaly eccentric . . . O asymptote spherical . . . O pole in infinity . . . O protosystem linear . . . O system holonomic . . . O space semimetrical . . . O space spherical . . . O space dielectrical . . ."

"Pleash . . . shir . . . yer shervet . . . pleash . . ."

The darkness teemed with husky whisperings, out of which boomed:

"The planetary bioplasm, its decaying mud, is the dawn of existence, the initial phase, and lo! from the bloody, dough-brained cometh copper. . . ."

"Brek—break—brabzel—be . . . bre . . . veryscope . . ."

"O class imaginary . . . O class powerful . . . O class empty . . . O class of classes . . ."

"Pleash . . . haff . . . look ar-round . . . shir . . ."

"Hush-sh . . ."

"You . . ."

"Sh-sh."

"Hear me. . . ."

"I hear. . . ."

"Can you touch . . . ?"

"Brek—break—brabzel . . ."

"No arms . . ."

"Sh-shame . . . you . . . you would see what a shiny and cold I am. . . ."

"L-let them re . . . turn my armor, my golden sword . . . my inheri . . . tance . . . dis . . . possessed . . . night. . . ."

"Behold the last efforts of the strutting croaking master of quartering and incarceration, for yea it riseth, thrice riseth the coming kingdom of the nonliving. . . ."

"I'm new . . . quite new . . . I never had a short in the skeleton. . . . I am still able . . . please . . ."

"Pleash . . ."

I did not know which way to look, asphyxiated by the merciless heat and those voices. They came from all sides. From the floor to the window slots below the ceiling rose heaps of twisted and tangled bodies; the little light that filtered in was reflected weakly in their dented metal.

"I had a temp, a temporary defect, but now I am all, am all right, I can see. . . ."

"What do you see . . . it is dark. . . ."

"Listen, please. I am invaluable, I am expensive. I indicate every power leak, I locate every stray current, every overload, just test me, please. . . . This . . . this shaking is temporary. . . . It has nothing in common with . . . please . . ."

"Pleash . . . shir . . ."

"And the dough-headed took their acid fermentation for a
soul, the stabbing of meat for history, the means of postponing
their decay for civilization. . . ."

"Please, me . . . only me . . . it is a mistake. . . ."

"Pleash . . . shir . . . haff . . ."

"I will save you. . . ."

"Who is that. . . ."

"What . . ."

"Who saves?"

"Repeat after me: the fire will not consume me utterly, and
the water will not turn me all to rust, both elements will be a
gate unto me, and I shall enter. . . ."

"Hush-sh-sh!"

"The contemplation of the cathode—"

"Cathodoplation—"

"I am here by mistake. . . . I think . . . I think, after
all . . ."

"I am the mirror of betrayal. . . ."

"Pleash . . . shir . . . yer shervet . . . haff a look ar-
round . . ."

"O flight of the transfinite, O flight of the nebulae . . . O
flight of the stars . . ."

"He is here!!!" something cried; and a sudden silence fell, a
silence almost as penetrating in its terrible tension as the many-
voiced chorus that had preceded it.

"Sir!!!" said something; I do not know why I was so sure, but
I felt that these words were directed to me, I did not respond.

"Sir, please . . . a moment of your time. Sir, I—am different.
I am here by mistake."

There was a stir.

"Silence! I am living!" This outshouted the rest. "Yes, I was
thrown in here, they dressed me in metal on purpose, so no one
would know, but please, only put your ear to me and you will
hear a pulse!"

"I also!" came a second voice over the first. "I also! Sir! I was
ill; during my illness I imagined that I was a machine, that was

my madness, but now I am well! Hallister, Mr. Hallister can vouch for me, please ask him, please get me out of here!"

"Pleash . . . pleash, shir . . ."

"Brek . . . break . . ."

"Your servant . . ."

The barracks buzzed and roared with rusty voices, at one point it was filled with a breathless scream, I began to retreat and stumbled backward into the sunlight, blinded, squinting; I stood awhile, shielding my eyes with my hand; behind me was a drawn-out grating sound; the robot had shut the door and bolted it.

"Sirrrr . . ." This still reached me through the wave of muffled voices from behind the wall. "Pleash . . . service . . . a mistake . . ."

I passed the glass annex. I did not know where I was going— I only wanted to get away from those voices, not to hear them; I jumped when I felt a hand on my shoulder. It was Marger, fair-haired, handsome, smiling.

"I do apologize, Mr. Bregg. It took forever. . . ."

"What will happen to them . . . ?" I interrupted, almost rudely, indicating the solitary barracks with my hand.

"I beg your pardon?" he blinked. "To whom?"

Suddenly he understood and was surprised:

"Ah, you went there? There was no need. . . ."

"Why no need?"

"That's scrap."

"How do you mean?"

"Scrap for recasting, after selection. Shall we go? We have to sign the official record."

"In a minute. Who conducts this selection?"

"Who? The robots."

"What? They do it themselves?"

"Certainly."

He fell silent under my gaze.

"Why aren't they repaired?"

"It wouldn't pay," he said slowly, with surprise.

"And what happens to them?"

"To the scrap? It goes there," he pointed at the thin, solitary column of the furnace.

In the office the forms were ready, spread out on the desk—the official record of the inspection, some other slips of paper—and Marger filled in the blanks in order, signed, and gave me the pen. I turned it over in my fingers.

"And is there no possibility of error?"

"I beg your pardon?"

"There, in that . . . scrap, as you call it, can they wind up there . . . even when they are still efficient, in working order—what do you think?"

He looked at me as if he did not understand what I was saying.

"That was the impression I got," I finished slowly.

"But that is not our concern," he replied.

"Then whose concern is it?"

"The robots'."

"But it is we who make the inspection."

"Ah, no," he smiled with relief at finally perceiving the source of my error. "The one has nothing to do with the other. We inspect the synchronization of processes, their tempo and efficiency, but we do not go into such details as selection. That is not our province. Apart from the fact that it is unnecessary, it also would be quite impossible, because today there are about eighteen automata for every living person; of these, five end their cycle daily and become scrap. That amounts to something on the order of two billion tons a day. You can see for yourself that we would be unable to keep track of this, and in any case the structure of our system is based on precisely the opposite relationship: the automata serve us, not we them. . . ."

I could not dispute what he said. Without another word I signed the papers. We were about to part when I surprised myself by asking him if humanoid robots were also produced.

"Not really," he said, and added reluctantly, "In their day they caused a bit of trouble. . . ."

"How so?"

"Well, you know engineers! They reached such a level of

perfection in their simulations that certain models could not be distinguished from live human beings. Some people could not tolerate that. . . ."

Suddenly I remembered the stewardess on the ship that I had taken from Luna.

"Could not tolerate that . . . ?" I repeated his words. "Was it, then, something like a . . . phobia?"

"I am no psychologist, but I suppose you could call it that. Anyway, this is ancient history."

"And are there still such robots?"

"Oh yes, they are found on short-range rockets. Did you meet one of them?"

I gave an evasive answer.

"Will you have time now to take care of your business?" He was concerned.

"My business . . . ?"

Then I remembered that I was supposed to have something to attend to in the city. We parted at the entrance to the station, where he had led me, all the while thanking me for extricating him from a difficult situation.

I wandered about the streets; I went to a realon but left before sitting through half of the ridiculous show, and I rode to Clavestra in the lowest spirits. I sent back the gleeder a kilometer from the villa and went the rest of the way on foot. Everything was in order. They were mechanisms of metal, wire, glass, one could assemble them and disassemble them, I told myself; but I could not shake off the memory of that hall, of the darkness and the distorted voices, that cacophony of despair which held too much meaning, too much of the most ordinary fear. I could tell myself that I was a specialist on that subject, I had tasted it enough, horror at the prospect of sudden annihilation has ceased to be fiction for me, as it was for them, those sensible designers who had organized the whole thing so well: robots took care of their own kind, did so to the very end, and man did not interfere. It was a closed cycle of precision instruments that created, reproduced, and destroyed themselves, and I had needlessly overheard the agony of mechanical death.

I stopped at the top of a hill. The view, in the slanting rays of the sun, was indescribably beautiful. Every now and then a gleeder, gleaming like a black bullet, sped along the ribbon highway, aimed at the horizon, where mountains rose in a bluish outline, softened by the distance. And suddenly I felt that I could not look—as if I did not have the right to look, as if there lay a horrible deception in this, squeezing at my throat. I sat down among the trees, buried my face in my hands; I regretted having returned. When I entered the house a white robot approached me.

"You have a telephone call," it said confidingly. "Long distance: Eurasia."

I walked after it quickly. The telephone was in the hall, so that while speaking I could see the garden through the glass door.

"Hal?" came a faraway but clear voice. "It's Olaf."

"Olaf . . . Olaf!" I repeated in a triumphant tone. "Where are you, friend?"

"Narvik."

"What are you doing? How is it going? You got my letter?"

"Of course. That's how I knew where to find you."

A moment of silence.

"What are you doing . . . ?" I repeated, less certain.

"What is there to do? I'm doing nothing. And you?"

"Did you go to Adapt?"

"I did. But only for a day. I stopped. I couldn't, you know . . ."

"I know. Listen, Olaf . . . I've rented a villa here. It might not be . . . but—listen! Come and stay here!"

He did not answer at once. When he did, there was hesitation in his voice.

"I'd like to come. And I might, Hal, but you know what they told us. . . ."

"I know. But what can they do to us? Anyway, to hell with them. Come on."

"What would be the point? Think, Hal. It could be . . ."

"What?"

"Worse."

"And how do you know that I'm not having a ball here?"

I heard his short laugh, really more a sigh: he laughed so quietly.

"Then what do you want with me there?"

Suddenly an idea hit me.

"Olaf. Listen. It's a kind of summer resort here. A villa, a pool, gardens. The only problem . . . but you must know what things are like now, the way they live, right?"

"I have a rough idea."

The tone said more than the words.

"There you are, then. Now pay attention! Come here. But first get hold of some . . . boxing gloves. Two pairs. We'll do some sparring. You'll see, it'll be great!" .

"Christ! Hal, Where am I going to find you boxing gloves? There probably haven't been any made for years."

"So have them made. Don't tell me it's impossible to make four stupid gloves. We'll set up a little ring—we'll pound each other. We two can, Olaf! You've heard about betrizating, I take it?"

"H'm. I'd tell you what I think of it. But not over the phone. Somebody might have delicate ears."

"Look, come. You'll do what I said?"

He was silent for a while.

"I don't know if there's any sense to it, Hal."

"All right. Then tell me, while you're at it, what plans you have. If you have any, then naturally I wouldn't think of bothering you with my whims."

"I have none," he said. "And you?"

"I came here to rest, educate myself, read, but these aren't plans, just . . . I simply couldn't see anything else ahead for me."

Silence.

"Olaf?"

"It appears that we have got off to an even start," he muttered. "What the hell. After all, I can leave at any time, if it turns out that . . ."

"Oh, stop it!" I said impatiently. "There is nothing to discuss. Pack a bag and come. When can you be here?"

"Tomorrow morning. You really want to box?"

"And you don't?"

He laughed.

"Hell, yes. And for the same reason you do."

"It's a deal, then," I said quickly. "I'll be expecting you. Take care."

I went upstairs. I looked through some things I had put in a separate suitcase and found the rope. A large coil. Ropes for a ring. Four posts, some rubber or springs, and we would be set. No referee. We wouldn't need one.

Then I sat down to the books. But it was as if my head were full of cement. When I had had that feeling in the past, I had chewed my way through the text like a bark beetle through ironwood. But I had never had this much trouble. In two hours I skimmed through twenty books and could not keep my attention on anything for longer than five minutes. I threw aside even the fairy tales. I decided not to indulge myself. I took what seemed to me the most difficult thing, a monograph on the analysis of metagens, and threw myself at the first equations as if, head lowered, I were charging a stone wall.

Mathematics, however, had certain beneficial properties, particularly for me, because after an hour I understood suddenly, my jaw dropped, I was struck with awe—this Ferret, how had he been able to do it? Even now, going back over the trail that he had blazed, I had moments when I lost my way; step by step I could still manage, but that man must have accomplished it in one leap.

I would have given all the stars to have in my head, for a month, something resembling the contents of his.

The signal sang out dinner, and at the same time something prodded me in the gut, reminding me that I was not alone here. For a second I considered eating upstairs. But shame overcame me. I threw under the bed the awful tight shirt that made me look like an inflated monkey, put on my priceless old loose-fitting sweater, and went down to the dining room. Apart from the exchange of a few trite civilities, there was silence. No conversation. They did not require words. They communicated in glances; she spoke to him with her head, her lashes, with her faint smile. And slowly a cold weight began to grow inside me, I felt my arms hungering, how they longed to seize something, and squeeze, and crush. Why was I so savage? I wondered with despair. Why, instead of thinking about Ferret's book, about the questions raised by Starck, instead of looking to my own affairs, why did I have to wrestle myself to keep from leering at that girl like a wolf?

But I did not become frightened until I closed behind me the door of my room upstairs. At Adapt they had told me, after the tests, that I was completely normal. Dr. Juffon had said the same thing. But could a normal person feel what I was feeling at that moment? Where did it come from? I was not a participant in it—I was a witness. Something was taking place, something irreversible, like the motion of a planet, an almost imperceptible, gradual emergence, still without form. I went to the window, looked out into the dark garden, and realized that this must have been in me ever since lunch, from the very first moment; it had just required a certain period of time. That was why I had gone to the city, why I had forgotten about the voices in the dark.

I was capable of doing anything. For that girl. I did not understand the how of it or the why. I did not know if it was love or madness. That did not matter. I only knew that everything had lost its importance for me. And I fought this—standing by the open window—as I had never fought anything before; I pressed my forehead to the cold window and feared myself.

I must do something, I mouthed. I must do something. It's because something's wrong with me. It will pass. She can't mean anything to me. I don't know her. She isn't even especially pretty. But at least I won't do anything. I won't—I pleaded with myself—at least I won't commit any . . . ye gods and little fishes!

I turned on the light. Olaf. Olaf would save me. I would tell him everything. He would take charge of me. We would go off somewhere. I would do what he told me, everything. He alone would understand. He would be arriving tomorrow. Good.

I paced the room. I could feel each one of my muscles, it was like being full of animals, they tensed, grappled with one another; suddenly I knelt at the bed, bit into the blanket, and made a strange sound, not like a sob, but dry, hideous; I did not want, I did not want to harm anyone, but I knew that it was useless to lie to myself, that Olaf couldn't help, no one could.

I got up. For ten years I had learned to make decisions at a moment's notice, decisions on which lives depended, my own and others', and I had always gone about it in the same way. I would go cold, my brain would turn into a machine made to calculate the for and the against, to separate and solve, irrevocably. Even Gimma, who did not like me, acknowledged my impartiality. And now, even if I had wanted to, I could not have acted differently, but only as then, in extremity, because this, too, was an extremity. I found my face in the mirror, the pale, almost white irises, narrowed pupils; I looked with hatred, I turned away, I could not think of going to bed. As I was, I swung my legs out over the window ledge. It was four meters to the ground. I jumped, landing almost without a sound. I ran silently in the direction of the pool. Past it, and onto the road. The phosphorescent surface led to the hills, wound among them like a shining snake, a viper, until it disappeared, a scar of light in the shadows. I tore along, faster and faster, to tire my heart, which pounded so steadily, so strongly; I ran for about an hour, until I saw the lights of some houses ahead. I had returned to my starting point. I was weary now, but for that reason I kept up the pace, telling myself silently: There! There! There! I kept running and finally came to a double row of hedges. I was back in front of the garden of the villa.

Breathing heavily, I stopped by the pool and sat down on the concrete edge; I lowered my head and saw the stars reflected. I did not want the stars. I had no use for them. I had been crazy, deranged, when I had fought for a place in the expedition, when I had let myself be turned into a bleeding sack in the gravirotors; what reason had I had, and why, why had I not realized that a man must be ordinary, completely ordinary, that otherwise it is impossible, and pointless, to live.

I heard a rustle. They went by me. He had his arm around her, they walked in step. He leaned over. The shadows of their heads merged.

I rose. He was kissing her. She, embracing his head. I saw the pale lines of her arms. Then a feeling of shame, of shame such as I had never known, horrible, sickening, cut through me like a knife. I, interstellar traveler, companion of Arder, having returned, stood in a garden and thought only of how to take a girl from some man, knowing neither him nor her, a bastard, an unmitigated bastard from the stars, worse, worse. . . .

I could not look. And I looked. At last they slowly went back, clinging to each other, and I, skirting the pool, set off again, then saw a large black shape and at the same time hit something with my hands. It was a car. Groping, I found the door. When I opened it, a light came on.

Everything that I did now was with a deliberate, concentrated haste, as if I was supposed to drive somewhere, as if I had to. . . .

The motor responded. I turned the wheel and, headlights on, drove out onto the road. My hands shook a little, so I tightened my grip on the wheel. Suddenly I remembered the little black box; I braked sharply and nearly skidded off the road, I jumped out, lifted the hood, and began feverishly to look for it. The engine was completely different, I couldn't find it. Perhaps at the very front. Wires. A cast-iron block. A cassette. Something unfamiliar, square—yes, that was it. Tools. I worked furiously, but with care; I hardly bloodied my hands. Finally I lifted out the black cube, heavy as if it were solid metal, and flung it into the bushes along the side of the road. I was free. I slammed the door and took off. The air began to whistle. More speed. The engine roared, the tires made a piercing hiss. A curve. I took it without slowing down, cut to the left, pulled out of the turn. Another curve, sharper. I felt an enormous force pushing me, along with the machine, to the outside of the bend. Still not enough. The next curve. At Apprenous they had special cars

for pilots. We did stunts in them, to improve reflexes. Very
good training. Developed a sense of balance, too. For example,
on a turn you throw the car onto the two outside wheels and
drive like that for a while. I could do that, at one time. And I
did it now, on the empty highway, careening through the darkness shattered by my headlights. Not that I wanted to kill
myself. It was simply that nothing mattered. If I showed no
mercy to others, then I could show none to myself. I took the
car into the turn and lifted it, so that for a moment it went on
its side, tires howling, and again I flung it, in the opposite
direction, fishtailed with a crash into something dark—a tree?
Then there was nothing but the roar of the engine picking up
speed, and the dials' pale reflections on the windshield, and the
wind whistling viciously. And then I saw, up ahead, a gleeder, it
tried to avoid me by taking the very edge of the road, a small
movement of the wheel carried me by it, the heavy machine
spun like a top, a dull thud, the clatter of torn metal, and darkness. The headlights were smashed, the engine died.

I took a deep breath. Nothing had happened to me, I was not
even bruised. I tried the headlights: nothing. The small front
lights: the left worked. In its weak glow, I started the engine.
The car, grinding, wobbled back onto the highway. A fine
machine, though: after all that I had put it through, it still
obeyed me. I headed back, slower now. But my foot pressed
the pedal, again something came over me when I saw a curve
coming up. And again I forced the maximum from the engine,
until, with squealing tires, thrown forward by the momentum,
I pulled up just before the hedge. I drove the machine into the
brush. Pushing aside the shrubbery, it came to rest against a
stump. I did not want anyone to know what I had done to it, so
I pulled down some branches and threw them over the hood and
the broken headlights. Only the front had been smashed; there
was just a small dent in the back, from the first collision with
the pole or whatever it had been there in the darkness.

Then I listened. The house was dark. Everything was still.
The great silence of the night reached up to the stars. I did not

want to return to the house. I walked away from the battered
car, and when the grass—the tall, damp grass—touched my
knees, I fell into it and lay thus until my eyes closed and I
slept.

I was wakened by a laugh. I recognized it. I knew who it was
before I opened my eyes, instantly awake. I was soaked, everything dripped with dew—the sun was still low. The sky, tufts
of white clouds. And opposite me, on a small suitcase, sat Olaf,
laughing. We leapt to our feet at the same time. His hand was
like mine—as large and as hard.

"When did you get here?"

"A moment ago."

"By ulder?"

"Yes. I slept like that, too, the first two nights."

"Yes?"

He stopped smiling. So did I. As though something stood between us. We studied each other.

He was my height, perhaps even a bit taller, but more slender.
In the strong light his hair, though dark, betrayed his Scan-
dinavian origin, and his stubble was completely blond. A bent
nose, full of character, and a short upper lip that revealed his
teeth; his eyes smiled easily, pale blue, darkening with merriment; thin lips, with a perpetual, slight curl to them, as if he
received everything with skepticism—perhaps it was that expression of his that made us keep our distance from each other.
Olaf was two years older than I; his best friend had been Arder.
Only when Arder died did we become close. For good, now.

"Olaf," I said, "you must be hungry. Let's get something to
eat."

"Wait," he said. "What is that?"

I followed his gaze.

"Ah, that . . . nothing. A car. I bought it—to remind
myself."

"You had an accident?"

"Yes. I was driving at night, you see. . . ."

"You, an accident?" he repeated.

"Well, yes. But it's not important. Anyway, nothing happened. Come on, you're not going to . . . with that suitcase . . ."

He picked it up. Said nothing. He did not look at me. The muscles of his jaw worked.

He senses something, I thought. He doesn't know what caused the accident, but he guesses.

Upstairs, I told him to choose one of the four vacant rooms. He took the one with the view of the mountains.

"Why didn't you want it? Ah, I know," he smiled. "The gold, right?"

"Yes."

He touched the wall with his hand.

"Ordinary, I hope? No pictures, television?"

"Rest assured." It was my turn to smile. "It's a proper wall."

I phoned down for breakfast. I wanted us to eat alone. The white robot brought in coffee. And a full tray, an ample breakfast. I watched with pleasure how he chewed, he chewed so that a tuft of hair above one ear moved. Finished, Olaf said:

"You still smoke?"

"I do. I brought two packs with me. What happens after that, I don't know. At present, I smoke. You want one?"

"One."

We smoked.

"How is it to be? Cards on the table?" he asked after a long pause.

"Yes. I'll tell you everything. And you me?"

"Always. But, Hal, I don't know if it's worth it."

"Tell me one thing: do you know what the worst of it is?"

"Women."

"Yes."

Again we were silent.

"It's on account of that?" he asked.

"Yes. You'll see at dinner. Downstairs. They are renting half of the villa."

"They?"

"A young couple."

The muscles of his jaw again moved under the freckled skin. "That's worse," he said.

"Yes. I've been here two days. I don't know how it could be, but . . . at the first conversation. Without any reason, without any . . . nothing, nothing. Nothing at all."

"Curious," he said.

"What is?"

"I did the same."

"Then why did you come here?"

"Hal, you've done a good deed. Do you understand?"

"For you?"

"No. For someone else. Because it would have ended badly."

"Why?"

"Either you know, or you won't understand."

"I do know. Olaf, what is this? Are we actually savages?"

"I don't know. We've been without women for ten years. Don't forget that."

"That doesn't explain everything. There is a kind of ruthlessness in me, I consider no one, you understand?"

"You still do, my friend," he said. "You still do."

"Well, yes; but you know what I mean."

"I know."

Again we were silent.

"Do you want to talk some more, or box?" he asked.

I laughed.

"Where did you get the gloves?"

"Hal, you would never guess."

"You had them made?"

"I stole them."

"No!"

"So help me. From a museum. I had to fly to Stockholm especially for them."

"Let's go, then."

He unpacked his modest belongings and changed. We both put on bathrobes and went downstairs. It was still early. Normally breakfast would not have been served for half an hour. "We'd better go out to the back of the house," I said. "No one will see us there."

We stopped in a circle of tall bushes. First we stamped down the grass, which was fairly short anyway.

"It'll be slippery," said Olaf, sliding his foot around the improvised ring.

"That's all right. It'll be harder."

We put on the gloves. We had a little trouble, because there was no one to tie them for us and I did not to want to call a robot.

He faced me. His body was completely white.

"You haven't got a tan yet," I said.

"Later I'll tell you what's been happening to me. I've had no time for the beach. Gong."

"Gong."

We began easily. A feint. Duck. Duck. I warmed up. I tapped, rather than punched. I did not really want to hit him. I was a good fifteen kilograms heavier, and his slightly longer reach did not offset my advantage, especially since I was also the better boxer. For that reason I gave him an opening several times, although I didn't have to. Suddenly he lowered his gloves. His face hardened. He was angry.

"Not this way," he said.

"What's wrong?"

"No games, Hal. Either we box or we don't."

"OK," I said, clenching my teeth, "we box!"

I began to move in. Glove hit glove with a sharp slap. He sensed that I meant business and put up his guard. The pace quickened. I feinted to the left and to the right, in succession, the last blow almost always landed on his chest—he was not fast enough. Unexpectedly he took the offensive, got in a nice right, I was knocked back a couple of steps. I recovered immediately. We circled, he swung, I ducked beneath the glove, backed off, and at half-distance landed a straight right. I put my weight behind it. Olaf went soft, for a moment loosened his guard, but then came back carefully, crouching. For the next minute he bombarded me with blows. The gloves struck my forearms with an appalling sound, but harmlessly. Once I barely dodged in time, his glove grazed my ear, and it was a roundhouse that would have decked me. Again we circled. He took a blow on the chest, a hard one, and his guard fell, I could have nailed him, but I did nothing, I stood as if paralyzed—she was at one of the windows, her face as white as the material covering her shoulders. A fraction of a second passed. The next instant, I was stunned by a powerful impact; I fell to my knees.

"Sorry!" I heard Olaf shout.

"Nothing to be sorry about . . . That was a good one," I mumbled, getting up.

The window was closed now. We fought for perhaps half a minute; suddenly Olaf drew back.

"What's the matter with you?"

"Nothing."

"Not true."

"All right. I've had enough. You aren't angry?"

"Of course not. It made no sense, anyway, to start right off . . . let's go."

We went to the pool. Olaf was a better diver than I. He could do fantastic things. I tried a full gainer with a twist, the way he did it, but succeeded only in smacking the water with my thighs. Sitting at the edge of the pool, I splashed water on my burning skin. Olaf laughed.

"You're out of practice."

"What do you mean? I never could do a twist right. You're great!"

"It never leaves you, you know. Today is the first time."

"Really?"

"Yes. This is terrific."

The sun was high now. We lay on the sand and closed our eyes.

"Where are . . . they?" he asked after a long silence.

"I don't know. Probably in their room. Their windows look out on the back of the house. I hadn't known that."

I felt him move. The sand was very hot.

"Yes, it was on account of that," I said.

"They saw us?"

"She did."

"She must have been frightened," he muttered, "don't you think?"

I did not answer. Again, a pause.

"Hal!"

"What?"

"They hardly fly now, do you know that?"

"I know."

"Do you know why?"

"They claim that there is no point in it. . . ."

I began to outline for him what I had read in Starck's book. He lay motionless, without a word, but I knew that he was listening intently.

When I finished, he did not speak right away.

"Have you read Shapley?"

"No. What Shapley?"

"No? I thought that you had read everything. . . . A twentieth-century astronomer. One of his things fell into my hands once, on precisely that subject. Quite similar to your Starck."

"What? That's impossible. Shapley could not have known. . . . But read Starck for yourself."

"I don't mean to. You know what this is? A smoke screen."

"A smoke screen?"

"Yes. I believe I know what happened."

"Well?"

"Betrization."

I sat up.

"You think so?"

He opened his eyes.

"It's obvious. They don't fly—and they never will. It will get worse. Pap. One great mess of pap. They can't stand the sight of blood. They can't think of what might happen when . . ."

"Hold on," I said. "That's impossible. There are doctors, after all. There must be surgeons. . . ."

"Then you don't know?"

"Know what?"

"The doctors only plan the operations. It's the robots that do them."

"That can't be!"

"I'm telling you. I saw it myself. In Stockholm."

"And if a doctor must intervene suddenly?"

"I'm not sure. There may be a drug that partly nullifies the effects of betrization, for a very short time, but they keep it under wraps like you can't imagine. The person who told me wouldn't say anything specific. He was afraid."

"Of what?"

"I don't know, Hal. I think that they have done a terrible thing. They have killed the man in man."

"You exaggerate," I said weakly. "Anyway . . ."

"It's really very simple. He who kills is prepared to be killed himself, right?"

I was silent.

"And therefore you could say that it is essential for a person to be able to risk—everything. We are able. They are not. That is why they are so afraid of us."

"The women?"

"Not only the women. All of them. Hal!"

He sat up suddenly.

"What?"

"Did you get a hypnagog?"

"Hypna—that machine for learning while you sleep? Yes."

"Have you used it?" he almost shouted.

"No, what's the problem . . . ?"

"You are lucky. Throw it into the pool."

"But why? What is it? Did you use one?"

"No. I had a hunch and listened to it while I was awake, although the instructions forbid that. Well, you'd never guess!"

I turned to him.

"What's in it?"

He looked at me grimly.

"Sweets. A regular confectionary, I'm telling you. That you should be calm, that you should be polite. That you should resign yourself to every unpleasantness, and if someone does not understand you or does not want to be good to you—a woman, in other words—it is your fault and not hers. That the greatest good is social equilibrium, stability, and so on and so on, in a circle, a hundred times. The conclusion: live quietly, write your memoirs, not for publication, of course, but just for yourself, engage in sports, and educate yourself. Mind your elders."

"A substitute for betrization," I muttered.

"Of course. And a lot more of the same: that one should never use force or even an aggressive tone toward anyone, and it is a great disgrace to strike anyone, a crime, even, for it causes a terrible shock. That under no circumstances should one fight, because only animals fight, that . . ."

"But wait," I said. "What if some wild animal escapes from a reserve . . . no . . . there are no wild animals any more. . . ."

"No wild animals," he said, "but there are robots."

"What is that supposed to mean? Are you saying that one could give them an order to kill?"

"Yes."

"How do you know?"

"I don't know for sure. But they have to be prepared for emergencies. Even a betrizated dog can go mad, can't it?"

"But, then, that . . . wait a minute! So they can kill, after all? By giving orders? Isn't it the same thing, whether I do the killing or give the order?"

"Not for them. But it would be only *in extremis*, you understand. In the face of a calamity, a threat, such as the mad dog. Ordinarily it does not happen. But if we . . ."

"We?"

"Yes, for example, you and I—if we were to . . . you know . . . then, of course, the robots would attend to us, not they. They cannot. They are good."

He was silent for a moment. His broad chest, reddened now by the sun and the sand, heaved.

"Hal. If I had known. If I had known this! If . . . I . . . had . . . known . . . this . . ."

"Stop it."

"Have you had anything happen to you yet?"

"Yes."

"You know what I'm talking about."

"Yes. There have been two. One invited me, as soon as I left the station, although not exactly like that. I got lost at that damned station. She took me home."

"She knew who you were?"

"I told her. At first she was frightened, but later . . . advances of a sort—out of pity or not, I don't know—and then she got really scared. I went to a hotel. The next day . . . do you know who I met? Roemer!"

"Don't tell me! He must be, what, a hundred and seventy?"

"No, it was his son. Even so, the man is nearly a hundred and fifty. A mummy. Horrible. I talked with him. And you know what? He envies us. . . ."

"There is nothing to envy."

"He does not understand that. Although, yes, there is. And then an actress. They call them realists. She was delighted with me: a true pithecanthropus! I went to her place, and escaped the next day. It was a palace. Magnificent. Flowering furniture, moving walls, beds that read your thoughts and wishes . . . yes."

"H'm. She wasn't afraid, eh?"

"No, she was afraid, but she drank something—I don't know what it was, some narcotic, maybe. Perto, something like that."

"Perto?"

"Yes. You know what it is? You've had it?"

"No," he said slowly. "I haven't. But that's the name of the thing that nullifies . . ."

"Betrization? No!"

"Thats what the person told me."

"Who?"

"I can't tell you; I gave my word."

"All right. So that is why . . . that is why she . . ."

I broke off.

"Sit down."

I sat.

"And what about you?" I said. "Here I keep talking about myself. . . ."

"Me? Nothing. That is—nothing has worked out for me. Nothing . . ." he repeated.

I was silent.

"What is this place called?" he asked.

"Clavestra. But the town is actually a few kilometers away. Say, let's go there. I wanted to have the car repaired. We'll come back cross-country—a little run. How about it?"

"Hal," he said slowly, "you old hothead . . ."

"What?"

His eyes were smiling.

"You think you can drive out the devil with athletics? You're an ass."

"Make up your mind, a hothead or an ass," I said. "What's wrong with it?"

"It won't work. Did you ever touch one of them?"

"Did . . . did I offend one? No. Why?"

"No, did you touch one of them?"

Finally I understood.

"There was no reason to. Why do you ask?"

"Don't."

"Why?"

"Because it's like striking an old woman. You understand?"

"More or less. You got into a fight?"

I tried not to show my surprise. Olaf had been one of the most self-controlled men on board.

"Yes. I made a perfect idiot of myself. It was on the first day. At night, to be exact. I couldn't get out of the post office—there was no door, only a kind of spinning thing. Have you seen one?"

"A revolving door?"

"No. I think it has to do with their controlling gravitation. In short, I spun around like a top, and some character who was with a girl pointed at me and laughed. . . ."

The skin on my face seemed to grow tighter.

"Old woman or not," I said, "he probably won't laugh any more."

"No. He has a broken collarbone."

"They didn't do anything to you?"

"No. Because I had just got out of the machine and he provoked me—I didn't hit him right away, Hal. No, I asked what was so funny, since I had been away for so long, and he laughed again, pointing upward, and said, 'Ah, from that monkey circus?' "

" 'Monkey circus'?"

"Yes. And then . . ."

"Hold on. Why 'monkey circus'?"

"I don't know. Perhaps he heard that astronauts are spun in centrifuges. I don't know because I wasn't talking to him by that time. . . . So, that was that. They let me go, only from now on the Luna Adapt will have to do a better job on its new arrivals."

"There are others returning?"

"Yes. Simonadi's group, in eighteen years."

"Then we have time."

"Plenty."

"You have to admit that they are easygoing," I said. "You break his collarbone and they let you off like that. . . ."

"I have the impression it was because of that 'circus,' " he said. "Even they are . . . toward us . . . you know. And they're not stupid. It would have caused a scandal. Hal, man—you don't know anything."

"Well?"

"Do you know the reason they didn't publicize our return?"

"There was something in the real. I didn't see it, but someone told me."

"Yes, there was. You would have died laughing if you had seen it. 'Yesterday, in the morning hours, a party of explorers returned to Earth from outer space. Its members are well. The scientific results of the expedition are now being studied.' The end, period."

"Are you serious?"

"Word of honor. And do you know why they did that? Because they fear us. That is also why they scattered us over the Earth."

"No. I don't understand that. They're not stupid. You said so yourself a moment ago. Surely they don't think that we are predators, that we will throw ourselves at people's throats!"

"If they thought that, they wouldn't have let us come. No, Hal. This doesn't have to do with us. More is at stake. Can't you see it?"

"Apparently I've grown stupid. Tell me."

"The public is not aware . . ."

"Of what?"

"Of the fact that the spirit of exploration is dead. That there are no expeditions, they know. But they don't think about it. They think that there are no expeditions because expeditions are unnecessary, and that's all. But there are some who see and know perfectly well what is going on, and what consequences it will have. Has already had."

"Well?"

"Pap. Pap and more pap for all eternity. No one will fly to the stars now. No one will risk a dangerous experiment now. No one will test a new medicine on himself now. What, they don't know this? They know! And if the word got out who we are, what we did, why we flew, what it was all about, then it would be impossible, you see, impossible to conceal the tragedy!"

"Pap and more pap?" I asked, using his expression; someone listening to our conversation might have found this funny, but I was in no mood to laugh.

"Of course. And you don't think it's a tragedy?"

"I don't know. Olaf, listen. For us that must be and will always be a great thing. The way we gave up those years—and everything—well, we believe this to be of the utmost importance. But perhaps it isn't. One has to be objective. Because—tell me yourself—what did we accomplish?"

"What do you mean?"

"Well, unpack the bags. Dump out everything you brought back from Fomalhaut."

"Are you crazy?"

"Not at all. What was the value of this expedition?"

"We were pilots, Hal. Ask Gimma, Thurber."

"Olaf, don't give me that. We were there together, and you know perfectly well what they did, what Venturi did before he died, what Thurber did—why are you looking at me like that? What did we bring back? Four loads of various analyses, spectral, elemental, et-ceteral, mineral samples, and then there is that soup or metaplasm or whatever that rotten stuff from Beta Arcturi was called. Normers verified his theory of gravimagnetic rotations, and it turned out, in addition, that on planets of type C Meoli there can exist not tri- but tetraploids of silicon, and on that moon where Arder nearly did himself in there is nothing but lousy lava and bubbles the size of skyscrapers. And was it in order to learn that that lava hardens into those goddamn big bubbles that we vomited ten years out of our lives and came back here to be side-show freaks? Then why in hell did we go there? For what? Maybe you can tell me. For what?"

"Not so loud," he said.

I was angry. And he was angry. His eyes had narrowed. I thought that we might fight yet, and my lips began to twitch into a grin. And then suddenly he, too, smiled.

"Still a hothead," he said. "You can drive a man into a fury, you know that?"

"Get to the point, Olaf. To the point."

"To the point? You haven't got to the point yet. And what if we had brought back an elephant that had eight legs and talked algebra, what then, would that have made you happy? What were you expecting on Arcturus? Paradise? A triumphal arch? What do you want? In ten years I didn't hear so much nonsense from you as now, in one minute."

I took a deep breath.

"Olaf, you are trying to make a fool of me. You know what I meant. I meant that people can live without it. . . ."

"I should think they can! Indeed, yes!"

"Wait. They can live, and even if it is as you say, that they have stopped flying because of betrization, still, was it worth it, was it right to pay such a price—that is the question before us, my friend."

"Is it? And suppose you marry. Why do you make a face? You can't get married? You can. I'm telling you, you can. And you will have children. And you will carry them to be betrizated with a song on your lips. Well?"

"Not with a song. But what could I do? I can't war against the whole world. . . ."

"Well, then, the blessing of the firmament upon you," he said. "And now, if you like, we can go to the city."

"Fine," I said. "Lunch will be in two and a half hours. We can make it."

"And if we don't make it, they won't give us anything to eat?"

"They will, but . . ."

I turned red. Pretending not to notice, he brushed the sand off his bare feet. We went upstairs, changed, and took the car to Clavestra. The traffic on the road was heavy. For the first time I saw colored gleeders, pink and pastel-lemon. We found a service station. I fancied I saw surprise in the glass eyes of the robot that examined the damage. We left the car there and returned on foot. It turned out that there were two Clavestras, an old and a new; in the old city was the local industrial center, where I had been the previous day with Marger. The new part was a fashionable summer resort, and there were people everywhere, almost exclusively young, teen-agers. In their gaudy, glittering outfits the boys looked dressed up as Roman soldiers, since the materials caught the sun like the half armor of that period. A lot of girls, most of them attractive, often in bathing suits more daring than anything I had seen so far. Walking with Olaf, I felt the eyes of the whole street on me. Colorful groups stopped under the palms at the sight of us. We were taller than anyone there, people stood and exchanged looks, it was extremely embarrassing.

When at last we got to the highway and turned south across the fields, in the direction of the house, Olaf wiped his forehead with a handkerchief. I was sweating a little, too.

"Damn them," he said.

"Save it for a better occasion. . . ."

He gave a sour smile.

"Hal!"

"What?"

"You know what it was like? A set in a movie studio. Romans, courtesans, and gladiators."

"We were the gladiators?"

"Exactly."

"Shall we run?" I said.

"Let's go."

We went over the fields. It was about eight kilometers. But we ended up too far to the right and had to double back a little. Even so, we had time to take a bath before lunch.

knocked on Olaf's door.

"If I know you, come on in," I heard him call.

He stood naked in the middle of the room and was spraying himself, from the flask that he held, with a pale yellow fluid that immediately set to form a fluffy mass.

"Liquid underwear?" I said. "How can you?"

"I didn't bring a spare shirt," he muttered. "You don't care for it?"

"No. You do?"

"My shirt got torn."

At my look of surprise, he added with a grimace:

"The guy who grinned."

I did not say another word. He put on his old trousers—I remembered them from the *Prometheus*—and we went downstairs. Only three places were set, and no one was in the dining room.

"There will be four of us," I addressed the white robot.

"No, sir. Mr. Marger has gone. The lady, yourself, and Mr. Staave make three. Shall I serve, or wait for the lady?"

"We'll wait," Olaf replied carelessly.

A terrific fellow. Just then, the girl entered. She had on the same skirt as the day before; her hair was a little damp, as if she had come from the water. I introduced Olaf to her; he was calm and dignified. I had never managed to be that dignified.

We talked a little. She said that every week her husband had to go away for three days in connection with his work, and that the water in the pool was not so warm as it could have been, despite the sun. But the conversation quickly died, and, try as I might, I could think of nothing to say. I ate in silence, with their sharply contrasting profiles before me. I noticed that Olaf was studying her, but only when I spoke to her and she looked in my direction. His face was without expression. As if he was thinking the whole time of something else.

Toward the end of the meal, the white robot approached and said that the water in the pool would be heated for the evening, in accordance with Mrs. Marger's wishes. Mrs. Marger thanked it and went to her room. The two of us were alone. Olaf looked at me, and again I reddened terribly.

"How is it," he said, putting to his lips the cigarette I had given him, "that a customer who could crawl into that stinking hole on Kereneia, an old space dog—an old rhinoceros, rather, a hundred and fifty—now starts to . . . ?"

"Please," I muttered, "if you really want to know, I'd crawl in there again . . ."

I didn't finish.

"All right. I'll stop. Word of honor. But, Hal, I have to say this: I understand you. And I'll bet you don't even know why. . . ."

I pointed my head in the direction in which she had gone.

"Why her?"

"Yes. Do you know?"

"No. And neither do you."

"But I do. Shall I tell you?"

"Yes. But without your jokes."

"You really have gone crazy!" exclaimed Olaf. "It is very simple. But you always did have that fault—you didn't see what was under your nose, only what was far removed, those Cantors, Corbasileuses. . . ."

"Don't preen."

"The style is sophomoric, I know, but our development was halted when they put those six hundred and eighty screws on us."

"Go on."

"She is exactly like a girl from our time. Doesn't have that red rubbish in her nose or those plates on her ears, and no shining cotton on her head; she doesn't drip with gold; she's a girl you could have met in Ceberto or Apprenous. I remember some just like her. That's all."

"I'll be damned," I said quietly. "Yes. Yes, but there is one difference."

"Well?"

"I told you already. At the very beginning. I never behaved like this before. And, to be perfectly honest, I never imagined myself . . . I thought I was the quiet type."

"Really, it's a shame I didn't take your picture when you came out of that hole on Kereneia. Then you could see what a quiet type you are. Man, I thought that you . . . Never mind!"

"Let's stow Kereneia, its caves and all of that," I said. "You know, Olaf, before I came here I went to a doctor, Juffon is his name, a very likable character. Over eighty, but . . ."

"That is our fate now," Olaf observed calmly. He exhaled and watched the smoke spread out above a clump of pale purple flowers that resembled hyacinths. He went on: "We feel most at home among the o-o-old folks. With lo-o-ong beards. When I think about it, I could scream. I tell you what. Let's buy ourselves a chicken coop, we can wring their necks."

"Come on, enough clowning. This doctor said a number of wise things to me. That we have no family, no friends of our own generation—which leaves only women, but nowadays it is harder to get one woman than many. And he was right. I can see that now."

"Hal, I know that you are much cleverer than I. You always liked the unprecedented. It had to be damned difficult, something that you couldn't manage at first, something you couldn't get without busting a gut three times over. Otherwise it didn't tickle your fancy. Don't give me that look. I'm not afraid of you, you know."

"Praise the Lord. That would make things complete."

"And so . . . what was I going to say? Ah. At first I thought that you wanted to be by yourself and that you hit the books because you wanted to be something more than a pilot and the guy who made the engine work. I waited for you to start putting on airs. And I must say that when you floored Normers and Venturi with those observations of yours and, all innocence, entered into those oh-so-highly-learned discussions, well, I thought that you had started. But then there was that explosion, you remember?"

"The one at night."

"Yes. And Kereneia, and Arcturus, and that moon. My friend, I still see that moon sometimes in my dreams, and once I actually fell out of bed because of it. Oh, that moon! Yes, but what —you see, my mind is going; I keep on forgetting—but then all that happened, and I saw that you were not out to be superior. That that was simply what you liked, and you couldn't be different. Remember how you asked Venturi for his personal copy of that book, the red one, what was it?"

"*The Topology of Hyperspace.*"

"Right. And he said, 'It is too difficult for you, Bregg. You lack the background. . . .'"

I laughed, because he did Venturi perfectly.

"He was right, Olaf. It was too difficult."

"Yes, then, but in time you figured it out, didn't you?"

"I did. But . . . without any real satisfaction. You know why. Venturi, that poor guy . . ."

"Not another word. It remains to be seen who should feel sorry for whom—in the light of subsequent events."

"He cannot feel sorry for anyone now. You were on the upper deck at the time?"

"I? On the upper deck? I was standing right beside you!"

"That's right. If he hadn't let it all into the cooling system, he might have got off with a few burns. The way Arne did. He had to go and lose his head."

"Indeed. No, you're incredible! Arne died anyway!"

"But five years later. Five years are five years."

"Years like those?"

"Now you're talking this way, but before, by the water, when I started to, you jumped down my throat."

"It was unbearable, yes, but it was magnificent, too. Admit it. You tell me—but, then, you don't need to talk. When you crawled out of that hole on Ke—"

"Enough, already, about that godforsaken hole!"

"It was only then that I understood what made you tick. We didn't know each other that well yet. When Gimma told me, a month later, that Arder would be flying with you, I thought—well, I don't know! I went to him but said nothing. He, of course, knew right away. 'Olaf,' he said to me, 'don't be angry. You are my best friend, but I'm flying with him this time, not with you, because . . .' Do you know what he said?"

"No." I had a lump in my throat.

" 'Because he alone went down. He alone. No one believed that it was possible to land there. He himself didn't believe it.' Well, did you believe that you would come back?"

I was silent.

"You see, you bastard? 'Either he'll return with me,' Arder said, 'or neither of us will return. . . .' "

"And I returned without him," I said.

"And you returned without him. I didn't recognize you. I was horrified! I was down below, at the pumps."

"Then that was you?"

"Yes. I saw—a stranger. A complete stranger. I thought I was hallucinating. Even your suit, all red."

"That was rust. A pipe had burst on me."

"What, you're telling me? I'm the one who patched that pipe later. The way you looked . . . But the clincher, afterward . . ."

"The thing with Gimma?"

"Yes. It isn't in the official records. And they cut it out of the tape, the following week; Gimma did it himself, I think. At the time I thought you were going to kill him. Christ."

"Don't talk about it," I said. I felt that in another minute I would start shaking. "Don't, Olaf. Please."

"No hysterics. Arder was closer to me than to you."

"Closer, not closer, what difference does it make? You're a

blockhead. If Gimma had given him a reserve, Arder would be sitting here with us now! Gimma hoarded everything; he was afraid of running out of transistors, but running out of men didn't bother him! I . . ."

I broke off.

"Olaf! This is insane. Let's forget it."

"Apparently, Hal, we can't forget it. At least, not so long as we are together. After that Gimma never again . . ."

"To hell with Gimma! Olaf! The end. Period. I don't want to hear another word!"

"And am I also forbidden to talk about myself?"

I shrugged. The white robot came to clear the table, but only looked in from the hall and left. Our raised voices must have frightened it off.

"Hal, tell me. What exactly is eating you?"

"Don't pretend."

"No, really."

"How can you ask? After all, it was because of me . . ."

"What was because of you?"

"The business with Arder."

"Wha-a-at?"

"Of course. Had I insisted from the first, before we took off, Gimma would have given . . ."

"Come on now! How were you to know that it was his radio that would go? It could have been something else."

"Could have been, could have been. But it was the radio."

"Hold on. And you walked around with this inside you for six years and never said a word?"

"What was there to say? I thought it was obvious; wasn't it?"

"Obvious! Ye gods! What are you saying, man? Come to your senses! Had you said that, any one of us would have thought you crazy. And when Ennesson's beam went out of focus, was that your fault, too? Well?"

"No. He . . . that can happen. . . ."

"I know it can. Don't worry, I know as much as you. Hal, I won't have any peace until you tell me . . ."

"What now?"

"That you are imagining things. This is complete nonsense. Arder himself would tell you so, if he were here."

"Thanks."

"Hal, I have a mind to . . ."

"Remember, I'm heavier."

"But I am angrier, you understand? Idiot!"

"Olaf, don't yell. We aren't alone here."

"All right. OK. Well, was it nonsense or not?"

"No."

Olaf inhaled until his nostrils went white.

"Why not?" he asked almost genially.

"Because, even before that, I had noticed Gimma's . . . tight-fistedness. It was my duty to foresee what might happen and confront Gimma immediately—and not when I returned with Arder's obituary. I was too soft. That is why not."

"I see. Yes. You were too soft. . . . No! I . . . Hal! I can't. I'm leaving."

He got up from the table abruptly; so did I.

"Are you crazy?" I cried. "He's leaving! All because . . ."

"Yes. Yes. Do I have to listen to your fantasies? No, thank you. Arder didn't reply?"

"Leave it be."

"He didn't reply, right?"

"He didn't reply."

"Could he have had a corona?"

I was silent.

"Could he have had any of a thousand other kinds of accidents? Or did he enter an echo belt? Did it kill his signal when he lost contact in the turbulence? Or did his emitters demagnetize above a sunspot and . . . ?"

"Enough."

"You won't admit I'm right? You ought to be ashamed of yourself."

"I didn't say anything."

"True. Well, then, could any of the things I said have happened?"

"Yes."

"Then why do you insist that it was the radio, the radio and nothing else, only the radio?"

"You may be right," I said. I felt terribly tired, I no longer cared.

"You may be right," I repeated. "The radio . . . it was simply the most likely thing. . . . No. Don't say anything else. We've already talked about it ten times more than was necessary."

Olaf walked up to me.

"Bregg," he said, "you poor old soldier . . . you have too much good in you, you know that?"

"What good?"

"A sense of responsibility. There should be moderation in everything. What do you intend to do?"

"About what?"

"You know."

"I have no idea."

"It's bad, is it?"

"Couldn't be worse."

"How about going away with me? Or somewhere—alone. If you like, I can help you arrange it. I can take your things or you can leave them, or . . ."

"You think I ought to hightail it?"

"I don't think anything. But when I see you lose control of yourself, just a little, as you did a moment ago . . . then . . ."

"Then?"

"Then I begin to wonder."

"I don't want to go away. You know what? I won't budge from here. And if . . ."

"What?"

"Never mind. That robot, at the service station, what did it say? When will the car be ready? Was it tomorrow or today? I've forgotten."

"Tomorrow morning."

"Good. Look: it's getting dark. We've chatted away the entire afternoon."

"God preserve us from such chats!"

"I was joking. Shall we go for a swim?"

"No. I'd like to read. Can you give me something?"

"Take whatever you want. Do you know how to work those grains of glass?"

"Yes. I hope you don't have that . . . that reading device with the sugary voice."

"No, all I have is an opton."

"Fine. I'll take it. You'll be in the pool?"

"Yes. But I'll go upstairs with you. I have to change."

I gave him a few books, mostly history, and one thing on the stabilization of population dynamics, since that interested him. And biology, with a long article on betrization. As for me, I started to change but couldn't find my trunks. I had mislaid them somewhere. No sign of them. I took Olaf's black trunks, put on my bathrobe, and went outside.

The sun had already set. From the west a bank of clouds was moving in, extinguishing the brighter part of the sky. I threw my robe on the sand, cool now after the heat of the day. I sat down, let my toes dangle in the water. The conversation had disturbed me more than I cared to admit. Arder's death stuck in me like a splinter. Olaf may have been right. Perhaps it was only the claim of a memory that had never been reconciled. . . .

I got up and made a flat dive, without any spring, head down. The water was warm. I had braced myself for cold and was taken by surprise. I surfaced. Too warm, like swimming in soup. I had just climbed out on the opposite side, leaving dark wet hand marks on the rail, when something pierced me in the heart. The story of Arder had carried me into a different world, but now, possibly because the water was warm—was supposed to be warm —I remembered the girl, and it was as if I had remembered something horrible, a misfortune that I could not overcome, yet had to.

And it may have been only my imagination. I examined the idea uncertainly, hunched over in the growing dusk. I could hardly see my own body, my tan hid me in the darkness. The clouds now filled the sky, and unexpectedly, too soon, it was night. From the house, a whiteness approached. Her bathing cap. Panic seized me. I got up slowly. I intended simply to run away, but she spotted me against the sky.

"Mr. Bregg?" she said in a small voice.

"It's me. You want to swim? I am in the way. I'm leaving. . . ."

"Why? You are not bothering me. Is the water warm?"

"Yes. For my taste, too warm," I said. She walked to the edge and jumped in lightly. I saw only her silhouette. Her bathing suit was dark. A splash. She surfaced near my feet.

"Terrible!" she cried, spitting out water. "What has he done? Some cold ought to be let in. Do you know how?"

"No. But I'll find out in a moment."

I dived over her head. I swam down, low, until I could touch the bottom, and I began to swim along it, touching the concrete every now and then. Underwater, as is usually the case, it was a little brighter than in the air, so that I was able to locate the inflow pipes. They were in the wall opposite the house. I swam to the surface, somewhat out of breath, since I had been under for a while.

"Bregg!" I heard her voice.

"Here. What's wrong?"

"I was frightened . . ." she said, more quietly.

"Of what?"

"You were gone so long."

"I know where it is now. We'll have it fixed in no time!" I called out and ran to the house. I could have spared myself the heroic dive; the taps were in full view, on a column near the veranda. I turned on the cold water and returned to the pool.

"It's done. You'll have to wait a little."

"Yes."

She stood below the springboard, I at the shallow end of the pool, as if I feared to draw near. Then I walked toward her, slowly, as though unintentionally. My eyes had grown accustomed to the dark. I was able to make out the features of her face. She regarded the water. Was very pretty in her white cap. And seemed taller without her clothes.

I stood like a post beside her; the situation grew awkward. Perhaps that is why I suddenly sat down. Clod! I berated myself. But I could think of nothing to say. The clouds thickened, it grew darker, but it did not look like rain. Quite cool.

"Are you cold?"

"No. Mr. Bregg?"

"Yes?"

"The water doesn't seem to be rising. . . ."

"Because I opened the outlet. That ought to be enough. I'll close it."

While I was coming back from the house it occurred to me that I could call out to Olaf. I nearly laughed aloud: it was so stupid. I was afraid of her.

I dived in flat and surfaced.

"There. Unless I overdid it—just tell me, I can let in some warm."

The water was visibly lower now, because the outlet was still open. The girl—I saw her slender shadow against the clouds— seemed to hesitate. Perhaps she no longer wanted to, perhaps she would go back; the thought flashed through me, and I felt a kind of relief. At that moment she jumped, feet first, and gave a faint cry, because the water was quite shallow there now—I hadn't had time to warn her. She must have hit bottom quite hard; she staggered but did not fall. I hurled myself toward her.

"Did you hurt yourself?"

"No."

"It's my fault. I'm an idiot."

We were standing in water up to our waists. She began to swim. I climbed out, ran to the house, shut off the outlet, and returned. I did not see her anywhere. I got in quietly and swam the length of the pool, then turned on my back and, moving my arms gently, sank to the bottom. I opened my eyes, saw the delicately rippled dark-glass surface of the water. I drifted upward slowly, began to tread water, and saw her. She was standing on the same side of the pool. I swam over to her. The springboard was at the other end; here it was shallow, I touched bottom immediately. The water, which I pushed aside as I walked, splashed noisily. I saw her face; she was looking at me; whether it was the momentum of my last steps—because if it is difficult to walk in water, it is not easy, either, to come to a sudden stop—or something else, I don't know, but I found myself beside her. Perhaps nothing would have happened had she withdrawn, but she remained where she was, her hand on the first rung of the ladder, and I was too close now to speak, to take refuge in conversation. . . .

I held her tightly. She was cold, slippery, like a fish, a strange, alien creature, and suddenly in this touch, so cool, lifeless—for she did not move at all—I found a place of heat, her mouth, I kissed her, I kissed and I kissed. . . . It was utter madness. She did not defend herself. Did not resist at all, was as if dead. I held her arms, lifted up her face, I wanted to see her, to look into her eyes, but it was already so dark, I had to imagine them. She did not tremble. There was only throbbing—from my heart or hers, I did not know. We stood like that, until slowly she began to free herself from my arms. I released her immediately. She went up the ladder. I followed her and again embraced her, from the side; she trembled. Now she trembled. I wanted to say something but could not find my voice. I just held her, pressed her to me, and we stood, and she freed herself again—not pushing me away, but as if I were not there at all. My arms dropped. She walked away. In the light that fell from my window I saw her pick up her robe and, without putting it on, start up the stairs. Lights were on at the door and in the hall. Drops of water gleamed on her shoulders and thighs. The door closed. She was gone.

I had—for a second—the urge to throw myself into the water and not come up. No, truly. Never before had such a thing entered my head. What served for a head. It all had been so senseless, impossible, and the worst of it was that I did not know what it meant and what I was supposed to do now. And why had she been that way . . . so . . . ? Had she been overwhelmed with fear? Ah, was it always fear, then, nothing but fear? It was something else. What? How could I discover what? Olaf. Then was I a fifteen-year-old kid, to kiss a girl and go running to him for advice?

Yes, I thought. I would. I went toward the house, picked up my robe, brushed the sand from it. The hall was brightly lit. I approached her door. Perhaps she would let me in, I thought. If she let me in, I would stop caring about her. Perhaps. And perhaps that would be the end of it. Or I'd get a slap in the face. No. They were good, they were betrizated, they were not able. She would give me a glass of milk; it would do me a world of good. I must have stood there for five minutes—and recalled the caves of Kereneia, the notorious hole Olaf had talked about. That wonderful hole! Probably an old volcano. Arder had got himself wedged between some boulders and could not get out, and the lava was rising. Not lava, actually; Venturi said it was a kind of geyser—but that was later. Arder . . . We heard his voice. On the radio. I went down and pulled him out. God! I would have preferred that ten times over to this door. Not the slightest sound. Nothing.

If only the door had had a handle. Instead, a plate. Nothing like that on mine upstairs. I did not know whether it functioned somehow as a lock, or whether I should press it; I was still the savage from Kereneia.

I raised a hand and hesitated. And if the door did not open? I pictured my retreat: it would give me something to think about for a long time. And I felt that the longer I stood, the less strength I had, as though everything were oozing out of me. I touched the plate. It did not yield. I pressed harder.

"Is that you, Mr. Bregg?" I heard her voice. She must have been standing on the other side of the door.

"Yes."

Silence. A half a minute. A minute.

The door opened. She stood in the doorway. Wearing a fluffy housecoat. Her hair fell over the collar. Not until now, incredibly, did I see that it was chestnut.

The door, only ajar. She held it. When I stepped forward, she backed away. By itself, without a sound, the door closed behind me.

An suddenly I realized how this must look. She watched, motionless, pale, holding the edges of her robe together, and there I was, opposite her, dripping, naked, in Olaf's black trunks, my sandy robe in my hand—gaping. . . .

And at the thought, I broke into a smile. I shook out the robe. Put it on, fastened it, sat down. I noticed two wet marks where I had been standing before. But I had absolutely nothing to say. What could I say? Suddenly it came to me. Like an inspiration.

"You know who I am?"

"I know."

"Ah, you do? That's good. From the travel office?"

"No."

"It doesn't matter. I am . . . wild, do you know that?"

"Yes?"

"Yes. Terribly wild. What is your name?"

"You don't know?"

"Your first name."

"Eri."

"I am going to carry you off."

"What?"

"Yes. Carry you off. You don't want to be?"

"No."

"No matter. I am. Do you know why?"

"I guess."

"You don't. I don't."

She was silent.

"Nothing I can do about it," I went on. "It happened the moment I saw you. The day before yesterday. At the table. Do you know that?"

"I know."

"But perhaps you think that I am joking?"

"No."

"How could you . . . ? No matter. Will you try to escape?"

She was silent.

"Don't," I asked. "It would be useless, you know. I would not leave you alone. I would like to, do you believe me?"

She was silent.

"You see, it isn't just because I am not betrizated. Nothing matters to me, you see. Nothing. Except you. I have to see you. I have to look at you. I have to hear your voice. I have to, and I care about nothing else. Nowhere. I don't know what will become of us. It will end badly, I suppose. But I don't care. Because something is worthwhile now. Because I speak and you listen. Do you understand? No. How could you? You have all done away with drama, in order to live quietly. I cannot. I do not need that."

She was silent. I took a deep breath.

"Eri," I said, "listen . . . but sit down."

She did not move.

"Please. Sit down."

Nothing.

"It won't hurt you to sit down."

Suddenly I understood. I clenched my teeth.

"If you don't want to, then why did you let me in?"

Nothing.

I got up. I took her by the shoulders. She did not resist. I sat her down in an armchair. I moved mine closer, so that our knees almost touched.

"You can do what you like. But listen. I am not to blame for this. And you most certainly are not. No one is. I did not want this. But that's how it is. It is, you understand, a beginning. I know that I am behaving like a madman. I know it. But I'll tell you why. You're not going to speak to me at all now?"

"It depends," she said.

"For that much, thank you. Yes. I know. I don't have any right and so on. Well, what I wanted to say—millions of years ago there were these lizards, brontosaurs, atlantosaurs. . . . Perhaps you have heard of them?"

"Yes."

"They were giants, the size of a house. They had exceptionally long tails, three times the length of their bodies. Consequently they were unable to move the way they might have wished—lightly and gracefully. I, too, have such a tail. For ten years, for reasons unknown, I poked around among the stars. Perhaps it was not necessary. But never mind. I can't undo it. That is my tail. You understand? I can't behave as though it never happened, as though it never was. I don't imagine that you are thrilled about this. About what I've told you and what I'm saying and have yet to say. But I see no help for it. I must have you, have you for as long as possible, and that is that. Will you say something?"

She looked at me. I thought that she turned even paler, but it could have been the lighting. She sat huddled in her fluffy robe as if she were cold. I wanted to ask her if she was cold, but again I was tongue-tied. I—oh, I was not cold.

"What would you . . . do . . . in my place?"

"Very good!" I said, encouragingly. "I imagine that I would put up a fight."

"I cannot."

"I know. Do you think that that makes it easier for me? I swear to you it doesn't. Do you want me to leave now, or can I say something else? Why are you looking at me that way? You know by now, surely, that I would do anything for you. Please don't look at me like that. The things I say, they do not mean the same as when other people say them. And you know what?"

I was terribly out of breath, as if I had been running for a long time. I held both her hands—had been holding them, for how long I did not know, perhaps from the beginning. I did not know. They were so small.

"Eri. You see, I never felt what I am feeling now. At this moment. Think of it. That terrible emptiness, out there. Indescribable. I didn't believe I would return. No one did. We used to talk about it, but only in that way. They are still there, Tom Arder, Arne, Venturi, and are now like stones, you know, frozen stones, in the darkness. And I, too, should have remained, but if I am here and hold your hands, and can speak to you, and you hear, then perhaps this is not so bad. So base. Perhaps it isn't,

Eri! Only don't look at me like that. I beg you. Give me a chance. Don't think that this is—merely love. Don't think that. It is more. More. You don't believe me. . . . Why don't you believe me? I'm telling you the truth. You don't, do you?"

She was silent. Her hands were like ice.

"You can't, is that it? It is impossible. Yes, I know it is impossible. I knew from the first moment. I have no business being here. There should be an empty space here. I belong there. It is not my fault that I came back. Yes. I don't know why I'm telling you all this. This doesn't exist. It doesn't, does it? If it doesn't concern you, then it doesn't matter. None of it. You thought that I could do with you as I liked? That isn't what I wanted, don't you understand? You are not a star. . . ."

Silence. The whole house was quiet. I bent my head over her hands, which lay limp in mine, and began to speak to them.

"Eri. Eri. Now you know you don't have to be afraid, right? That nothing threatens you. But this is—so big. Eri. I didn't know. . . . I swear to you. Why does man fly to the stars? I cannot understand. Because this is here. But maybe you have to go there first, to understand it. Yes, that's possible. I'll go now. I'm going. Forget all this. You'll forget?"

She nodded.

"You won't tell anyone?"

She shook her head.

"Truly?"

"Truly."

It was a whisper.

"Thank you."

I left. Stairs. A cream-colored wall; another, green. The door of my room. I opened the window wide, I breathed in. How good the air was. From the moment I left her, I was completely calm. I even smiled—not with my mouth, not with my face. My smile was inside, pitying, toward my own stupidity, that I had not known, and it was so simple. Bent over, I went through the contents of the sports bag. Among the ropes? No. Some packages, was that it, no, wait a minute. . . .

I had it. I straightened up, and suddenly I was embarrassed.

The lights. I couldn't, like that. I went to turn them off and found Olaf standing in the doorway. He was dressed. Hadn't he gone to bed?

"What are you doing?"

"Nothing."

"Nothing? What do you have there? Don't hide it!"

"It's nothing."

"Show me!"

"No. Go away."

"Show me!"

"No."

"I knew it. You bastard!"

I did not expect the blow. My hand opened, dropping it, it clattered on the floor, and then we were fighting, I held him beneath me, he flung me off, the desk toppled, the lamp hit the wall with a crash that shook the house. Now I had him. He couldn't break away, he only twisted, I heard a cry, her cry, and released him, and jumped back.

She was standing at the door.

Olaf got up on his knees.

"He wanted to kill himself. Because of you!" he croaked. He held his throat. I turned my face away. I leaned against the wall, my legs trembled under me. I was so ashamed, so horribly ashamed. She looked at us, first at one, then at the other. Olaf still held his throat.

"Go, both of you," I said quietly.

"You'll have to finish me off first."

"For pity's sake."

"No."

"Please, go," she said to him. I stood silent, my mouth open. Olaf looked at her, dumbstruck.

"Girl, he . . ."

She shook her head.

Keeping his eyes on us, he edged out of the room.

She looked at me.

"Is it true?" she asked.

"Eri . . ."

"You must?"

I nodded yes. And she shook her head.

"You mean . . . ?" I said. And again, stammering, "You mean . . . ?" She was silent. I went to her and saw that she was cringing, that her hands were shaking as she clutched the loose edge of her fluffy robe.

"Why? Why are you so afraid?"

She shook her head.

"No?"

"No."

"But you are trembling."

"It's nothing."

"And . . . you'll go away with me?"

She nodded twice, like a child. I embraced her, as gently as I was able. As if she were made of glass.

"Don't be afraid . . ." I said. "Look. . . ."

My own hands shook. Why had they not shaken then, when I slowly turned gray, waiting for Arder? What reserves, what innermost recesses had I reached at last, in order to learn my worth?

"Sit down," I said. "You are still trembling? But no, wait."

I put her on my bed, covered her up to the neck.

"Better?"

She nodded, better. Was she mute only with me, or was this her way?

I knelt by the bed.

"Tell me something," I whispered.

"What?"

"About yourself. Who you are. What you do. What you desire. No—what you desired before I landed on you like a ton of bricks."

She gave a small shrug, as if saying, "There is nothing to tell."

"You don't want to speak? Why, is it that . . . ?"

"It's not important," she said. It was as if she had struck me with those words. I drew back.

"You mean . . . Eri . . . you mean . . ." I stammered. But I understood now. I understood perfectly.

I jumped up and began to pace the room.

"Not that way. I can't, that way. I can't. No, I . . ."

I gaped. Again. Because she was smiling. The smile was so faint, it was barely perceptible.

"Eri, what . . . ?"

"He is right," she said.

"Who?"

"That man, your friend."

"Right about what?"

It was difficult for her to say it. She looked away.

"That you are not wise."

"How do you know he said that?"

"I heard him."

"Our conversation? After dinner?"

She nodded. Blushed. Even her ears went pink.

"I could not help hearing. Your voices were awfully loud. I would have gone out, but . . ."

I understood. The door of her room was in the hallway. What an idiot I had been! I thought. I was stunned.

"You heard everything?"

She nodded.

"And you knew that it was about you?"

"Mhm."

"But how? Because I never mentioned . . ."

"I knew before that."

"How?"

She moved her head.

"I don't know. I knew. That is, at first I thought I was imagining it."

"And when, later?"

"I don't know. Yes, during the day. I felt it."

"You were afraid?" I asked glumly.

"No."

"No? Why not?"

She gave a wan smile.

"You are exactly, exactly like . . ."

"Like what?"

"Like in a fairy tale. I did not know that one could be that way . . . . and if it were not for the fact that . . . you know . . . I would have thought it was a dream."

"It isn't, I assure you."

"Oh, I know. I only said it that way. You know what I mean?"

"Not exactly. It seems I am dense, Eri. Yes, Olaf was right. I am a blockhead. An out-and-out blockhead. So speak plainly, won't you?"

"All right. You think that you are frightening, but you're not at all. You only . . ."

She fell silent, as if unable to find the words. I had been listening with my mouth half open.

"Eri, child, I . . . I didn't think that I was frightening, no. Nonsense. I assure you. It was only when I arrived, and listened, and learned various things . . . but enough. I've said enough. Too much. I have never in my life been so talkative. Speak, Eri. Speak." I sat on the bed.

"I have nothing to say, really. Except . . . I don't know. . . ."

"What don't you know?"

"What is going to happen?"

I leaned over her. She looked into my eyes. Her eyelids did not flicker. Our breaths mingled.

"Why did you let me kiss you?"

"I don't know."

I touched her cheek with my lips. Her neck. I lay with my head upon her shoulder. Never before had I felt like this. I had not known that I could feel this way. I wanted to weep.

"Eri," I whispered voicelessly, mouthing the words. "Eri. Save me."

She lay motionless. I could hear, as if at a great distance, the rapid beating of her heart. I sat up.

"Could . . ." I began, but hadn't the courage to finish. I got up, picked up the lamp, set the desk right, and stumbled over something—the penknife. It lay on the floor. I threw it into the suitcase. I turned to her.

"I'll put out the light," I said. "OK?"

She did not answer. I touched the switch. The darkness was complete, even in the open window, no lights, not even distant lights, were visible. Nothing. Black. As black as out there. I closed my eyes. The silence hummed. "Eri," I whispered. She did not reply. I sensed her fear. I groped toward the bed. I listened for her breath, but the ringing silence drowned out everything, as if it had materialized in the darkness and now was the darkness. I ought to leave, I thought. Yes. I would leave at once. But I bent forward and with a kind of clairvoyance found her face. She held her breath.

"No," I murmured, "really . . ."

I touched her hair. I stroked it with the tips of my fingers; it was still foreign to me, still unexpected. I so wanted to understand all this. But perhaps there was nothing to understand? Such silence. Was Olaf asleep? Surely not. He sat, he listened. Was waiting. Go to him, then? But I couldn't. This was too improbable, uncertain. I couldn't. I couldn't. I lay my head on her shoulder. One movement and I was beside her. I felt her entire body stiffen. She shrank away. I whispered:

"Don't be afraid."

"No."

"You are trembling."

"I'm just . . ."

I held her. The weight of her head slipped into the crook of my arm. We lay thus, side by side, and there was darkness and silence.

"It's late," I whispered, "very late. You can sleep. Please. Go to sleep. . . ."

I rocked her, with only the slow flexing of my arm. She lay quietly, but I felt the warmth of her body and her breath. It was rapid. And her heart was beating like an alarm. Gradually, gradually, it began to subside. She must have been very tired. I listened at first with my eyes open, then shut them, it seemed to me that I could hear better that way. Was she already asleep? Who was she? Why did she mean so much to me? I lay in that darkness; a breeze came through the window and stirred the curtains, so that they made a soft rustling sound. I was filled, motionless, with amazement. Ennesson. Thomas. Venturi. Arder. What had it all been for? For this? A pinch of dust. There where the wind never blows. Where there are no clouds or sun, or rain, where there is nothing, exactly as if nothing were possible or even imaginable. And I had been there? Really? Why? I no longer knew anything, everything dissolved into the formless darkness—I froze. She twitched. Slowly turned over on her side. But her head remained on my arm. She murmured something, very softly. And went on sleeping. I tried hard to picture the chromosphere of Arcturus. A seething vastness, above which I flew and flew, as if revolving on a monstrous, invisible carousel of fire, with tearing, swollen eyes, and repeated in a lifeless voice: Probe, zero, seven—probe, zero, seven—probe, zero, seven—a thousand times, so that afterward, at the very thought of those words, something in me shuddered, as if I had been branded with them, as if they were a wound; and the reply was a crackling in the earphones, and the giggling-squawking into which my receiver translated the flames of the prominence, and that was Arder, his face, his body, and the rocket, turned to incandescent gas. . . . And Thomas? Thomas was lost, and no one knew that he . . . And Ennesson? We never got along—I couldn't stand him. But in the pressure chamber I struggled with Olaf, who did not want to let me go because it was too late. How all-fired noble of me. But it was not nobility, it was simply a matter of price. Yes. Because each one of us was priceless, human life had the highest value where is could have none, where such a thin, practically nonexistent film separated it from annihilation. That wire or contact in Arder's radio. That weld in Venturi's reactor, which Voss failed to detect—but perhaps it opened suddenly, that did happen, after all, fatigue in metal—and Venturi ceased to exist in maybe five seconds. And Thurber's return? And the miraculous rescue of Olaf, who got lost when his directional antenna was punctured—when, how? No one knew. Olaf came back, by a miracle. Yes, one-in-a-million odds. And I had luck. Extraordinary, impossible luck. My arm ached, a wonderful ache. Eri, I said in my mind, Eri. Like the song of a bird. Such a name. The song of a bird . . . We used to ask Ennesson to do bird calls. He could do them. How he could do them, and when he perished, along with him went all those birds. . . .

But things grew confused, I sank, I swam through the darkness. Right before I fell asleep it seemed to me that I was there, at my place, in my bunk, deep down, at the iron bottom, and near me lay little Arne—I awoke for a moment. No. Arne was not alive, I was on Earth. The girl breathed quietly.

"Bless you, Eri," I said, inhaling the fragrance of her hair, and slept.

I opened my eyes, not knowing where or even who I was. The dark hair flowing across my arm—the arm had no feeling, as if it were a foreign thing—astonished me. This, for a fraction of a second. Then I realized everything. The sun had not yet risen; the dawn—milk-white, without a trace of pink, clean, the air sharp—stood at the windows. In this earliest light I studied her face, as if seeing it for the first time. Sound asleep, she breathed with her lips tightly closed; she must not have been very comfortable on my arm, because she had placed a hand beneath her head, and now and then, gently, her eyebrows moved, as if in continual surprise. The movement was slight, but I watched intently, as if upon that face my fate were written.

I thought of Olaf. With extreme care I began to free my arm. The care turned out to be unnecessary. She was in a deep sleep, dreaming of something. I stopped, tried to guess, not the dream, but only whether or not it was bad. Her face was almost childlike. The dream was not bad. I disengaged myself, stood up. I was in the bathrobe I had been wearing when I lay down. Barefoot, I went out into the corridor, closed the door quietly, very slowly, and with the same caution looked into his room. The bed was untouched. He sat at the table, his head on his arms, and slept. Hadn't undressed, as I'd thought. I don't know what woke him up—my gaze? He started, gave me a sharp look, straightened, and began to stretch.

"Olaf," I said, "in a hundred years I . . ."

"Shut your mouth," he suggested kindly. "Hal, you always did have unhealthy tendencies."

"Are you beginning already? I only wanted to say . . ."

"I know what you wanted to say. I always know what you're going to say, a week in advance. Had there been a need for a chaplain on board the *Prometheus*, you would have filled the bill. A damned shame I didn't see that before. I would have knocked it out of you. Ha! No sermons. No solemnities, swearing, oaths, and the like. How is it? Good, yes?"

"I don't know. I suppose. I don't know. If you mean . . . well, nothing happened."

"No, first you should kneel," he said. "You must speak from a kneeling position. You dunce, did I ask you about that? I am talking about your prospects and so on."

"I don't know. And I don't think she does, either. I landed on her like a ton of bricks."

"Yes. It's a problem," Olaf observed. He undressed, looked for his trunks. "What do you weigh? A hundred and ten kilos?"

"Something like that. If you're looking for your trunks, I have them."

"For all your holiness, you always liked to pinch things," he mumbled, and when I started to pull them off, "Idiot, leave them on. I have another pair in the suitcase. . . ."

"How do divorces work? Do you happen to know?" I asked.

Olaf looked at me over the open suitcase. He winked.

"No, I do not. And how would I? I have heard that it's as easy as sneezing. And you don't even have to say *Gesundheit*. Is there a decent bathroom here, with water?"

"I don't know. Probably not. There's only the kind—you know."

"Yes. The invigorating wind with the smell of mouthwash. An abomination. Let's go to the pool. Without water, I don't feel washed. She's asleep?"

"Asleep."

"Then let's blast off."

The water was cold, superb. I did a half gainer with a twist: a good one. My first. I surfaced, snorting and choking, I had water in my nose.

"Watch out," shouted Olaf from the side of the pool, "you'll have to be careful now. Remember Markel?"

"Yes. Why?"

"He had gone to the four ammoniated moons of Jupiter. When he returned and set down on the training field, and got out of the rocket, laden with trophies like a Christmas tree, he tripped and broke his leg. So watch out. I'm telling you."

"I'll try. Damned cold, this water. I'm coming out."

"Quite right. You could catch a cold. I didn't have one for ten years. The moment I landed on Luna I started coughing."

"Because it was so dry there," I said with a serious expression. Olaf laughed and splashed water in my face, jumping in a meter away.

"Dry, exactly," he said, surfacing. "A good way to put it. Dry, but not too cozy."

"Ole, I'm going."

"OK. We'll see each other at breakfast? Or would you prefer not to?"

"Of course we will."

I ran upstairs, drying myself on the way. At the door I held my breath. I peered in carefully. She was still sleeping. I took advantage of this and quickly changed. I had time to shave, too, in the bathroom.

I stuck my head into the room—I thought that she had said something. When I approached the bed on tiptoe, she opened her eyes.

"Did I sleep here?"

"Yes. Yes, Eri."

"I had the feeling that someone . . ."

"Yes, Eri, I was here."

She stared at me, as though gradually it was all coming back to her. First, her eyes widened a little—with surprise?—then she closed them, opened them again, then furtively, very quickly, though even so I noticed, she looked under the blanket—and her face turned pink.

I cleared my throat.

"You probably want to go to your own room, right? Perhaps I should leave, or . . ."

"No," she said. "I have my robe."

She pulled it tightly around herself, sat up on the bed.

"So . . . it's real, then?" she said quietly, as if parting with something.

I was silent.

She got up, walked across the room, came back.

She lifted her eyes to my face; in them was a question, uncertainty, and something else that I could not define.

"Mr. Bregg . . ."

"My name is Hal. My first name."

"Mr. . . . Hal, I . . ."

"Yes?"

"I really don't know. . . . I would like . . . Seon . . ."

"What?"

"Well . . . he . . ."

She could not or did not wish to say "my husband." Which?

"He will be back the day after tomorrow."

"And?"

"What is going to happen?"

I swallowed.

"Should I have a talk with him?" I asked.

"What do you mean?"

Now it was my turn to look at her with surprise, not understanding.

"Yesterday you said . . ."

I waited.

"That you . . . would take me away."

"Yes."

"And he?"

"Then I shouldn't talk to him?" I asked, feeling stupid.

"Talk? You want to do it yourself?"

"Who else?"

"It has to be . . . the end?"

Something was choking me; I cleared my throat.

"Really, there's no other way."

"I thought it would be . . . a mesk."

"A what?"

"You don't know?"

"I understand nothing. No. I don't know. What is that?" I said, feeling an ominous chill. Again I had hit upon one of those sudden blanks, a mire of misunderstanding.

"It is like this. A man . . . a woman . . . if someone meets a person . . . if he wants, for a certain period of time . . . You really know nothing about this?"

"Wait, Eri. I don't know, but I think I'm beginning to. Is it something provisional, a kind of temporary suspension, an episode?"

"No," she said, and her eyes grew round. "You don't know what it is. . . . I don't exactly know how it works myself," she admitted. "I've only heard about it. I thought that that was why you . . ."

"Eri, I'm completely in the dark. Damned if I understand any of this. Does it have . . . ? In any case, it is connected in some way with marriage, right?"

"Well, yes. You go to an office, and there, I'm not exactly sure, but anyway, after that it's . . . it's . . ."

"It's what?"

"Independent. So that nothing can be said. No one. Including him . . ."

"So it is, after all . . . it is a kind of legalization—well, hell!—a legalization of infidelity?"

"No. Yes. That is, it is not infidelity then—no one speaks of it like that. I know what that means; I learned about it. There is no infidelity because, well, because after all Seon and I are only for a year."

"Wha-a-at?" I said, because I thought that I was not hearing correctly. "And what does that mean, for a year? Marriage for a year? For one year? Why?"

"It is a trial."

"Ye gods and little fishes! A trial. And what is a mesk? A notification for the following year?"

"I don't know what you mean. It is . . . it means that if the couple separates after a year, well, then the other arrangement becomes binding. Like a wedding."

"The mesk?"

"Yes."

"And if not, then what?"

"Then nothing. It has no significance."

"Aha, I think I see now. No. No mesk. Till death do us part. You know what that means?"

"I do. Mr. Bregg?"

"Yes."

"I'm completing my graduate studies in archeology this year. . . ."

"I understand. You're letting me know that by taking you for an idiot I'm only making an idiot of myself."

She smiled.

"You put it too strongly."

"Yes. I'm sorry. Well, Eri, may I talk to him?"

"About what?"

My jaw fell. Here we go again, I thought.

"Well, what do you, for Christ's . . ." I bit my tongue. "About us."

"But that just isn't done."

"It isn't? Ah. Well, all right. And what is done?"

"One goes through the separation procedure. But, Mr. Bregg, really . . . I . . . can't do it this way."

"And in what way can you?"

She gave a helpless shrug.

"Does this mean we are back where we began yesterday evening?" I asked. "Don't be angry with me, Eri, for speaking like this, I am doubly handicapped, you see. I'm not familiar with all the formalities, customs, with what should be done and what shouldn't, even on a daily basis, so when it comes to things like . . ."

"No, I know. I know. But he and I . . . I . . . Seon . . ."

"I understand," I said. "Look here. Let's sit down."

"I think better when I stand."

"Please. Listen, Eri. I know what I should do. I should take

you, as I said, and go away somewhere—and I don't know how
I have this certainty. Perhaps it only comes from my boundless
stupidity. But it seems to me that eventually you could be happy
with me. Yes. At the same time I—observe—am the type who
. . . well, in a word, I don't want to do that. To force you. Thus
the whole responsibility for my decision—let's call it that—falls
on you. In other words, to make me be a swine not from the
right side, but only from the left. Yes. I see that clearly. Very
clearly. So now tell me just one thing—what do you prefer?"

"The right."

"What?"

"The right side of the swine."

I began to laugh. Perhaps a little hysterically.

"My God. Yes. Good. Then I can talk to him? Afterward.
That is, I would come back here alone. . : ."

"No."

"It isn't done like that? Perhaps not, but I feel I ought to,
Eri."

"No. I . . . please, please. Really. No!"

Suddenly tears fell from her eyes. I put my arms around her.

"Eri! No. It's no, then. I'll do whatever you want, but don't
cry. I beg you. Because . . . don't cry. Stop, all right? But then
. . . cry if you . . . I don't . . ."

"I didn't know that it could be . . . so . . ." she sobbed.

I carried her around the room.

"Don't cry, Eri. . . . You know what? We will go away for
. . . a month. How about that? Then later, if you want, you can
return."

"Please," she said, "please."

I put her down.

"Not like that? I don't know anything. I thought . . ."

"Oh, the way you are! Should do, shouldn't do. I don't want
this! I don't!"

"The right side grows larger all the time," I said with an unexpected coldness. "Very well, then, Eri. I won't consult you
any more. Get dressed. We'll eat breakfast and go."

She looked at me with her tear-streaked face. Was strangely

intent. Frowned. I had the impression that she wanted to say something and that it would not be flattering to me. But she only sighed and went out without a word. I sat at the table. This sudden decision of mine—like something out of a romance about pirates—had been a thing of the moment. In fact I was as resolute as a weather vane. I felt like a heel. How could I? How could I? I asked myself. Oh, what a mess!

In the half-open doorway stood Olaf.

"Old man," he said, "I am very sorry. It is the height of indiscretion, but I heard. Couldn't help hearing. You should close your door, and besides, you have such a healthy voice. Hal—you surpass yourself. What do you want from the girl, that she should throw herself into your arms because once you went down into that hole on . . . ?"

"Olaf!" I snarled.

"Only calm can save us. So the archeologist has found a nice site. A hundred and sixty years, that's already antiquity, isn't it?"

"Your sense of humor . . ."

"Doesn't appeal to you. I know. Nor does it to me. But where would I be, old man, if I couldn't see through you? At your funeral, that's where. Hal, Hal . . ."

"I know my name."

"What is it you want? Come, Chaplain, fall in. Let's eat and take off."

"I don't even know where to go."

"By chance, I do. Along the shore there are still some small cabins to rent. You two take the car. . . ."

"What do you mean—you take the car . . . ?"

"What else? You prefer the Holy Trinity? Chaplain . . ."

"Olaf, if you don't stop it . . ."

"All right. I know. You'd like to make everybody happy: me, her, that Seol or Seon—no, it won't work. Hal, we'll leave together. You can drop me off at Houl. I'll take an ulder from there."

"Well," I said, "a nice vacation I'm giving you!"

"I'm not complaining, so don't you. Perhaps something will come of it. But enough for now. Come on."

Breakfast took place in a strange atmosphere. Olaf spoke more than usual, but into the air. Eri and I hardly said a word. Afterward, the white robot brought the gleeder, and Olaf took it to Clavestra to get the car. The idea came to him at the last minute. An hour later the car was in the garden, I loaded it with my belongings, Eri also brought her things—not all her things, it seemed to me, but I didn't ask; we did not, in fact, converse at all. And so, on a sunny day that grew very hot, we drove first to Houl—a little out of our way—and Olaf got out there; it was only in the car that he told me he had rented a cottage for us.

There was no farewell as such.

"Listen," I said, "if I let you know . . . you'll come?"

"Sure. I'll send you my address."

"Write to the post office at Houl," I said.

He gave me his firm hand. How many hands like that were left on Earth? I held it so hard that my fingers cracked, then, not looking back, I got behind the wheel. We drove for less than an hour. Olaf had told me where to find the little house. It was small—four rooms, no pool—but at the beach, right on the sea. Passing rows of brightly colored cottages scattered across the hills, we saw the ocean from the road. Even before it appeared, we heard its muffled, distant thunder.

From time to time I glanced at Eri. She was silent, stiff, only rarely did she look out at the changing landscape. The house— our house—was supposed to be blue, with an orange roof. Touching my lips with my tongue, I could taste salt. The road turned and ran parallel to the sandy shoreline. The ocean, its waves seemingly motionless because of the distance, joined its voice to the roar of the straining engine.

The cottage was one of the last along the road. A tiny garden, its bushes gray from the salt spray, bore the traces of a recent storm. The waves must have come right up to the low fence: here and there lay empty shells. The slanting roof jutted out in front, like the fancifully folded brim of a flat hat, and gave a great deal of shade. Behind a large, grassy dune the neighboring cottage could be seen, some six hundred paces away. Below, on the half-moon beach, were the tiny shapes of people.

I opened the car door.

"Eri."

She got out without a word. If only I knew what was going on behind that furrowed forehead. She walked beside me to the door.

"No, not like that," I said. "You're not supposed to walk across the threshold."

"Why?"

I lifted her up.

"Open . . ." I asked her. She touched the plate with her fingers and the door opened.

I carried her in and put her down.

"It's a custom. For luck."

She went first to look at the rooms. The kitchen was in the rear, automatic and with one robot, not really a robot, only an electrical imbecile to do the housework. It could set the table. It carried out instructions but spoke only a few words.

"Eri," I said, "would you like to go to the beach?"

She shook her head. We were standing in the middle of the largest room, white and gold.

"Then what would you like, maybe . . ."

Before I could finish, again the same movement.

I could see now what was in store. But the die was cast and the game had to be played out.

"I'll bring our things," I said. I waited for her to reply, but she sat on a chair as green as grass and I realized that she would not speak. That first day was terrible. Eri did nothing obvious, did not go out of her way to avoid me, and after lunch she even tried to study a little—I asked her then if I could stay in her room, to look at her. Promising that I would not utter a word and would not disturb her. But after fifteen minutes (how quick of me!) I realized that my presence was a tremendous burden to her; the line of her back betrayed this, her small, cautious movements, their hidden effort; so, covered with sweat, I beat a hasty retreat and began to pace back and forth in my own room. I did not know her yet. I could see, however, that the girl was not stupid, far from stupid. Which, in the present situation, was

both good and bad. Good, because even if she did not understand, she could at least guess what I was and would not see in
me some barbarous monster or wild man. Bad, because in that
case the advice that Olaf had given me at the last moment was
worthless. He had quoted to me an aphorism that I knew, from
Hon: "If the woman is to be like fire, then the man must be like
ice." In other words, he felt that my only chance was at night,
not during the day. I did not want this, and for that reason had
been wearing myself out, but I understood that in the short time
I had I could not hope to get through to her with words, that
anything I said would remain on the outside—for in no way
would it weaken her rectitude, her well-justified anger, which
had shown itself only once, in a short outburst, when she began
to shout, "I don't! I don't!" And the fact that she had then
controlled herself so quickly I also took to be a bad sign.

In the evening she began to be afraid. I tried to keep low, step
softly, like Voov, that small pilot who managed—the perfect
man of few words—to say and do everything he wanted without
speaking.

After dinner—she ate nothing, which alarmed me—I felt
anger growing inside me; at times I almost hated her for my own
torment, and the great injustice of this feeling only served to
intensify it.

Our first real night together: when she fell asleep in my arms,
still all hot, and her ragged breath began, in single, ever-weaker
sighs, to pass into oblivion, I was certain that I had won.
Throughout she had struggled, not with me but with her own
body, which I came to know, the delicate nails, the slender
fingers, the palms, the feet, whose every part and curve I un-
locked and brought to life, as it were, with my kisses, my breath,
stealing my way into her—against her—with infinite patience
and slowness, so that the transitions were imperceptible, and
whenever I felt a growing resistance, like death, I would retreat,
would begin to whisper to her mad, senseless, childish words,
and again I would be silent and only caress her, and I besieged
her with my touch, for hours, and felt her open and her stiffness
give way to the trembling of a last defense, and then she trem-

bled differently, conquered now, but still I waited and, saying nothing, for this was beyond words, drew from the darkness her slender arms, and breasts, the left breast, for there beat the heart, faster and faster, and her breath grew more violent, more desperate, despairing, and the thing took place; this was not even pleasure, but the mercy of annihilation and dissolving, a storming of the last wall of our bodies, so that in violence they could be one for a few seconds, our battling breaths, our fervor passed into mindlessness, she cried out once, weakly, in the high voice of a child, and clutched me. And then her hands slid away from me, furtively, as if in great shame and sadness, as if suddenly she understood how horribly I had tricked her. And I began everything again, the kisses placed in the bends of the fingers, the mute appeals, the whole tender and cruel progression. And everything was repeated, as in a hot black dream, and at one point I felt her hand, buried in my hair, press my face to her naked shoulder with a strength I had not expected in her. And later, exhausted, breathing rapidly, as if to expel from herself the accumulated heat and sudden fear, she fell asleep. And I lay motionless, like one dead, taut, trying to figure out whether what had happened meant everything or nothing. Just before I fell asleep it seemed to me that we were saved, and only then came peace, a great peace, as great as that on Kereneia, when I lay on the hot sheets of cracked lava with Arder, whose mouth I could see breathing behind the glass of his suit although he was unconscious, and I knew that it had not been in vain, yet I hadn't the strength then even to open the valve of his reserve cylinder; I lay paralyzed, with the feeling that the greatest thing of my life was behind me now and that if I were to die right there, nothing would change, and my immobility was like the unutterable silence of triumph.

But in the morning everything began again. In the early hours she was still ashamed, or perhaps it was contempt, I do not know whether it was directed at me or whether it was herself she despised for what had taken place. Around lunchtime I succeeded in persuading her to take a short drive. We rode along the huge beaches, with the Pacific stretched before us in the sun, a roaring colossus furrowed by crescents of white-and-gold foam, filled to the horizon with the tiny colored sheets of sail-boats. I stopped the car where the beaches ended, ended in an unexpected wall of rock. The road made a sharp turn here, and, standing a meter from the edge, one could look straight down upon the violent surf. We returned for lunch. It was as on the previous day, and everything in me cringed at the thought of the night, because I did not want it. Not like that. When I was not looking at her, I felt her eyes on me. I was puzzled by her re-newed frowns, her sudden stares, and then—how or why I do not know—just before dinner, as we sat at the table, suddenly, as though someone had opened my skull with a single blow, I understood everything. I wanted to punch myself in the head—what a self-centered fool I had been, what a self-deceiving bas-tard—I sat, stunned, motionless, a storm within me, beads of sweat on my forehead. I felt extremely weak.

"What is the matter?" she asked.

"Eri," I croaked, "I . . . only now. I swear! Only now do I understand, only now, that you went with me because you were afraid, afraid that I . . . yes?"

Her eyes widened with surprise, she looked at me carefully, as if suspecting a trick, a joke.

She nodded.

I jumped up.

"Let's go."

"Where?"

"To Clavestra. Pack your things. We'll be there"—I looked at my watch—"in three hours."

She stood without moving.

"You mean it?" she said.

"Eri, I didn't know. Yes, it sounds unbelievable. But there are limits. Yes, there are limits. Eri, it is still not clear to me how I could have done such a thing—because I blinded myself, I guess. Well, I don't know, it doesn't matter, it has no im-portance now."

She packed—so quickly. . . . Everything inside me broke and crumbled, but on the surface I was perfectly, almost perfectly, calm. When she sat down beside me in the car, she said: "Hal, forgive me."

"For what? Ah!" I understand. "You thought that I knew?"

"Yes."

"All right. Let's not talk about it any more."

And again I drove at a hundred; houses flashed by, purple, white, sapphire, the road twisted and turned, I increased our speed, the traffic was heavy, then let up, the cottages lost their colors, the sky became a dark blue, the stars appeared, and we sped along in the whistling wind.

The surrounding countryside grew gray, the hills lost their volume, became outlines, rows of dark humps, the road stood out against the dusk as a wide, phosphorescent band. I recognized the first houses of Clavestra, the familiar turn, the hedges. At the entrance I stopped the car, carried her things into the garden, to the veranda.

"I don't want to go inside. You understand."

"I understand."

I did not say good-bye to her, but simply turned away. She touched my arm; I flinched as if I had been struck.

"Hal, thank you."

"Don't say anything. Just don't say anything."

I fled. I jumped into the car, took off; the roar of the engine saved me for a while. It was laughable. Obviously she had been afraid that I would kill him. After all, she had seen me try to kill Olaf, who was as innocent as a lamb, simply because he had not let me—and anyway! Anyway, nothing. There in the car I howled, I could permit myself anything, being alone, and the engine covered my madness—and again I do not know at what point it was that I realized what I had to do. And once more, as the first time, peace came. Not the same. Because the fact that I had taken advantage of the situation so terribly and had forced her to go with me, and that everything had taken place on account of that—it was worse than anything I could have imagined, because it robbed me even of my memories, of that night, of everything. Alone, with my own hands, I had destroyed all, through a boundless egoism, a lie that had not let me see what was at the very surface, the most obvious thing. Yes, she told the truth when she said that she did not fear me. She did not fear for herself. For him.

Lights flew by, flowed, moved slowly to the rear, the landscape was indescribably beautiful, and I—torn, pierced—hurtled, tires squealing, from one turn to the next, toward the Pacific, toward the cliff there; at one point, when the car veered more sharply than I expected and went off the edge of the road with its right wheels, I panicked for a fraction of a second, then burst into crazy laughter—that I was afraid to die here, having decided to do it in another place—and the laughter turned suddenly into sobbing. I must do it quickly, I thought, I'm no longer myself. What's happening to me is worse than terrible, it's disgusting. And I also told myself that I ought to be ashamed. But the words had no weight or meaning. It had got completely dark, the road practically deserted, because few drove at night, when I noticed, not far behind me, a black gleeder. It went lightly and without effort in the places where I had had to employ all my skill with brake and accelerator. Because gleeders hold the road with magnetic forces, or gravitational, God knows. The point is that it could have passed me with no difficulty, but it kept to the rear, some eighty meters behind me, sometimes a little closer, sometimes farther back. On sharp bends, when I skidded across the road and cut from the left, it kept its distance, though I did not believe that it could not keep up with me. Perhaps the driver was afraid. But, then, there would be no driver. Anyway, what did the gleeder matter to me?

It mattered, because I felt that it did not hang back by chance. And suddenly came the thought that it was Olaf, that Olaf, who didn't trust me in the least (and rightly!), had stayed in the vicinity and was waiting to see how things turned out. Yes, there was my deliverer, good old Olaf, who once again would not let me do what I wanted, who would be my big brother, my comforter; and at that thought something took hold of me, and for a second I could not see the road through my red fury.

Why don't they leave me alone? I thought, and began to squeeze every last shred out of the machine, every possibility, as if I did not know that the gleeder could go at twice the speed. Thus we raced through the night, among the hills with scattered lights, and above the shrill whistling of the wind I could hear now the roar of the invisible, spreading, immense Pacific, as though the sound rose from bottomless depths.

Drive, then, I thought. Drive. You don't know what I know. You spy on me, trail me, won't leave me be, fine; but I'll fool you, I'll give you the slip before you know what's happened; and no matter what you do it won't help, because a gleeder can't go off the road. So that even at the last second I'll have a clear conscience. Excellent.

I went by the cottage where we had stayed; its three lit windows stabbed me as I passed, as if to prove to me that there is no suffering that cannot be made still greater, and I began the last stretch of road, parallel to the ocean. Then the gleeder, to my horror, suddenly increased its speed and began to overtake me. I blocked its way brutally, veering to the left. It fell back, and thus we maneuvered—whenever it tried to pass me I blocked the left lane with the car, maybe five times altogether. Suddenly, though I was barring the way, it began to pull in front of me; the body of my car practically brushed the glistening black hull of that windowless, seemingly unoccupied projectile. I was certain, then, that it could only be Olaf, because no other man would have attempted such a thing—but I could not kill Olaf. I could not. Therefore I let him by. He got in front of me, and I thought that now he would in turn try to cut me off, but instead he stayed some fifteen meters ahead. Well, I thought, that's all right. And I slowed down, in the small hope that he might increase the distance between us, but he did not; he, too, slowed down. It was about two kilometers to that last turn at the cliff when the gleeder slowed down even more and kept to the center, so that I could not pass it. I thought I might be able to do it now, but there was no cliff yet, only sandy beach, the car's wheels would sink in the sand after a hundred meters, I wouldn't even make it to the ocean—it would be idiotic. I had no choice, I had to drive on. The gleeder slowed down still more and I saw that it would stop soon; the rear of its black body glowed, as though splashed with burning blood, from the brake lights. I tried to slip around it with a sudden swerve, but it blocked my way. He was faster and more agile than I—but, then, a machine was driving the gleeder. A machine always has faster reflexes. I slammed on the brakes, too late, there was a terrible crash, a black mass loomed up before the windshield, I was thrown forward and lost consciousness.

I opened my eyes, awakened from a dream, a senseless dream—I dreamed that I was swimming. Something cold and wet ran down my face, I felt hands, they shook me, and I heard a voice.

"Olaf," I mumbled. "Why, Olaf? Why . . . ?"

"Hal!"

I roused myself; I propped myself up on one elbow and saw her face over me, close, and when I sat up, too stunned to think, she slumped slowly onto my knees, her shoulders heaving—and still I did not believe it. My head was huge, as if filled with cotton.

"Eri," I said; my lips were curiously large, heavy, and somehow very remote.

"Eri, it's you. Or am I only . . ."

And suddenly strength came to me, I caught her by the arms, lifted her, got to my feet, and staggered with her; we both fell on the still warm, soft sand. I kissed her wet, salty face and wept—it was the first time in my life—and she wept. We said nothing for a long time; gradually we began to be afraid—of what, I can't say—and she looked at me with lunatic eyes.

"Eri," I repeated. "Eri . . . Eri . . ."

That was all I knew. I lay down on the sand, suddenly weak, and she grew alarmed, tried to pull me up, but hadn't the strength.

"No, Eri," I whispered. "No, I'm all right, it's only this. . . ."

"Hal. Say something! Say something!"

"What should I say . . . Eri . . ."

My voice calmed her a little. She ran off somewhere and returned with a flat pan, again poured water on my face—bitter, the water of the Pacific. I had intended to drink much more of it, flashed a thought, senseless; I blinked. I came to. Sat up and touched my head.

There was not even a cut; my hair had cushioned the impact, so I had only a lump the size of an orange, a few abrasions, still a ringing in my ears, but I was all right. At least, as long as I sat. I tried to stand up, but my legs didn't seem cooperative.

She knelt in front of me, watching, her arms at her sides.

"It's you? Really?" I asked. Only now did I understand; I turned and saw, through the nauseating vertigo brought on by that movement, two tangled black shapes in the moonlight, a dozen or so meters away at the edge of the road. My voice failed me when I returned my eyes to her.

"Hal . . ."

"Yes."

"Try to get up. I'll help you."

"Get up?"

Apparently my head was still not clear. I understood what had happened, and I didn't understand. Had that been Eri in the gleeder? Impossible.

"Where is Olaf?" I asked.

"Olaf? I don't know."

"You mean he wasn't here?"

"No."

"You alone?"

She nodded.

And suddenly an awful, inhuman fear gripped me.

"How were you able? How?"

Her face trembled, her lips quivered, she couldn't say the words.

"I ha-a-ad to. . . ."

Again she wept. Then quieted, grew calm. Touched my face. My forehead. With light fingers felt my skull. I repeated breathlessly:

"Eri . . . it's you?"

Raving. Later, slowly, I stood up, she supported me as best she could; we walked to the road. Only there did I see what shape the car was in; the hood, the entire front, everything was folded like an accordion. The gleeder, on the other hand, was hardly damaged—now I appreciated its superiority—only a small dent in the side, where it had taken the main impact. Eri helped me get in, backed away the gleeder until the wreck of my car fell over on its side with a long clattering of metal, then took off. We were going back. I was silent, the lights swam by. My head wobbled, still large and heavy. We got out in front of the cottage. The windows were still lit up, as if we had left only for a moment. She helped me inside. I lay down on the bed. She went to the table, walked around it, walked to the door. I sat up:

"You're leaving!"

She ran to me, knelt by the side of the bed, and shook her head in denial.

"No?"

"No."

"And you'll never leave me?"

"Never."

I embraced her. She put her cheek to my face, and everything was drained from me—the burning embers of my obstinacy and anger, the madness of the last few hours, the fear, the despair; I lay there empty, like one dead, and only pressed her to me more tightly, as if my strength had returned, and there was silence, the light gleamed on the golden wallpaper of the room, and somewhere far away, as in another world, outside the open windows, the Pacific roared.

It may seem strange, but we said nothing that evening, or that night. Not a single word. Not until late the following day did I learn how it had been. As soon as I had driven off, she'd guessed the reason and panicked, didn't know what to do. First she thought to summon the white robot, but realized that it could not help; and he—she referred to him in no other way— he could not help, either. Olaf, perhaps. Olaf, certainly, but she did not know where to find him, and anyway there wasn't time. So she took the house gleeder and drove after me. She quickly caught up with me, then kept behind me for as long as there was a chance that I was only returning to the cottage.

"Would you have got out then?" I asked.

She hesitated.

"I don't know. I think I would have. I think so now, but I don't know."

Then, when she saw that I did not stop but kept driving, she got even more frightened. The rest I knew.

"No. I don't understand it," I said. "This is the part I don't understand. How were you able to do it?"

"I told myself that . . . that nothing would happen."

"You knew what I wanted to do? And where?"

"Yes."

"How?"

After a long pause:

"I don't know. Perhaps because by now I know you a little."

I was silent. I still had many things to ask but didn't dare. We stood by the window. With my eyes closed, feeling the great open space of the ocean, I said:

"All right, Eri, but what now? What is going to happen?"

"I told you already."

"But I don't want it this way," I whispered.

"It can't be any other way," she replied after a long pause. "Besides . . ."

"Besides?"

"Never mind."

That very day, in the evening, things got worse, again. Our trouble returned and progressed, and then retreated. Why? I do not know. She probably did not know, either. As if it was only in the face of extremity that we became close, and only then that we were able to understand each other. And a night. And another day.

On the fourth day I heard her talking on the telephone and was terribly afraid. She cried afterward. But at dinner was smiling again.

And this was the end and the beginning. Because the following week we went to Maë, the main city of the district, and in an office there, before a man dressed in white, we said the words that made us man and wife. That same day I sent a telegram to Olaf. The next day I went to the post office, but there was nothing from him. I thought that perhaps he had moved, and hence the delay. To tell the truth, even then, at the post office, I felt a twinge of anxiety, because this silence was not like Olaf, but what with all that had happened, I thought about it only for a moment and said nothing to her. As if it were forgotten.

or a couple joined only by the violence of my madness, we suited each other above expectation. Our life together was subject to a curious division. When it came to a difference in attitudes, Eri was able to defend her position, but then the matter in question was usually of a general nature; she was, for example, a staunch advocate of betrization and defended it with arguments not taken from books. That she opposed my views so openly I considered a good sign; but these discussions of ours took place during the day. In the light of day she did not dare—or did not wish—to speak about me objectively, calmly, no doubt because she did not know which of her words would amount to pointing out some personal fault of mine, some absurdity of "the character from the pickle jar," to use Olaf's expression, and which an attack leveled at the basic values of my time. But at night—perhaps because the darkness attenuated my presence somewhat—she spoke to me about myself, that is, about us, and I was glad of these quiet conversations in the dark, for the dark mercifully hid my frequent amazement.

She told me about herself, about her childhood, and in this way I learned for the second time—for the first time, really, since with concrete, human content—how finely wrought was this society of constant, delicately stabilized harmony. It was considered a natural thing that having children and raising them during the first years of their life should require high qualifications and extensive preparation, in other words, a special course of study; in order to obtain permission to have offspring, a married couple had to pass a kind of examination; at first this seemed incredible to me, but on thinking it over I had to admit that we, of the past, and not they, should be charged with having paradoxical customs: in the old society one was not allowed to build a house or a bridge, treat an illness, perform the simplest administrative function, without specialized education, whereas the matter of utmost responsibility, bearing children, shaping their minds, was left to blind chance and momentary desires, and the community intervened only when mistakes had been made and it was too late to correct them.

So, then, obtaining the right to a child was now a distinction not awarded to just anyone. Furthermore, parents could not isolate children from their contemporaries; specially selected groups were formed, for both sexes, and in these the most divergent temperaments were represented. So-called difficult children were given additional, hypnagogic treatment, and the education of all children was begun very early. Not reading and writing, which came much later, but the education of the youngest, introducing them—through special games—to the functioning of the world, Earth, to the richness and variety of life in society; four- and five-year-olds were instilled, in precisely this way, with the principles of tolerance, coexistence, respect for other beliefs and attitudes, the unimportance of the differing external features of the children (and hence the adults) of other races. All of which seemed quite fine to me, with one single but fundamental reservation, because the immovable cornerstone of this world, its all-embracing rule, was betrization. The whole aim of a child's upbringing was to make it accept betrization as a fact of life no less unquestionable than birth or death. When I heard how ancient history was taught, even from Eri, I had difficulty containing my indignation. According to this portrayal, those were times of animality and barbaric, uncontrolled procreation, of catastrophe both economic and military, and the undeniable achievements of past civilization were presented as an expression of the strength and determination that permitted people to overcome the benightedness and the cruelty of the period: those achievements, then, came about as it were in spite of the prevailing tendency to live at the cost of others. What once took untold effort, they said, and was attainable only by a few, the road to it bristling with danger and the necessity for sacrifice, compromise—material success purchased only by moral defeat—was now common, easy, and certain.

It was not so bad as long as one dealt in generalizations; I could go along with the condemnation of various aspects of the past, such as, say, war; and the lack—the complete lack—of politics, of friction or tension, of international conflict—though a surprising lack, giving instant rise to the suspicion that such things existed but went unmentioned—I had to admit was an accomplishment, not a loss; but it was bad indeed when this re-evaluation touched me personally. Because it was not only Starck who abandoned, in his book (written, *nota bene*, a half century before my return), the exploration of space. Here Eri, as an archeology graduate, had much to teach me. The first betrizated generations radically changed their attitude toward astronautics, but though the signs changed from plus to minus, the interest in it remained intense. The consensus, then, was that a tragic error had been committed, an error that reached its culmination in the very years during which our expedition was planned, because at that time similar expeditions were mounted in huge numbers. It was not that the yield of these expeditions had been so small, that the penetration of space in a radius of many light years from the solar system had led only to the discovery, on a few planets, of primitive and strange forms of vegetation, not to contact with any highly developed civilization. Nor was it considered the worst thing that the terrible length of the voyage would change the crew of the spacecraft, those representatives of Earth—to an increasing degree, as the destinations became more remote—into a group of wretched, mortally weary creatures who, after landing here and there, would require much care and convalescence; or that the decision to send forth such enthusiasts was thoughtless and cruel. The crux of the matter was that man wanted to conquer the universe without having attended to his own problems on Earth, as though it were not obvious that heroic flights would do nothing· to alleviate the sea of human suffering, injustice, fear, and hunger on the globe.

But, as I say, only the first betrizated generation thought this

way, because afterward, in the natural course of things, came
oblivion and indifference; children marveled when they learned
of the romantic period of astronautics, and possibly felt even
a little fear toward their ancestors, who were as strange to them
and as incomprehensible as the ancestors who engaged in wars
of plunder and voyages for gold. It was the indifference that
appalled me the most, far more than the condemnation—our
life's work had become wrapped in silence, buried, and forgotten.

Eri did not try to kindle enthusiasm in me for this new world,
she made no effort to convert me; she simply told me of it in
speaking about herself, and I—precisely because she spoke about
herself and was herself testimony to it—could not shut my eyes
to its virtues.

It was a civilization that had rid itself of fear. Everything that
existed served the people. Nothing had weight but their well-
being, the satisfaction of their basic as well as their most sophis-
ticated needs. Everywhere—in all walks of life where the presence of man, the fallibility of his passions, and the slowness of
his reflexes could create even the smallest risk—man was re-
placed by nonliving devices, automata.

It was a world that had shut out danger. Threat, conflict, all
forms of violence—these had no place in it; a world of tran-
quillity, of gentle manners and customs, easy transitions, undra-
matic situations, every bit as amazing as my or our (I am
thinking of Olaf) reaction to it.

For we, in the course of ten years, had gone through so many
horrors, everything that was inimical to man, that wounded
him and crushed him, and we had returned, sick of it, so very
sick of it; any one of us, hearing that the return would be delayed, that there would be a few more months in space to en-
dure, would probably have leapt at the speaker's throat. And
now we—no longer able to stand the constant risk, the blind
chance of a meteorite hit, that endless suspense, the hell we
went through when an Arder or an Ennesson failed to return
from a reconnaissance flight—we immediately began to refer
to that time of terror as the only proper thing, as right, as giving
us dignity and purpose. Yet even now I shuddered at the mem-

ory of how, sitting, lying, hanging in the oddest positions above the circular radio-cabin, we waited, waited, in a silence broken only by the steady buzz of the signal from the ship's automatic scanner, seeing, in the leaden bluish light, drops of sweat run down the forehead of the radio operator frozen in the same waiting—while the clock, its alarm set, moved soundlessly, until finally the moment when the hand touched the red mark on the dial, the moment of relief. Relief . . . because then it was possible to go out and explore and die alone, and that truly seemed easier than waiting. We pilots, the nonscientists, made up the old guard; our time had stopped three years before the actual start of the expedition. In those three years we went through a succession of tests of increasing psychological stress. There were three main stages, three stations, which we called the Ghost Palace, the Wringer, and the Coronation.

The Ghost Palace: One was locked inside a small container, cut off completely from the world. No sound, ray of light, puff of air, or vibration from without reached the interior. Resembling a small rocket, the container was equipped with a mock-up of the same controls, supplies of water, food, and oxygen. And one had to stay there, idle, with absolutely nothing to do, for a month—which seemed an eternity. No one came out the same. I, one of the toughest of Dr. Janssen's subjects, began in my third week to see the strange things that others had observed as early as the fourth or fifth day: monsters without faces, shapeless crowds that oozed from the dully glowing dials to enter into senseless conversations with me, to hover above my sweating body, my body that was losing its outline, was changing, growing larger, and that finally—the most frightening thing—began to assume an independence, first in spasms of individual muscles, then, after a tingling and a numbness, contractions, and finally movements, while I watched, amazed, not understanding. But for the preliminary training, but for the theoretical briefing, I would have sworn that my arms, head, neck were possessed by demons. The upholstered interior of the container had seen things that defied description—Janssen and his staff, with the appropriate equipment, were monitoring what took place in there, but none of us knew that at the time. The feeling of isolation had to be genuine and complete. Therefore the disappearance of some of the doctor's assistants was a mystery to us. It was only during the voyage that Gimma told me that they had simply cracked. One of them, a certain Gobbek, had apparently tried to force open the container, unable to watch the torment of the man inside.

But that was only the Ghost Palace. Because then came the Wringer, with its tumblers and centrifuges, its hellish accelerating machine that could produce 400 g's—an acceleration, never used, of course, that would have turned a man into a puddle, but 100 g's was enough to make a subject's entire back sticky with blood forced out through the skin.

The last test, the Coronation, I passed with flying colors. This was the final sieve, the final station for weeding us out. Al Martin, a strapping fellow who back then, on Earth, looked the way I do today, a giant, one hunk of iron muscle, and as calm as you could want—he came back to Earth from the Coronation in such a state that they immediately removed him from the center.

The Coronation was quite a simple matter. They put a man in a suit, took him up into orbit, and at an altitude of some hundred thousand kilometers, where the Earth shines like the Moon enlarged fivefold, simply tossed him out of the rocket into space, and then flew away. Hanging there like that, moving his arms and legs, he had to wait for their return, wait to be rescued; the spacesuit was reliable and comfortable, it had oxygen, air conditioning, a heater, and it even fed the man, with a paste squeezed out every two hours from a special mouthpiece. So nothing could happen, unless maybe there was a malfunction in the small radio attached to the outside of the suit, which automatically signaled the location of the wearer. There was only one thing missing in the suit, a receiver, which meant that the man could hear no voice but his own. With the void and the stars around him, suspended, weightless, he had to wait. True, the wait was fairly long, but not that long. And that was all.

Yes, but people went insane from this; they would be dragged in writhing in epileptic convulsions. This was the test that went most against what lay in a man—an utter annihilation, a doom, a death with full and continuing consciousness. It was a taste of eternity, which got inside a man and let him know its horror. The knowledge, always held to be impossible and impalpable, of the cosmic abyss extending in all directions, became ours; the never-ending fall, the stars between the useless, dangling legs, the futility, the pointlessness of arms, mouth, gestures, of movement and no movement, in the suit an earsplitting scream, the wretches howled, enough.

No need to dwell on what was only, after all, a test, an introduction, intentional, planned with care, with safety precautions: physically, none of the "coronated" were harmed, and the rocket from the base retrieved every one. True, we were not told that, either, to keep the situation as authentic as possible.

The "Coronation" went well for me. I had my own system. It was very simple and completely dishonest—we were not supposed to do it. When they threw me out the hatch, I closed my eyes. Then I thought about various things. The only thing you needed, and needed in plenty, was will power. You had to tell yourself not to open those miserable eyes no matter what. Janssen, I think, knew about my trick. But there were no repercussions.

All this, however, took place on Earth or in its proximity. Afterward came a space not contrived and not created in the laboratory, a space that killed in fact, without pretending, and that sometimes spared—Olaf, Gimma, Thurber, myself, those seven from the *Ulysses*—and even let us return. Whereupon we, who longed most of all for peace, seeing our dream come true, and to perfection, immediately scorned it. I believe it was Plato who said, "O wretched one—you will have what you wanted."

ne night, very late, we lay spent; Eri's head, turned to one side, rested in the crook of my arm. Raising my eyes to the open window, I saw the stars in the gaps among the clouds. There was no wind, the curtain hung frozen like some pale phantom, but now a desolate wave approached from the open ocean, and I could hear the long rumble announcing it, then the ragged roar of the breakers on the beach, then silence for several heartbeats, and again the unseen water stormed the night shore. But I hardly noticed this steadily repeated reminder of my presence on Earth, for my eyes were fixed on the Southern Cross, in which Beta had been our guiding star; every day I took bearings by it, automatically, my thoughts on other things; it had led us unfailingly, a never-fading beacon in space. I could almost feel in my hands the metal grips I would shift to bring the point of light, distinct in the darkness, to the center of the field of vision, with the soft rubber rim of the eyepiece against my brows and cheeks. Beta, one of the more distant stars, hardly changed at all when we reached our destination. It shone with the same indifference, though the Southern Cross had long since disappeared to us because we had gone deep into its arms, and then that white point of light, that giant star, no longer was what it had seemed at the beginning, a challenge; its immutability revealed its true meaning, that it was a witness to our transience, to the indifference of the void, the universe —an indifference that no one is ever able to accept.

But now, trying to catch the sound of Eri's breathing between the rumbles of the Pacific, I was incredulous. I said to myself silently: It's true, it's true, I was there; but my wonder remained.

Eri gave a start. I began to move away, to make more room for her, but suddenly I felt her gaze on me.

"You're not asleep?" I whispered. And leaned over, wanting to touch her lips with mine, but she put the tips of her fingers on my mouth. She held them there for a moment, then moved them along the collarbone to the chest, felt the hard hollow between my ribs, and pressed her palm to it.

"What's this?" she whispered.

"A scar."

"What happened?"

"I had an accident."

She became silent. I could feel her looking at me. She lifted her head. Her eyes were all darkness, without a glimmer in them; I could see the outline of her arm, moving with her breath, white.

"Why don't you tell me anything?"

"Eri . . . ?"

"Why don't you want to talk?"

"About the stars?" I suddenly understood. She was silent. I did not know what to say.

"You think I wouldn't understand?"

I looked at her closely, through the darkness, as the ocean's roar ebbed and flowed through the room, and did not know how to explain it to her.

"Eri . . ."

I tried to take her in my arms. She freed herself and sat up in bed.

"You don't have to talk if you don't want to. But tell me why, at least."

"You don't know? You really don't?"

"Now, maybe. You wanted . . . to spare me?"

"No. I'm simply afraid."

"Of what?"

"I'm not sure. I don't want to dig it all up. It's not that I'm denying any of it. That would be impossible, anyway. But talking about it would mean—or so it seems to me—shutting myself up in it. Away from everyone, everything, from what is . . . now."

"I understand," she said quietly. The white smudge of her face disappeared, she had lowered her head. "You think that I don't value it."

"No, no," I tried to interrupt her.

"Wait, now it's my turn. What I think about astronautics, and the fact that I would never leave Earth, that's one thing. But it has nothing to do with you and me. Though actually it does: because we are together. Otherwise, we wouldn't be, ever. For me—it means you. That is why I would like . . . but you don't have to. If it is as you say. If you feel like that."

"I'll tell you."

"But not today."

"Today."

"Lie back."

I fell on the pillows. She tiptoed to the window, a whiteness in the gloom. Drew the curtain. The stars vanished, there was only the slow roar of the Pacific, returning repeatedly with a dreary persistence. I could see practically nothing. The moving air betrayed her steps, the bed sagged.

"Did you ever see a ship of the class of the *Prometheus*?"

"No."

"It's large. On Earth, it would weigh over three hundred thousand tons."

"And there were so few of you?"

"Twelve. Tom Arder, Olaf, Arne, Thomas—the pilots, along with myself. And the seven scientists. If you think that it was empty there, you are wrong. Propulsion takes up nine-tenths of the mass. Photoaggregates. Storage, supplies, reserve units. The actual living quarters are small. Each of us had a cabin, in addition to the common ones. In the middle part of the body—the control center and the small landing rockets, and the probes, even smaller, for collecting samples from the corona . . ."

"And you were over Arcturus in one of those?"

"Yes. As was Arder."

"Why didn't you fly together?"

"In one rocket? It's riskier that way."

"How?"

"A probe is a cooling system. A sort of flying refrigerator. Just enough room to sit down in. You sit inside a shell of ice. The ice melts from the shield and refreezes on the pipes. The air compressors can be damaged. All it takes is a moment, because outside the temperature is ten, twelve thousand degrees. When the pipes stop in a two-man rocket, two men die. This way, only one. Do you understand?"

"I understand."

She put her hand on that unfeeling part of my chest.

"And this . . . happened there?"

"No, Eri; shall I tell you?"

"All right."

"Only don't think . . . No one knows about this."

"This?"

The scar stood out under the warmth of her fingers—as if returning to life.

"Yes."

"How is that possible? What about Olaf?"

"Not even Olaf. No one knows. I lied to them, Eri. Now I have to tell you, since I've started. Eri . . . it happened in the sixth year. We were on our way back then, but in cloudy regions you can't move quickly. It's a magnificent sight; the faster the ship travels, the stronger the luminescence of the cloud. We had a tail behind us, not like the tail of a comet, more a polar aurora, thin at the sides, deep into the sky, toward Alpha Eridanus, for thousands and thousands of kilometers. . . . Arder and Ennesson were gone by then. Venturi was dead, too. I would wake at six in the morning, when the light was changing from blue to white. I heard Olaf speaking from the controls. He had spotted something interesting. I went down. The radar showed a spot, slightly off our course. Thomas came, and we wondered what the thing could be. It was too big for a meteor, and, anyway, meteors never occur singly. We reduced speed. This woke the rest. When they joined us, I remember, Thomas said it had to be a ship. We often joked like that. In space there must be ships from other systems, but two mosquitoes released at opposite ends of the Earth would stand a better chance of meeting. We had reached a gap now in the cloud, and the cold, nebular dust became so dispersed that you could see stars of the sixth magnitude with the naked eye. The spot turned out to be a planetoid. Something like Vesta. A quarter of a billion tons, perhaps more. Extraordinarily regular, almost spherical. Which is quite rare. Two milliparsecs off the bow. It was traveling, and we—followed. Thurber asked me if we could get closer. I said we could, by a quarter of a milliparsec.

"We drew nearer. Through the telescope it looked like a porcupine, a ball bristling with spines. An oddity. Belonged in a museum. Thurber started arguing with Biel about its origin, whether tectonic or not. Thomas butted in, saying that this could be determined. There would be no loss of energy, we hadn't even begun to accelerate. He would fly there, take a few specimens, return. Gimma hesitated. Time presented no problem—we had some to spare. Finally he agreed. No doubt because I was present. Although I hadn't said a thing. Perhaps because of that. Because our relationship had become . . . but that's another story. We stopped; a maneuver of this kind takes time, and meanwhile the planetoid moved away, but we had it on radar. I was worried, because from the time we started back we had nothing but trouble. Breakdowns, not serious but hard to fix—and happening without any apparent reason. I'm not superstitious, but I believe in series. Still, I had no argument against his going. It made me look childish, but I checked out Thomas's engine myself and told him to be careful. With the dust."

"The what?"

"Dust. In the region of a cold cloud, you see, planetoids act like vacuum cleaners. They remove the dust from the space in their path, and this goes on over a long period of time. The dust settles in layers, which can double the size of the planetoid. A blast from a jet nozzle or even a heavy step is enough to set up a swirling cloud of dust that hangs above the surface. May not sound serious, but you can't see a thing. I told him that. But he knew it as well as I did. Olaf launched him off the ship's side, I went up to navigation and began to guide him down. I saw him approach the planetoid, maneuver, turn his rocket, and descend to the surface, like on a rope. Then, of course, I lost sight of him. But that was five kilometers. . . ."

"You picked him up on radar?"

"No, on the optical, that is, by telescope. Infrared. But I could talk to him the whole time. On the radio. Just as I was thinking that I hadn't seen Thomas make such a careful landing in a long time—we had all become careful on the way back—I saw a small flash, and a dark stain began to spread across the surface of the planetoid. Gimma, standing next to me, shouted. He thought that Thomas, to brake at the last moment, had hit the flame. That's an expression we use. You give one short blast of the engine, naturally not in such circumstances. And I knew that Thomas would never have done that. It had to be lightning."

"Lightning? There?"

"Yes. You see, any body moving at high speed through a cloud builds up charge, static electricity, from friction. There was a difference in potential between the *Prometheus* and the planetoid. It could have been billions of volts. More, even. When Thomas landed, a spark leapt. That was the flash, and because of the sudden heat the dust rose, and in a minute the entire surface was covered by a cloud. We couldn't hear him —his radio just crackled. I was furious, mainly at myself, for having underestimated. The rocket had special lightning conductors, pronged, and the charge should have passed quietly into St. Elmo's fire. But it didn't. It was exceptionally powerful. Gimma asked me when I thought the dust would settle. Thurber didn't ask; it was clear that it would take days."

"Days?"

"Yes. Because the gravity was extremely low. If you dropped a stone, it would fall for several hours before hitting the ground. Think how much longer it would take dust to settle after being thrown up a hundred meters. I told Gimma to go about his business, because we had to wait."

"And nothing could be done?"

"No. If I could be sure that Thomas was still inside his rocket, I would have taken a chance—turned the *Prometheus* around, got close to the planetoid, and blasted the dust off to all four corners of the galaxy—but I could not be sure. And finding him? The surface of the planetoid had an area equal to, I don't know, that of Corsica. Besides, in the dust cloud you could walk right by him at arm's length and not see him. There was only one solution. He had it at his fingertips. He could have taken off and returned."

"He didn't do that?"

"No."

"Do you know why?"

"I can guess. He would have had to take off blind. I could see that the cloud reached, well, not quite a kilometer above the surface, but he didn't know that. He was afraid of hitting an overhang or a rock. He might have landed on the bottom of some deep gorge. So we hung there a day, two days; he had enough oxygen and provisions for six. Emergency rations. No one was in a position to do anything. We paced and thought up ways of getting Thomas out of this mess. Emitters. Different wavelengths. We even threw down flares. They didn't work, that cloud was as dark as a tomb. A third day—a third night. Our measurements showed that the cloud was settling, but I wasn't sure it would finish coming down in the seventy hours left to Thomas. He could last without food far longer, but not without oxygen. Then I got an idea. I reasoned this way: Thomas's rocket was made primarily of steel. Provided there were no iron ores on that damned planetoid, it might be possible to locate him with a ferromagnetic indicator—a device for finding iron objects. We had a highly sensitive one. It could pick up a nail at a distance of three-quarters of a kilometer. A rocket at several kilometers. Olaf and I went over the apparatus. Then I told Gimma and took off."

"Alone."

"Yes."

"Why?"

"Because without Thomas there were only the two of us, and the *Prometheus* had to have a pilot."

"And they agreed to it?"

I smiled in the darkness.

"I was the First Pilot. Gimma could not give me orders, only suggest, I would weigh the chances and say yes or no. Most of the time, of course, I said yes. But in emergencies the decision was mine."

"And Olaf?"

"Well, you know Olaf a little by now. As you might imagine, I couldn't take off right away. But when it came down to it, I was the one who had sent Thomas out. Olaf couldn't deny that. So I took off. Without a rocket, of course."

"Without a rocket . . . ?"

"Yes, in a suit, with a gas shooter. It took a while, but not so very long. I had some trouble with the detector, which was practically a chest, awkward to handle. Weightless, of course, but when I was entering the cloud, I had to be careful not to hit anything. I ceased to see the cloud as I approached it; first the stars began to disappear, a few at a time, on the periphery, then half the sky got black; I looked back and saw the *Prometheus* glowing in the distance—she had special equipment that made the hull luminous. Looked like a long white pencil with a ball at one end, the photon headlight. Then everything winked out. The transition was so abrupt. Maybe a second of black mist, then nothing. My radio was disconnected; instead, I had the detector hooked up to the earphones. It took me only a few minutes to fly to the edge of the cloud, but over two hours to drop to the surface—I had to be careful. The electric flashlight was useless, as I had expected. I began the search. You know what stalactites look like in caves. . . ."

"Yes."

"Something like that, only more outlandish. I'm talking about what I saw later, when the dust settled, because during my search I couldn't see a thing, as if someone had poured tar over the window of my suit. The box I had on straps. I moved the antenna and listened, then walked with both arms extended—

I'd never stumbled so much in my life. No harm, thanks only to the low gravity. With just a little visibility, of course, a man could have regained his balance ten times over. But this way —it's hard to explain to someone who's never experienced it— the planetoid was all jagged peaks, with boulders piled up around them, and wherever I put my foot I began falling, in that drunken slow motion, and I couldn't jump back up: that would send me soaring for a quarter of an hour. I simply had to wait, keep trying to walk on. The rubble slid beneath me, debris, pillars, shards of rock, everything was barely held in place, the force that held them was unusually weak—which does not mean that if a boulder landed on a man, it would not kill him. The mass would act then, not the weight; there would be time to jump clear, of course, if you could see the thing falling . . . or at least hear it. But, then, there was no air, so it was only by the vibration under my feet that I could tell whether I had again sent some rock structure toppling, and I could do nothing but wait for a fragment to come out of the pitch-dark and begin to crush me. . . . I wandered about for hours and no longer thought that my idea of using the detector was brilliant. I also had to be careful because now and then I would find myself in the air, that is, floating, as in some clownish dream. At last I caught a signal. I must have lost it eight times, I don't remember exactly, but by the time I found the rocket, it was night on the *Prometheus.*

"The rocket stood at an angle, half-buried in that fiendish dust. The softest, most delicate stuff you can imagine. Almost insubstantial. The lightest fluff on Earth would offer more resistance. The particles were so incredibly small. . . . I checked inside the rocket; he was not there. I've said that it stood at an angle, but I wasn't at all sure; it was impossible to find the vertical without using special equipment, and that would've taken at least an hour, and a conventional plumb line, weighing practically nothing, was useless, since the bob wouldn't have held the string tight. . . . I wasn't surprised, then, that he hadn't tried to take off. I entered. I saw immediately that he had jury-rigged something to determine the vertical but that it hadn't worked. There was plenty of food left, but no oxygen. He must have transferred it all to the tank on his suit and left."

"Why?"

"Yes, why. He had been there three days. In that type of rocket you have only a seat, a screen, the control, levers, and a hatch at the rear. I sat there for a while. I realized that I would never be able to find him. For a second I thought that possibly he had gone out just as I landed, that he'd used his gas shooter to return to the *Prometheus* and was sitting on board now, while I wandered over these drunken stones. . . . I jumped out of the rocket so energetically that I flew upward. No sense of direction, nothing. You know how it is when you see a spark in total darkness? The eyes fantasize, there are rays, visions. Well, with the sense of balance, something similar can happen. In zero gravity there's no problem, a person accustoms himself. But when gravity is extremely weak, as on that planetoid, the inner ear reacts erratically, if not irrationally. You think you're zooming up like a Roman candle, then plummeting, and so on, all the time. And then the sensations of spinning and shifting, of the arms, legs, torso—as if the parts of your body changed places and your head wasn't where it belonged. . . .

"That was how I flew, until I collided with a wall, bounced off it, caught on something, was sent rolling, but managed to grab hold of a projecting rock. . . . Someone lay there. Thomas."

She was silent. In the darkness the Pacific roared.

"No, not what you think. He was alive. He sat up at once. I switched on the radio. At that short distance we could communicate perfectly.

" 'Is that you?' I heard him say.

" 'It's me,' I said. A scene from a ridiculous farce, it was so farfetched. Yet that's how it was. We got to our feet.

" 'How do you feel?' I asked.

" 'Fine. And you?'

"This surprised me a little, but I said:

" 'Very well, thank you. And everyone at home, too, is in good health.'

"Idiotic, but I thought that he was talking this way to show that he was holding up, you know?"

"I understand."

"When he stood close to me, I saw him as a patch of denser darkness in the light of my shoulder lamp. I ran my hands over his suit—it was undamaged.

" 'Do you have enough oxygen?' I asked. That was the most important thing.

" 'Who cares?' he said.

"I wondered what to do next. Start up his rocket? That would be too risky. To tell the truth, I wasn't even very pleased. I was afraid—or, rather, unsure—it is difficult to explain. The situation was unreal, I sensed something strange in it, what exactly I didn't know, I was not even fully aware of how I felt. Only that I wasn't pleased by this miraculous discovery. I tried to figure out how the rocket could be saved. But that, I thought, was not the most important thing. First I had to see what shape he was in. We stood there, in a night without stars.

" 'What have you been doing all this time?' I asked. This was important. If he had tried to do anything at all, even to take a few mineral samples, that would be a good sign.

" 'Different things,' he said. 'And what have you been doing, Tom?'

" 'What Tom?' I asked and went cold, because Arder had been dead a year, and he knew that very well.

" 'But you're Tom. Aren't you? I recognize your voice.'

"I said nothing; with his gloved hand he touched my suit and said:

" 'Nasty, isn't it? Nothing to see, and nothing there. I had pictured it differently. What about you?'

"I thought that he was imagining things in connection with Arder. . . . That had happened to more than one of us.

" 'Yes,' I said, 'it isn't too interesting here. Let's go, what do you say, Thomas?'

" 'Go?' He was surprised. 'What are you talking about, Tom?'

"I no longer paid attention to his 'Tom.'

" 'You want to stay here?' I said.

" 'And you don't?'

"He is pulling my leg, I thought, but enough of these stupid jokes.

" 'No,' I said. 'We must get back. Where is your pistol?'

" 'I lost it when I died.'

" 'What?'

" 'But I didn't mind,' he said. 'A dead man doesn't need a pistol.'

" 'Well, well,' I said. 'Come, I'll strap you to me and we'll go.'

" 'Are you crazy, Tom? Go where?'

" 'Back to the *Prometheus.*'

" 'But it isn't here. . . .'

" 'It's out there. Let me strap you up.'

" 'Wait.'

"He pushed me away.

" 'You speak strangely. You're not Tom!'

" 'That's right. I'm Hal.'

" 'You died, too? When?'

"I now saw what was up, and I decided to go along with his game.

" 'Oh,' I said, 'a few days ago. Now let me strap you. . . .'

"He didn't want to. We began to banter back and forth, first as if good-naturedly, but then it grew more serious; I tried to take hold of him, but couldn't, in the suit. What was I to do? I couldn't leave him, not even for a moment—I would never find him a second time. Miracles don't happen twice. And he wanted to remain there, as a dead man. Then, when I thought I had convinced him, when he seemed ready to agree—and I gave him my gas shooter to hold—he put his face close to mine, so that I could almost see him through the double glass, and shouted, 'You bastard! You tricked me! You're alive!' —and he shot me."

For some time now I had felt Eri's face pressed to my back. At these last words she jerked, as if a current had passed through her, and covered the scar with her hand. We lay in silence for a while.

"It was a very good suit," I said. "It wasn't pierced at all. It bent into me, broke a rib, tore some muscles, but wasn't pierced. I didn't even lose consciousness, but my right arm wouldn't move for a while and a warm sensation told me I was bleeding. For a moment, however, I must have been in a muddle, because when I got up Thomas was gone. I searched for him, groping on all fours, but instead of him I found the shooter. He must have thrown it down immediately after firing. With the shooter I made it back to the ship. They saw me the moment I left the dust cloud. Olaf brought the ship up and they pulled me in. I said that I had not been able to find him. That I had found only the empty rocket, and that the shooter had fallen from my hand and gone off when I stumbled. The suit was double-layered. A piece of the metal lining came away. I have it here, under my rib."

Again, silence and the thunder of a wave, crescendoing, as if gathering itself for a leap across the entire beach, undaunted by the failure of its innumerable predecessors. Breaking, it surged, was dashed, became a soft pulse, closer and quieter, then completely still.

"You flew away . . . ?"

"No. We waited. After two more days the cloud settled, and I went down a second time. Alone. You understand why, apart from all the other reasons?"

"I understand."

"I found him quickly; his suit gleamed in the darkness. He lay at the foot of a pinnacle. His face was not visible, the glass was frosted on the inside, and when I lifted him up I thought, for a moment, that I was holding an empty suit—he weighed almost nothing. But it was he. I left him and returned in his rocket. Later, I examined it carefully and found out what had happened. His clock had stopped, an ordinary clock—he had lost all sense of time. The clock measured hours and days. I fixed it and put it back, so no one would suspect."

I embraced her. My breath stirred her hair. She touched the scar, and suddenly what had been a caress became a question.

"Its shape . . ."

"Peculiar, isn't it? It was sewed up twice, the stitches broke the first time. . . . Thurber did the sewing. Because Venturi, our doctor, was dead by then."

"The one who gave you the red book?"

"Yes. How did you know that, Eri—did I tell you? No, that's impossible."

"You were talking to Olaf, before—you remember. . . ."

"That's right. But imagine your remembering that! Such a small thing. I'm really a swine. I left it on the *Prometheus*, with everything else."

"You have things there? On Luna?"

"Yes. But it isn't worth dragging them here."

"It is, Hal."

"Darling, it would turn the place into a memorial museum. I hate that sort of thing. If I bring them back, it will only be to burn them. I'll keep a few small things I have, to remember the others by. That stone . . ."

"What stone?"

"I have a lot of stones. There's one from Kereneia, one from Thomas's planetoid—only don't think that I went around collecting! They simply got struck in the ridges of my boots; Olaf would pry them out and put them away, complete with labels. I couldn't get that idea out of his head. This is not important but . . . I have to tell you. Yes, I ought to, actually, so you won't think that everything there was terrible and that nothing ever happened except death. Try to imagine . . . a fusion of worlds. First, pink, at its lightest, most delicate, an infinity of pink, and within it, penetrating it, a darker pink, and, farther off, a red, almost blue, but much farther off, and all around, a phosphorescence, weightless, not like a cloud, not like a mist— different. I have no words for it. The two of us stepped from the rocket and stared. Eri, I don't understand that. Do you know, even now I get a tightness in the throat, it was so beautiful. Just think: there is no life there, no plants, animals, birds, nothing; no eyes to witness it. I am positive that from the creation of the world no one had gazed upon it, that we were the first, Arder and I, and if it hadn't been for the gravimeter's breaking down and our landing to calibrate it, because the quartz shattered and the mercury ran out, then no one, to the end of the world, would have stood there and seen it. Isn't that strange? One had an urge to—well; I don't know. We couldn't leave. We forgot why we had landed, we stood just like that, stood and stared."

"What was it, Hal?"

"I don't know. When we returned and told the others, Biel wanted to go, but it wasn't possible. Not enough power in reserve. We'd taken plenty of shots, but nothing came out. In the photographs it looked like pink milk with purple palisades, and Biel went on about the chemiluminescence of the silicon hydride vapors; I doubt that he believed that, but in despair, since he would never be able to investigate it, he tried to come up with some explanation. It was like . . . like nothing. We have no referents. No analogies. It possessed immense depth, but was not a landscape. Those different shades, as I said, more and more distant and dark, until your eyes swam. Motion—none, really. It floated and stood still. It changed, as if it breathed, yet remained the same; perhaps the most important thing was its enormity. As if beyond this cruel black eternity there existed another eternity, another infinity, so concentrated and mighty, so bright, that if you closed your eyes you would no longer believe in it. When we looked at each other . . . you'd have to know Arder. I'll show you his photograph. There was a man—bigger than I am, he looked like he could walk through any wall without even noticing. Always spoke slowly. You heard about that . . . hole on Kereneia?"

"Yes."

"He got stuck there, in the rock, hot mud was boiling under him, at any moment it could come gushing up through the tube where he was trapped, and he said, 'Hal, hold on. I'll take one more look around. Perhaps if I remove the bottle—no. It won't, my straps are tangled. But hold on.' And so on. You would have thought that he was talking on the telephone, from his hotel room. It was not a pose, he was like that. The most level-headed among us: always weighing. That was why he flew with me afterward, not with Olaf, who was his friend—but you heard about that."

"Yes."

"So . . . Arder. When I looked at him there, he had tears in his eyes. Tom Arder. He wasn't ashamed of them, either, not then or later. Whenever we talked about it—and we did from time to time, coming back to it—the others would get angry. They thought we were putting on an act, pretending or something. Because we became so . . . beatific. Funny, isn't it? Anyway. We looked at each other and the same thought entered our minds, even though we did not know if we would be able to calibrate the gravimeter properly—our only chance of finding the *Prometheus*. Our thought was this, that it had been worth it. Just to be able to stand there and behold that majesty."

"You were standing on a hill?"

"I don't know. Eri, it was a different kind of perspective. We looked as if from a great height, yet it was not an elevation. Wait a moment. Have you seen the Grand Canyon, in Colorado?

"I have."

"Imagine that that canyon is a thousand times larger. Or a million. That it is made of red and pink gold, almost completely transparent, that through it you can see all the strata, geological folds, anticlines and synclines; that all this is weightless, floating and seeming to smile at you. No, that doesn't do it. Darling, both Arder and I tried terribly hard to tell the others, but we failed. The stone is from there. . . . Arder picked it up for luck. He always had it with him. He had it with him on Kereneia. Kept it in a box for vitamin pills. When it began to crumble he wrapped it in cotton. Later—after I returned without him—I found the stone under the bed of his cabin. It must have fallen there. I think Olaf believed that that was the reason, but he didn't dare say this, it was too stupid. . . . What could a stone have to do with the wire that caused the failure of Arder's radio . . . ?"

EIGHT

n the meantime Olaf made no sign. I was uneasy, then guilty. Afraid that he had done something crazy. Because he was still alone, and more so, even, than I had been. I did not want to involve Eri in unpredictable events, and that would happen if I began the search myself; therefore, I decided to go to Thurber first. I wasn't sure I was going to ask him for advice—I only wanted to see him. I had got the address from Olaf; Thurber was at the university center in Malleolan. I wired him that I was coming, and parted with Eri for the first time. Over the last few days she had been reticent and nervous; I attributed this to concern for Olaf. I promised I'd be back as soon as I could, probably in two days, and that I wouldn't do anything until I had consulted her.

Eri drove me to Houl, where I caught a nonstop ulder. The beaches of the Pacific were deserted now, on account of the approaching autumn storms; the colorful crowds of young people had vanished from the local resorts, so I was not surprised to be practically the only passenger in the silver projectile. The flight, in clouds that made everything unreal, lasted almost an hour and was over at dusk. The city rose through the gathering darkness like a many-colored fire—the tallest buildings, goblet-shaped, blazed in the midst like thin, motionless flames, their outlines, against white clouds, shaped like giant butterflies joined by arches at the highest levels; the lower levels of the streets, running into one another, made twisting, colored rivers. It might have been the mist, or an effect of the glasslike construction material, but the city looked, from above, like a cluster of concentric gems, a crystal island, jewel-studded, rising up from the ocean, whose mirror surface repeated more and more faintly the shining tiers, right to the last, now barely visible, as if beneath the city lay its incandescent ruby skeleton. It was hard to believe that this fairy tale of mingled flame and color was the home of several million people.

The university complex stood outside the city. My ulder landed in a huge park, on a concrete platform. Only the pale silver glow across the sky, above the blank wall of trees, showed the proximity of the city. A long avenue led to the main building, which was dark, as though deserted.

No sooner did I open the huge door than the interior was flooded with light. I found myself in a vaulted hall with pale blue tiles. A network of soundproof passages took me to a corridor, plain and austere—I opened one door, then another, but the rooms were all empty, as if the people had departed long ago. I went upstairs, up a flight of real stairs. There must have been an elevator somewhere, but I didn't feel like looking for it. Besides, stairs that didn't move were a novelty. At the top, heading in both directions, was another corridor with vacant rooms; on the door of one I saw a small piece of paper with the words "In here, Bregg." I knocked, and heard the voice of Thurber.

I went in. He was sitting hunched in the light of a low-hanging lamp. Behind him was the darkness of a wall-to-wall window. The desk at which he worked was littered with papers and books—real books—and on another, smaller, desk nearby lay entire handfuls of those crystal "grains of corn" plus various pieces of equipment. In front of him he had a stack of paper and with a pen—a fountain pen! —he was making notes in the margins.

"Have a seat," he said, not looking up. "I'll be done in a minute."

I took a low chair by the desk but immediately moved it to the side, because the light made a blur of his face and I wanted to get a good look at him.

He worked in his characteristic way, slowly, frowning into the glare of the lamp. This was one of the simplest rooms I had seen so far, with dull walls, an old door, no decoration, and none of that tiresome gold. On either side of the door was a square, blank screen, and the wall near the window was filled with metal cabinets; rolls of maps or technical drawings leaned against one of these—that was all. I considered Thurber. Bald, solidly built, heavy; he was writing, now and then would wipe his eyes with the edge of his hand. They were always watering. Gimma (who liked to reveal others' secrets, especially those that a person tried hardest to keep hidden) once told me that Thurber was afraid of going blind. Which explained why he was always the first to turn in when we changed acceleration, and why—in later years— he let others do things for him that he had once insisted on doing himself.

He gathered the papers with both hands, tapped the desk with them to get the edges even, then put them in a briefcase, closed it, and only then, lowering his large hands with those thick fingers that looked as though they had difficulty bending, said:

"Welcome, Hal. How goes it?"

"I'm not complaining. Are you . . . alone?"

"You mean is Gimma here? No, he isn't; he left yesterday. For Europe."

"You're working . . . ?"

"Yes."

There was a pause. I didn't know how he would take what I had to say to him—I wanted first to find out what he thought of this world that we had come to. True, knowing him, I didn't expect a flood of words. He kept most of his opinions to himself.

"Have you been here long?"

"Bregg," he said, without moving, "I doubt that that interests you. You're stalling."

"Possibly," I said. "Then I'm to say what's on my mind?"

I was beginning to feel again that awkwardness, something between irritation and shyness, that always came over me in his presence. I suspect the others felt the same thing. You never knew when he was joking and when he was being serious; for all his composure, the attention that he gave you, he was hard to figure out.

"No," he said. "Perhaps later. Where did you come from?"

"Houl."

"Directly?"

"Yes . . . why do you ask?"

"That is good," he said, as if he hadn't heard my question. He looked at me for maybe five seconds without moving, as if wanting to make sure of my presence. His expression said nothing—but I knew, now, that something had happened. But would he tell me? He was unpredictable. While I wondered how I ought to begin, he studied me carefully, as though I had appeared before him in some unfamiliar form.

"What's Vabach doing?" I asked, when this silent scrutiny got to be too much.

"He went with Gimma."

That was not what I meant, and he knew it, but, then, I hadn't come to ask about Vabach. Again, a silence. I was beginning to regret my decision.

"I hear that you got married," he said suddenly, almost carelessly.

"Yes," I said, perhaps too dryly.

"It's done you good."

I searched for something else to talk about. Apart from Olaf, nothing came to mind, but I didn't want to ask about him yet. I was afraid of Thurber's smile—the way he used to demolish Gimma with it, and not only Gimma—but he only raised his brows a little and asked:

"What plans do you have?"

"None," I replied, and it was the truth.

"And would you like to do something?"

"Yes. But not just anything."

"You haven't done anything so far?"

I was definitely blushing now. I was angry.

"Nothing. Thurber . . . I didn't come here to talk about myself."

"I know," he said quietly. "It's Staave, isn't it?"

"Yes."

"There was a certain element of risk in this," he said, pushing himself gently away from the desk. His chair obediently turned toward me.

"Oswamm feared the worst, especially later, when Staave threw away his hypnagog. . . . You did, too, didn't you?"

"Oswamm?" I said. "Which Oswamm? Wait—the one from Adapt?"

"Yes. He was worried most about Staave. I pointed out to him his error."

"What do you mean?"

"But Gimma vouched for both of you . . ." he concluded, as though he had not heard me.

"What?" I said, rising from the chair. "Gimma?"

"Of course, he knew nothing," Thurber went on, "and told me so."

"Then why the hell did he vouch for us?" I burst out, confounded.

"He felt that he had to," Thurber explained laconically. "That the director of an expedition should know his men . . ."

"Nonsense."

"I'm only repeating what he said to Oswamm."

"Yes?" I said. "And what was Oswamm afraid of? That we would mutiny?"

"You never had the urge?" Thurber asked quietly.

I reflected.

"No," I said finally. "Never seriously."

"And you'll let your children be betrizated?"

"And you?" I asked slowly.

He smiled for the first time, twitching his bloodless lips. He said nothing.

"Listen, Thurber . . . you remember that evening, after the last flight over Beta . . . when I told you . . ."

He nodded indifferently. Suddenly my calm vanished.

"I did not tell you everything then, you know. We were all there together, but not on an equal footing. I took orders from the two of you—you and Gimma—I wanted it that way. We all did. Venturi, Thomas, Ennesson, and Arder, who didn't get a reserve tank because Gimma was saving it for a rainy day. Fine. Only what gives you the right now to speak to me as though you had been sitting in that chair the whole time? You were the one who sent Arder down on Kereneia in the name of science, Thurber, and I pulled him out in the name of his poor ass, and we returned, and now it turns out that the ass is the thing that counts, the other doesn't. So maybe now I should be asking you how you feel and vouching for you, not the other way around? What do you think? I know what you think. You brought back a pile of facts and you can bury yourself in them to the end of your days, knowing that none of these polite people will ask, 'What did this spectral analysis cost? One man, two men? Wouldn't you say, Professor Thurber, that the price was a bit high?' No one will say that to you because they do not keep accounts with us. But Venturi does. And Arder, and Ennesson. And Thomas. What will you use for payment, Thurber? Setting Oswamm straight about me? And Gimma—vouching for Olaf and me? The first time I saw you, you were doing the same thing you are doing today. That was in Apprenous. You sat in the midst of your papers and stared, like now: taking a break from more important matters, in the name of science. . . ."

I got up.

"Thank Gimma for taking our side. . . ."

Thurber stood, too. For perhaps a second we looked each other in the eye. He was shorter, but you didn't notice it. His height didn't matter. The calmness of his gaze was beyond words.

"Am I allowed to speak, or has sentence been passed?" he asked.

I mumbled something unintelligible.

"Then sit," he said and, without waiting, lowered himself heavily into his chair.

I sat down.

"But you have done something," he said in a tone that suggested we had been talking about the weather. "You read Starck, believed him, felt cheated, and now you are looking for someone to blame. If it means such a great deal to you, I can take the blame. But that is not the issue. Starck convinced you—after those ten years? Bregg, I knew you were a hothead, but I never thought you stupid." He paused for a moment, and, strangely, I experienced something like relief—and a hope for liberation. I didn't have time to analyze it, because he continued.

"Contact with galactic civilizations? Whoever said anything about that? None of us, not one of the scholars, not Merquier, not Simonadi, not Rag Ngamieli—no one; no expedition counted on any such contact, and therefore all that talk about fossils flying through space and the perpetually delayed galactic mail, it's a refutation of an argument that no one ever made. What can one get from the stars? And of what use was Amundsen's expedition? Or Andree's? None. The only clear benefit lay in the fact that they had proved a possibility. That it could be done. Or, more precisely, that it was, for a given time, the most difficult attainable thing. I don't know if we even did that much, Bregg. I really don't. But we were there."

I was silent. Thurber did not look at me now. He rested his fists on the edge of the desk.

"What did Starck prove to you—the futility of cosmodromia? As if we did not know that ourselves! And the poles! What was at the poles? Those who conquered them knew that there was nothing there. And the Moon? What did Ross's group seek in the crater Eratosthenes? Diamonds? And why did Bant and Jegorin cross the face of Mercury—to get a tan? And Kellen and Offshagg—the only thing they knew for certain, when they flew to the cold cloud of Cerber, was that they could die there. Don't you know what Starck is really saying? That a human being must eat, drink, and clothe himself; and the rest is madness. Every man has his Starck, Bregg. Every period in history has had one. Why did Gimma send you and Arder? To collect samples from the corona. Who sent Gimma? Science. Cut and dried, isn't it? The study of the stars. Bregg, do you think we wouldn't have gone if there had been no stars? I say we would have. We would have wanted to examine that emptiness, to provide an explanation for it, Geonides or someone else would have told us what valuable measurements and experiments we could carry out on the way. Do not misunderstand me. I am not saying that the stars are only an excuse. Neither was the pole; Nansen and Andree needed it. . . . Everest meant more to Mallory and Irving than the air itself. You say that I ordered you 'in the name of science'? You know that isn't true. You were testing my memory. Shall I test yours? Do you remember Thomas's planetoid?"

I started.

"You lied to us then. You flew down a second time, knowing that he was dead. True?"

I was silent.

"I guessed immediately. I never discussed it with Gimma, but I think he also guessed. Why did you do it, Bregg? That was not Arcturus or Kereneia, and there was no one to save. What purpose did you have, man?"

I was silent. Thurber gave a faint smile.

"You know what our problem is, Bregg? The fact that we made it and are sitting here. Man always comes back empty-handed. . . ."

He stopped. His smile became an almost meaningless scowl. For a moment he breathed more loudly, gripping the desk with both hands. I looked at him, as if seeing him for the first time; it struck me that he was old, and the realization was a shock. I had never thought of him that way, as if he were ageless. . . .

"Thurber," I said quietly, "listen . . . this is, well . . . only a eulogy over the graves of—the insatiable. There are none like them now. And will not be again. So—after all—Starck wins. . ."

He showed his flat yellow teeth, but it was not a smile.

"Bregg, give me your word that you will repeat to no one what I am about to tell you."

I hesitated.

"To no one," he repeated, with emphasis.

"All right."

He stood, went over to the corner, picked up a tube of paper, and returned with it to the desk.

The paper rustled as it unrolled in his hands. I saw what looked like a gutted fish, red lines, like blood.

"Thurber!"

"Yes," he replied quietly, rolling the paper back up with both hands.

"A new expedition?"

"Yes," he repeated. And went back to the corner and leaned the tube against the wall, like a rifle.

"When? Where?"

"Not soon. To the Center."

"Sagittarius . . ." I whispered.

"Yes. The preparations will take a long time. But thanks to anabiosis . . ."

He continued, but only single words and expressions came through to me—"loop flight," "nongravitational acceleration"— and the excitement I felt when I saw the drawing of the giant rocket gave way to an unexpected languor, from which, as through a descending gloom, I examined the hands resting on my knees. Thurber stopped, glanced at me, went to his desk, and began to gather papers, as if giving me time to digest the news. I should have been firing questions at him—which of us, of the old guard, would be flying; how many years the expedition would last; its objectives—but I asked nothing. Not even why the whole thing was being kept a secret. I looked at his huge, thick hands, which showed his age more distinctly than did his face, and I felt a small measure of satisfaction, as unexpected as it was base—that he, in any case, would not be flying. I would not live to see their return, not even if I broke Methuselah's record. It didn't matter. Was unimportant. I got up. Thurber rustled his papers.

"Bregg," he said, without looking up, "I still have work to do. If you like, we can have dinner together. You can spend the night in the dormitory; it's empty now."

I mumbled, "All right," and walked to the door. He had started to work as if I were no longer there. I stood awhile in the doorway, then left. I was not aware of exactly where I was, until the steady clap of my own footsteps reached me. I halted. I was in the middle of the long corridor, between two rows of identical doors. The echo of my steps could still be heard. An illusion? Someone following me? I turned and saw a tall figure disappear through a door at the far end. It happened so quickly that I did not get a good look at him, saw just a movement, a back, and the closing door. There was nothing for me to do here. No sense in walking farther—the corridor came to a dead end. I turned back, walked past an enormous window through which I could see the glow of the city, silver on the vast black park, and again stopped in front of the door marked "In here, Bregg," where Thurber was working. I no longer wanted to see him. I had nothing to say to him, nor he to me. Why had I come in the first place? Suddenly, with surprise, I remembered why. I would go back inside and ask about Olaf—but not now. Not just yet. I wasn't tired, I felt perfectly fine, but something was happening to me, something I didn't understand. I went to the stairs. Opposite them stood the last of the doors, the one into which the unknown person had disappeared a moment ago. I recalled that I had looked into that same room at the beginning, when I entered the building; I recognized the patch of peeling paint. There had been nothing at all in that room. What could the person have been looking for?

I was certain that he had not been looking for anything, that he was only hiding from me, and I stood undecided for some time in front of the stairs, the empty white motionless stairs. Slowly, very slowly, I turned. I felt an odd uneasiness; not an uneasiness exactly, for I was not afraid of anything; it was the way one feels after an injection of an anesthetic—tense, yet collected. I took two steps and strained my ears; it seemed to me that I heard—on the other side of the door—the sound of breathing. Impossible. I decided to go, but couldn't, I had given too much attention to that ridiculous door to walk away. I opened it and looked inside. Under a small ceiling lamp, in the middle of the empty room, stood Olaf. In the same old clothes, and with his sleeves rolled up, as if he had just put down his tools.

We looked at each other. Seeing that I wasn't going to speak, he spoke.

"How are you, Hal?"

His voice was not altogether steady.

I didn't want to play games, I was just surprised by this unexpected meeting, and perhaps, too, the shock of Thurber's words had not yet left me; in any case I said nothing in reply. I went over to the window, which had the same view, the black park and the glow of the city, and turned and sat on the sill. Olaf didn't move. He stood in the center of the room; from the book in his hand a single sheet of paper slipped and glided to the floor. We bent at the same time; I picked up the sheet and saw on it the blueprint of the rocket, the one that Thurber had shown me a moment ago. At the bottom of the sheet were comments in Olaf's handwriting. So that was it, I thought. He hadn't written because he would be flying, he'd wanted to spare me that knowledge. I would tell him that he was mistaken, that I didn't care about the expedition. I'd had enough of the stars, and anyway I knew everything from Thurber, so he could talk to me with a clear conscience.

I looked carefully at the lines of the drawing in my hand, as if approving the streamlined shape of the rocket, but said nothing; I merely returned the paper, which he took from me with a certain reluctance, folded in two, and put inside the book. All this took place in total silence, not by design, I am sure, but because it was acted out in silence the scene took on a symbolic significance, as though I had learned of his participation in the expedition and, by returning the drawing, accepted this step, without enthusiasm, but also without regret. When I tried to catch his eye he looked away, only to glance at me a moment later—the picture of uncertainty and confusion. Even now, when I knew everything? The silence in the small room became unbearable. I heard him breathe a little faster. His face was haggard and his eyes not as bright as when I had seen him last, as though he had been working hard and sleeping little, but there was another expression in them, too, one I did not recognize.

"I'm fine . . ." I said slowly. "And you?"

The instant I said these words I realized that the time for them had passed; they would have suited when I entered, but now they sounded almost hostile, or even sarcastic.

"Did you see Thurber?" he asked.

"Yes."

"The students have gone. . . . There's no one here now, they gave us the whole building . . ." he began awkwardly.

"So that you could work out the plan for the expedition?" I prompted him, and he answered eagerly.

"Yes, Hal. Well, but you know the kind of work it is. Right now there are only a handful of us, but we have fantastic machines, these robots, you know. . . ."

"That's good."

After these words, however, there was another silence. And, oddly enough, the longer it lasted, the greater grew Olaf's anxiety, his exaggerated stiffness, for he still stood in the center of the room, as if nailed to the floor, under the light, prepared for the worst. I decided to end this.

"Listen," I said very softly. "What exactly did you imagine? The coward's way doesn't work, you know. . . . Did you really think I wouldn't find out if you didn't tell me?"

I broke off, and he remained silent, with his head hung to one side. I had gone too far, no doubt, since he was not to blame—in his shoes I probably would have done the same. Nor did I hold against him his month-long silence; it was that attempt to escape, to hide from me in this deserted room, when he saw me stepping out of Thurber's office—but I couldn't tell him this directly, it was too stupid and ridiculous. I raised my voice, called him a damned fool, but even then he didn't defend himself.

"So you think there's nothing left to discuss?" I snapped.

"That depends on you. . . ."

"How so, on me?"

"On you," he repeated stubbornly. "It was important, who would be the one to tell you. . . ."

"You really believe that?"

"That was how it seemed to me. . . ."

"It makes no difference," I muttered.

"What do you intend to do?" he asked quietly.

"Nothing."

Olaf looked at me suspiciously.

"Hal, look, I . . ."

He didn't finish. I felt I was torturing him with my presence, yet I couldn't forgive him for running away; and to leave like that, at that moment, without a word, would have been worse than the uncertainty that had brought me there. I didn't know what to say; everything that united us was forbidden. I looked at him in the same moment that he glanced at me—each of us, even now, was counting on the other to help.

I got up from the sill.

"Olaf . . . it's late. I'm going. Don't think that I'm angry with you; nothing of the sort. We'll get together, anyway, perhaps you'll drop in on us." I said this with effort; each word was unnatural, and he knew it.

"What . . . you're not staying the night?"

"I can't, you see, I promised . . ."

I did not say her name. Olaf mumbled:

"As you wish. I'll see you out."

We left the room together and went down the stairs; outside it was completely dark. Olaf walked beside me without a word; suddenly he stopped. And I stopped.

"Stay," he whispered, as if ashamed. I could see only the vague blur of his face.

"All right," I agreed unexpectedly and turned around. He was not prepared for that. He stood for a while, then took me by the arm and led me to another, lower, building. In an empty room, where a few lights had been left on, we ate dinner on a counter, without even sitting down. During the entire time we exchanged perhaps ten words. Then went upstairs.

The room to which he led me was almost perfectly square, decorated in dull white, with a wide window that must have overlooked the park from a different direction, because I could see no trace of the city's glow above the trees; there was a freshly made bed, two chairs, and a third chair, larger, by the window. Through the narrow opening of a doorway the tiles of a bathroom glistened. Olaf stood at the door with his arms hanging, as if waiting for me to speak, but I said nothing, just walked around the room and touched the pieces of furniture mechanically, as though temporarily taking possession of them; he asked quietly:

"Can I . . . do anything for you?"

"Yes," I said. "Leave me alone."

He continued to stand there, not moving. His face turned red, then pale, and suddenly he smiled—smiled to hide the insult, because it had sounded like an insult. At this helpless, pathetic smile, something within me broke; in a convulsive effort to tear away the mask of indifference I had been wearing, since I had no other, I ran to him as he turned to leave, grabbed his hand, and squeezed it, as if asking his forgiveness with this violent clasp, and he, without looking at me, replied with a similar squeeze and went out. His firm grip still tingled in my hand when he had closed the door after himself, closed it carefully and quietly, as though leaving a sickroom. I was left alone, as I had wanted.

The building was filled with an absolute silence. I did not even hear Olaf's retreating footsteps; in the glass of the window my own heavy shape was weakly reflected; from an unknown source flowed heated air; through the outline of my reflection I saw the edge of trees submerged now in complete darkness. Again I ran my eyes around the room, then went to the large chair by the window.

An autumn night. I couldn't even think of sleeping. I stood at the window. The darkness that lay beyond it had to be full of coolness and the whisper of leafless branches brushing against one another. Suddenly I wanted to be there, in it, wandering through the darkness, through its unpremeditated chaos. Without another thought I left the room. The corridor was deserted. I tiptoed to the stairs—an unnecessary caution, probably, for Olaf must have gone to bed some time ago, and Thurber, if he was working, was on a different floor, in a distant wing of the building. I ran downstairs, no longer muffling my footsteps, slipped outside, and began to walk quickly. I chose no particular direction, just walked, avoiding the glow of the city as much as possible. The paths of the park soon took me beyond its boundary, marked by a hedge; I found myself on the road, walked it for a while, then made a sudden stop. I didn't want to walk down a road; roads led to houses, people, and I wanted to be alone. I remembered: Olaf had told me, back in Clavestra, about Malleolan, the new city in the mountains, built after our departure; the few kilometers of road that I had walked certainly seemed full of bends, curves, no doubt skirting slopes, but in the darkness I couldn't see if this was the case. The road, typically, was not illuminated, the surface itself glowed with a weak phosphorescence, too weak to light up the vegetation on the sides. So I left the road, felt my way in the dark, found myself in low, dense shrubbery that led up to a hill without trees—without trees, because the wind gusted freely here. Several times, pale, winding fragments of the road I had abandoned came into view, far below, and then that last light vanished; I stopped a second time; not so much with my helpless eyes as with my whole body, my face to the wind, I tried to get to know the land, alien to me, like another planet; I wanted to reach one of the peaks surrounding the valley where the city lay, but how to find the right direction? Suddenly, when the whole enterprise seemed hopeless, I heard a drawn-out, distant roar, like that of waves, yet different, coming from high up and to the right—the noise of wind blowing through a forest, a forest much higher than where I stood. I headed in that direction. A slope overgrown with dry grass led me to the first trees. I picked my way through these phantoms, raising my arms to protect my face from the branches. Soon the slope became less steep, the trees thinned out, and again I had to choose a direction; listening intently in the darkness, I waited patiently for the next strong gust of wind. And the wind came, from the high ground in the distance I heard its long whistle; yes, the wind of that night was my ally; I went straight, disregarding the fact that I was now losing altitude, descending sharply into a black ravine.

At the bottom of this was a steep incline; I began climbing gradually upward, a trickling rivulet showed me the way. At one point I stopped seeing it; anyway it probably was running beneath a layer of stones; the sound of the water diminished as I went higher, until it died away altogether, and once more the forest surrounded me, tall trees, pine, almost entirely devoid of undergrowth. The ground was covered by a pillow-soft layer of old pine needles, and in places it was slippery with moss. This blind wandering went on for more than three hours; the roots I tripped over were twisted more and more frequently around erratic boulders that jutted through the shallow soil. I was afraid that the summit would turn out to be covered by forest and that in that labyrinth would end my barely begun excursion into the mountains, but I was fortunate—through a small, bare pass I reached a field of rubble, which grew steeper and steeper. Finally, I could hardly stay on my feet, the stones began slipping from under me with a rattling sound; hopping from one foot to the other, not without repeated falls, I made it to the side of a narrow gully and now could climb more quickly. I stopped from time to time, to try to distinguish my surroundings, but the total darkness made that impossible. I saw neither the city nor its glow, nor any trace of the shining road that I had left. The gully led me to a bare area with patches of dry grass; that I was now high up I knew from the ever-widening starry sky, and the other mountain ridges began to draw level with the one I was climbing. A few hundred steps more and I came to the first clusters of dwarf pines.

Had someone in the darkness suddenly stopped me and asked where I was going and why, I would not have been able to answer; but there was no one, and the loneliness of that night march gave me a feeling, even if temporary, of relief. The angle of the slope increased, walking became more and more difficult, but I forged ahead, trying only to keep straight, as if I had a definite goal. My heart pounded, my lungs labored, and I fought upward in a frenzy, feeling instinctively that this exhausting effort was precisely what I needed. I pushed aside the twisted branches of the dwarf pines, sometimes became entangled, pulled free, and went on. Clusters of needles brushed my face, my chest, caught on my clothing; my fingers stuck together from the resin. In an open space a sudden wind hit me; rushing out of the dark, it rampaged, whistling high above, where I guessed was a pass. Then the next thicket of dwarf pines swallowed me up; in it were islands of warm, motionless air permeated with its strong fragrance. Indistinct obstacles rose in my path, erratic rocks, loose stones underfoot. I must have been walking for several hours now, and still I felt a reservoir of strength in me, sufficient to bring me to despair; the gully, leading to some pass, possibly to the summit, narrowed so that I could see both its edges high against the sky, blocking out the stars with their dark ridges.

The region of mist was far below me, but the cool night had no moon, and the stars gave little light. I was surprised, then, at the appearance, around me and above me, of elongated whitish shapes. They lay in the darkness without illuminating it, as though they had absorbed radiance during the day; the first loose crunch beneath my feet told me that I was on snow.

A thin layer of it covered the rest of the steep slope. I would have been frozen to the bone, lightly dressed as I was, but the wind fell unexpectedly, and now I could hear distinctly the sound of crunching snow with every step.

At the pass itself there was hardly any snow. Huge windswept rocks stood silhouetted above the scree. I stopped, my heart hammering, and looked in the direction of the city. It was hidden behind the slope; only a patch of reddish gray, from the lights, betrayed its position in the valley. Above me quivered the stars, sharply visible. I went on a few steps more and sat down on a saddle-shaped boulder. Now the glow was gone. Ahead of me, in the darkness, were the mountains, ghostlike, their peaks whitened by snow. Looking hard at the eastern edge of the horizon, I could make out the first streaks of daybreak. Against it, the outline of a ridge broken in two. And all at once, in my immobility, something began to happen; formless shadows around me—or within me?—shifted, receded, altered in proportions. I was so preoccupied with this that for a moment it was

as if I had lost my vision, and when I regained it, everything
was different. The skies of the east, barely gray above the invisible valley, deepened even more the blackness of the rock, yet
I could have pointed out every irregularity, every indentation;
I knew intimately the scene that the day would unfold to me,
because it had been inscribed in me for all time, and not in vain.
Here was the immutability that I had desired, that had remained
untouched while my world crumbled and perished in a century-
and-a-half gulf of time. It was in this valley that I had spent my
boyhood years—in the old wooden hostel on the grassy slope,
opposite, of the Cloud Catcher. Of that house not even the
foundation stones would be left, the last boards must long since
have rotted away, but the rocky ridge stood unchanged, as if
it had been waiting for this meeting—could a vague unconscious
memory have guided me through the night to this very spot?

The shock of recognition instantly freed me of all my weak-
ness, so desperately concealed, concealed first with a pretense of
calm, then by the intentional frenzy of my mountaineering.
I reached down and, not embarrassed by the trembling of my
fingers, took some snow and put it into my mouth. The cold
melting on my tongue did not quench my thirst but made me
more awake. I sat and ate snow, still not believing, now waiting
to have my surmise confirmed by the first rays of the sun. Long
before the sun appeared, from above the slowly fading stars,
came a bird, which folded its wings, made itself smaller, and,
alighting on a slanted sheet of rock, began to walk toward me.
I froze, afraid of scaring it away. The bird went around me and
moved away, and just when I thought that it hadn't noticed me,
it returned from the other side and circled the boulder where I
was sitting. We regarded each other for a while, until I said
quietly:

"And where did you come from?"

Seeing that it didn't fear me, I resumed eating snow. It cocked
its head, peered at me with its black beads of eyes, then suddenly, as if it had had enough of me, spread its wings and flew
away. And I, resting against the rough rock, hunched over, my
hands numb from the snow, waited for the dawn, and the whole

night came back to me in a violent, incomplete synopsis—
Thurber and his words, the silence between Olaf and me, the
view of the city, the red mist and the breaks in the mist made
by funnels of light, gusts of hot air, the inhaling and exhaling
of a million, the hanging squares, malls, avenues, skyscrapers
with wings of fire, the different levels with different colors, the
uninspired conversation with the bird at the pass, and how I
ate snow—and all these pictures were and were not themselves,
as in dreams sometimes, they were both a reminder and an
avoidance of the thing I dared not touch. Because, throughout,
I had tried to find in myself an acceptance of what I could not
accept. But that had been before, like a dream. Now, clear-
headed and alert, awaiting the day, in air almost silver, in the
presence of the slowly revealed mountain slopes, the gullies,
the scree, which emerged from the night in silent confirmation
of the reality of my return, for the first time I—alone but not a
stranger to the Earth—now subject to her and her laws—for the
first time I could, without protest, without regret, think of those
setting out for the golden fleece of the stars. . . .

The snow of the summit caught fire in gold and white, it
stood above the purple shadows of the valley, stood powerful
and eternal, and I, not closing my tear-filled eyes, got up slowly
and began to walk across the stones, to the south, to my home.

Zakopane—Cracow, 1960